ANTHONY BERKELEY

The Wychford Poisoning Case

WITH AN INTRODUCTION
BY TONY MEDAWAR

COLLINS
CRIME
CLUB

COLLINS CRIME CLUB

An imprint of HarperCollins*Publishers*
1 London Bridge Street
London SE1 9GF

www.harpercollins.co.uk

HarperCollins*Publishers*
1st Floor, Watermarque Building, Ringsend Road
Dublin 4, Ireland

This paperback edition 2021

1

First published in Great Britain by
W. Collins Sons & Co. Ltd 1926

A catalogue record for this book is
available from the British Library

ISBN 978-0-00-833388-1

Typeset in Bulmer MT Std by
Palimpsest Book Production Ltd, Falkirk, Stirlingshire

Printed and bound in Great Britain by
CPI Group (UK) Ltd, Croydon CR0 4YY

MIX
Paper from
responsible sources
FSC
www.fsc.org   FSC™ C007454

Anthony Berkeley was a pen name of Anthony Berkeley Cox (1893–1971), one of the most important figures in the history of detective fiction. Founder of the prestigious (and still flourishing) Detection Club for British crime writers, he was one of the most innovative authors of the Golden Age and beyond. Many of his novels feature the amateur criminologist Roger Sheringham, most famously in *The Poisoned Chocolates Case* (1929), and under the pseudonym Francis Iles he pioneered the increasingly popular psychological crime novel. He retired from writing books in 1939, although he continued to write stories, articles and reviews until his death in 1971.

INTRODUCTION

ANTHONY BERKELEY COX—or Anthony Berkeley as he is best known—was born on 5 July, 1893 in Watford, a town near London. His father was a doctor and his mother was descended from the Earl of Monmouth, a courtier to Queen Elizabeth I. At school, Berkeley was what we would now call a high achiever—Head of House, prefect, Colour Sergeant in the Officer Training Corps and an expert marksman. In 1911, he left school to read Classics at University College, Oxford, but his university career was cut short by the First World War and, between 1914 and 1918, Berkeley served in France in the 7th Northamptonshire Regiment, reaching the rank of Lieutenant, and also in the Royal Air Force.

After the war, Berkeley spent a couple of years 'trying to find out what nature had intended him to do in life' before he discovered that he had the most extraordinary knack for writing comic stories for the many weekly magazines and newspapers that carried such fiction in the 1920s. Thankfully, Berkeley also decided to try his hand at something more serious, a detective mystery.

His first attempt, *The Layton Court Mystery*, was published anonymously in 1925 by Herbert Jenkins. The book marked the debut of Roger Sheringham, a man with more than a hint of his creator about him—in particular, like Berkeley, he was an Oxford man and his health had been compromised during the war. *The Layton Court Mystery* features a closed circle of suspects and a suitably unpleasant victim who is found dead in a locked room; the murderer's identity comes as a devastating surprise. In dedicating the novel to his father, Berkeley explained that he had 'tried to make the gentleman who eventually solves the mystery behave as nearly as possible as he might be expected to do in real life. That is to say, he is very far removed from a sphinx and he does make a mistake or two occasionally.'

Sheringham's tendency to make 'a mistake or two occasionally' may very well have been inspired by E.C. Bentley's famous novel *Trent's Last Case*, published a dozen years earlier. Certainly, fallibility was to become something of a trademark for Roger Sheringham.

The Layton Court Mystery sold well and, enthused by the sales figures, Anthony Berkeley decided to focus on writing novels and to make Roger Sheringham the central figure of a series of mysteries. Sheringham's second case, also published anonymously (the byline of the jacket was simply 'By the author of *The Layton Court Mystery*'), was *The Wychford Poisoning Case*.

The Wychford Poisoning Case (1926) is the rarest of Berkeley's detective fiction. It was the first of his novels to be published by Collins but, unlike other Sheringham mysteries, has not until now been reissued, even in a paperback edition. It is unclear why this was but it has been suggested that it may have been because Berkeley felt acute embarrassment at a brief, irrelevant but bizarre scene in which an annoying young woman is subjected to corporal punishment. Whether or not the scene was meant ironically or simply as comic relief, it reads oddly today and, as with the casual anti-semitism that pollutes some Golden Age mysteries, leaves modern readers uncomfortable. Sexist aberrations aside, the novel is strong and the explanation of the poisoning is characteristically unexpected and outrageous. It is also noteworthy for being dedicated to Berkeley's long-standing friend, the aristocratic Edmée Elizabeth Monica de la Pasture under her rather more prosaic pseudonym, E.M. Delafield.

Unlike *The Layton Court Mystery*, *The Wychford Poisoning Case* is based on a real-life murder—that of James Maybrick, a Liverpool businessman, in 1889. Like many other writers of the era, Berkeley had a deep interest in what has come to be called 'true crime', writing essays on various different cases over the years—indeed, *The Wychford Poisoning Case* would not be the only occasion on which Berkeley would draw on what he called 'the far more absorbing criminological dramas of real life'. *The Wychford Poisoning Case* is also notable for the innovative consideration of psychology as a method of crime detection, pioneered some fifteen years earlier by Edwin Balmer and William MacHarg with their stories of Luther Trant. This was an approach that Anthony Berkeley would eventually perfect with *Malice Aforethought* (1931), in which he gave an ingenious study of a murderer, and in two other novels, all of which were published under a different pen name, Francis Iles.

The first two Sheringham mysteries sold well and the detective's popularity was such that his name would be included in the title of the third, *Roger Sheringham and the Vane Mystery* (1927), which for the first time in the series was published as by Anthony Berkeley.

In all, Sheringham appears in ten novel-length detective stories, one of which, *The Silk Stocking Murders* (also reissued in this Detective Club series), is dedicated by Berkeley to none other than A.B. Cox! Sheringham is also mentioned in passing in two of Berkeley's non-series novels, *The Piccadilly Murder* (1929) and *Trial and Error* (1937), and appears in a novella and a number of short stories, including two recently discovered 'cautionary' detective problems published during the Second World War.

Though undoubtedly one of the 'great detectives' of the Golden Age, Roger Sheringham is not a particularly original creation. As already noted, there is much of E.C. Bentley's Philip Trent about Sheringham, as there is about many other Golden Age detectives, including Margery Allingham's Albert Campion and Dorothy L. Sayers' Lord Peter Wimsey. And, emulating Bentley's iconoclastic approach to the genre, Berkeley delighted in turning its unwritten rules upside down. Thus, while Sheringham's cases conform, broadly, to the principal conventions of the detective story—there is always a crime and there is always at least one detective—the mysteries are distinctive and memorable for the way in which they drove the evolution of crime and detective stories. Each of the novels brings something new and fresh to what Berkeley had previously dismissed as the 'crime-puzzle'. Several do have what can be described as twist endings but that is to diminish Berkeley's ingenuity and undervalue his importance in the history of crime and detective fiction.

While other luminaries wrought their magic consistently—Agatha Christie in making the most likely suspect the least likely suspect, and John Dickson Carr in making the impossible possible—Anthony Berkeley delighted in finding different ways to structure the crime story. 'Anthony Berkeley is the supreme master not of "the twist" but of the "double twist",' wrote Milward Kennedy in the *Sunday Times*, but his focus was not so much on adding a twist at the end but on twisting the genre itself.

Astonishingly, it is more than 75 years since the publication of Berkeley's final novel, *As for the Woman* (1939), which appeared under the pen name of Francis Iles. And yet his influence lives on. Berkeley did much to shape the evolution of crime fiction in the 20th century and to transform the 'crime puzzle' into the novel of psychological suspense. In the words of one of his peers, Anthony Berkeley Cox—more than most—'deserves to become immortal'.

TONY MEDAWAR
September 2016

To
E. M. DELAFIELD
Most Delightful of Writers

My dear Elizabeth,

There is only one person to receive the dedication of the book which has grown out of those long criminological discussions of ours. You will recognise in it many of your own ideas, which I have unblushingly annexed; but I hope you will also recognise the attempt I have made to substitute for the materialism of the usual crime-puzzle of fiction those psychological values which are (as we have so often agreed) the basis of the universal interest in the far more absorbing criminological dramas of real life. In other words I have tried to write what might be described as a psychological detective story.

In any case I offer you the result as a small expression of my admiration of your work and of my gratitude for the gift of your friendship.

CONTENTS

CHAPTER I

MARMALADE AND MURDER

'KEDGEREE,' said Roger Sheringham oracularly, pausing beside the silver dish on the sideboard and addressing his host and hostess with enthusiasm, 'kedgeree has often seemed to me in a way to symbolise life. It can be so delightful or it can be so unutterably mournful. The crisp, dry grains of fish and rice in your successful kedgeree are days and weeks so easily surmountable, so exquisite in their passing; whereas the gloomy, sodden mass of an inferior cook—'

'I warned you, darling,' observed Alec Grierson to his young wife. 'You can't say I didn't warn you.'

'But I like it, dear,' protested Barbara Grierson *(née* Shannon). 'I like hearing him talk about fat, drunken cooks; it may be most useful to me. Go on, Roger!'

'I don't think you can have been attending properly, Barbara,' said Roger in a pained voice. 'I was discoursing at the moment upon kedgeree, not cooks.'

'Oh! I thought you said something about the gloomy mass of a sodden cook. Never mind. Go on, whatever it was. I ought to warn you that your coffee's getting cold, though.'

'And you might warn him at the same time that it's past ten o'clock already,' added her husband, applying a fresh match to his after-breakfast pipe. 'Hadn't you better start eating that kedgeree instead of lecturing on it, Roger? I was hoping to be at the stream before this, you know. I've been ready for the last half-hour.'

'Vain are the hopes of men,' observed Roger sadly, carrying a generously loaded plate to the table. 'In the night they spring up and in the morning, lo! cometh the sun and they are withered and die.'

1

'In the morning cometh Roger not, who continueth frowsting in bed,' grumbled Alec. 'That'd be more to the point.'

'Cease, Alexander,' Roger retorted gently. 'The efforts of your admirable cook engage me.'

Alec picked up his newspaper and began to study its contents with indifferently concealed impatience.

'Did you sleep well, Roger?' Barbara wanted to know.

'Did he sleep well?' growled her husband, with heavy sarcasm. 'Oh, *no*!'

'Thank you, Barbara; very well indeed,' Roger replied serenely. 'Really, you know, that cook of yours is a culinary phenomenon. This kedgeree's a dream. I'm going to have some more.'

'Finish the dish. Now then, aren't you sorry you wouldn't come and stay with us before?'

'Not in the least. In fact, I'm still congratulating myself that I resisted the awful temptation. One of the wisest things I ever did in all my life, compact with wisdom though it has been.'

'Oh? Why?'

'For any number of reasons. How long have you been married now? Just over a year? Exactly. It takes precisely twelve months for a married couple to get sufficiently used to each other without having to be maudlin in public, to the extreme embarrassment of middle-aged bachelors and unsympathetic onlookers such as myself.'

'Roger!' exclaimed his indignant hostess. 'I'm sure Alec and I have never said a single—'

'Oh, I'm not talking about words. I'm talking about expressive glances. My dear Barbara, the expressive glances I've had to sit and writhe between in my time! You wouldn't believe it.'

'Well, I should have thought you'd have enjoyed that sort of thing,' Barbara laughed. 'All's copy that comes into your mill, isn't it?'

'I don't write penny novelettes, Mrs Grierson,' returned Roger with dignity.

'Don't you?' Barbara replied innocently.

An explosive sound burst from Alec. 'Good for you, darling. Had him there.'

'You are pleased to insult me, the two of you,' said Roger pathetically. 'Helpless and in your power, speechless with kedgeree—'

'No, not speechless!' came from the depths of Alec's paper. 'Never that.'

'Speechless with kedgeree, squirming with embarrassment in the presence of your new relationship to each other—'

'Roger, how can you! When you yourself were Alec's best man, too!'

'You put me between you and insult me. The very first morning of my visit, too. What are the trains back to London?'

'There's a very good one in about half an hour. And now tell me all the other reasons why you wouldn't come down here before.'

'Well, for one thing I set a certain value on my comfort, Barbara, and other regrettable experiences, over which we will pass with silent shudders, have shown me very clearly that it takes a wife a full twelve months to learn to run her house with sufficient dexterity and knowledge to warrant her asking guests down to it.'

'Roger! This place has always gone like clockwork ever since I took it over. Hasn't it, Alec?'

'Clockwork, darling,' mumbled her husband absently.

'But then, you're a very exceptional woman, Barbara,' said Roger mildly. 'In the presence of your husband I can't say less than that. He's bigger than me.'

'Roger, I don't think I'm liking you very much this morning. Have you finished the kedgeree? Well, you'll find some grilled kidneys in that other dish. More coffee?'

'Grilled kidneys?' said Roger, rising with alacrity. 'Oh, I *am* going to enjoy my stay here, Barbara. I suspected it at dinner last night. Now I know.'

'Are you going to be *all* the morning over brekker, Roger?' demanded Alec in desperation.

'Most of it, Alexander, I hope,' Roger replied happily.

For nearly two minutes the silence was unbroken.

'Anything in the paper this morning, dear?' Barbara asked casually.

'Only this Bentley case,' replied her husband without looking up.

'The woman who poisoned her husband with arsenic? Anything fresh?'

'Yes, the magistrates have committed her for trial.'

'Anything said about her defence, Alec?' asked Roger.

Alex consulted the paper. 'No; defence reserved.'

'Defence!' said Barbara with a slight sniff. 'What a hope! If ever a person was obviously guilty—!'

'There,' said Roger, 'speaks the voice of all England—with two exceptions.'

'Exceptions? I shouldn't have thought there was a single exception. Who?'

'Well, Mrs Bentley, for one.'

'Oh—Mrs Bentley. She knows what she did all right.'

'Oh, no doubt. But she couldn't have thought she was being *obviously* guilty, could she? I mean, she's a curious sort of person if she did.'

'But she is rather a curious sort of person in any case, isn't she? Ordinary people don't feed their husbands on arsenic. And who's the other exception?'

'Me,' said Roger modestly.

'You? Roger! Do you mean to say you think she's not guilty?'

'Not exactly. It was just the word "obviously" that I was taking exception to. After all, she hasn't been tried yet, you know. We haven't heard yet what she's got to say about it all.'

'What can she say? I suppose she'll fake up some sort of story, but really, Roger! All I can say is that if they don't hang her, no husband's life will ever be safe again.'

'Then let's hope they do,' remarked Alec humorously. 'Speaking entirely from the personal point of view, of course.'

'Prejudice, thy name is woman,' Roger murmured. 'Second name, apparently, bloodthirstiness. It's wonderful. We're all being women over this affair. Marmalade, please, Alexander.'

'I know you're a perverse old devil, Roger,' Alec was constrained to protest as he passed the dish across, 'but you can't mean to say that you really think she's innocent?'

'I don't think anything of the sort, Alexander. What I *am* trying to do (which apparently no one else is) is to preserve an open mind. I repeat—she hasn't been tried yet!'

'But the coroner's jury brought it in murder against her.'

'Even coroner's juries have been known to be fallible,' Roger pointed out mildly. 'And they didn't bring it in quite as bluntly as that. Their exact words, as far as I remember, were that Bentley died from the administration of arsenic, and the majority were of the opinion that the arsenic had been administered with the intention of taking away life.'

'That comes to the same thing.'

'Possibly. But it isn't conclusive.'

'You seem to know a lot about this case, Roger,' Barbara remarked.

'I do,' Roger agreed. 'I've tried to read every word that's been written about it. I find it an uncommonly interesting one. After you with that paper, Alec.'

Alec threw the paper across. 'Well, there was a lot of new evidence brought before the magistrates yesterday. You'd better read it. If you can keep an open mind after that, call the rest of us oysters.'

'I do that already,' Roger replied, propping the paper up in front of him. 'Thank you, Oyster Alexander.'

CHAPTER II

STATING THE CASE

'Alec,' said Roger, as he settled his back comfortably against a shady willow and pulled his pipe out of his pocket. 'Alec, I would reason with you.'

It was a glorious morning at the beginning of September. The two men had managed after all to put in a couple of hours' fishing in the little trout-stream which ran through the bottom of the Grierson's estate, in spite of Roger's lingering over his kedgeree and kidneys. Twenty minutes ago they had broken off for the lunch of sandwiches and weak whisky-and-water which they had brought with them, and these having now been despatched Roger was feeling disposed to talk.

For once in a while Alec was not unwilling to encourage him. 'About the Bentley case?' he said. 'Yes, I've been meaning to ask you about that. What've you got up your sleeve?'

'Oh, nothing up my sleeve,' Roger said, cramming tobacco into the enormous bowl of his short-stemmed pipe. 'Nothing as definite as that. But I must say I am most infernally interested in the case, and there's one thing about it that strikes me very forcibly. Look here, would it bore you if I ran through the whole thing and reviewed all the evidence? I've got it all at my fingers' tips, and it would help to clarify it in our minds, I think. Just facts. I mean, without all the prejudice.'

'Not a bit,' Alec agreed readily. 'We've got half an hour to smoke our pipes in anyhow, before we want to get going again.'

'I think you might have put it a little better than that,' Roger said with reproach. 'However! Now let me see, what's the beginning of the story? The Bentley *ménage*, I suppose. No, further back than that. Wait a minute, I've got some notes here.'

6

He plunged his hand into the breast-pocket of the very disreputable, very comfortable sports' coat he was wearing and drew out a small note-book, which he proceeded to study for a minute or two.

'Yes. We'd better go over the man's whole life, I think. Well, John Bentley was the eldest of three brothers, and at the time of his death he was forty-one years old. At the age of eighteen he entered his father's business of general import and export merchants, specialising in machine-tools, and spent six years in the London office. When he was twenty-four his father sent him over to France to take charge of a small branch which was being opened in Paris, and he remained there for twelve years, including the period of the war, in which he was not called upon to serve. During that time he had married, at the age of thirty-four, a Mademoiselle Jacqueline Monjalon, the daughter of a Parisian business acquaintance, since dead; his bride was only eighteen years old. Is that all clear?'

'Most lucid,' said Alec, puffing at his pipe.

'Two years after his marriage, Bentley was recalled to London by his father to assume gradual control of the whole business, which was then in a very flourishing condition, and this he proceeded to do. There was another brother in the business, the second one; but this gentleman had not been able to elude his duties to his country and had been conscripted in 1916, subsequently serving for eighteen months in France till badly wounded in the final push. From a certain wildness which I seem to trace in some of his statements to the press and else-where, I should diagnose a dose of shell-shock as well.'

'Diagnosis granted,' Alex agreed: 'I noticed that. Hysterical kind of ass, I thought. Go on.'

'Well, when our couple returned from France, they bought a large and comfortable house in the town of Wychford, which lies about fifteen miles south-east of London and possesses an excellent train-service for the tired businessman. Thence, of course, friend John would travel up to town every day except

Saturdays, a day on which nobody above the rank of assistant-manager dare show his face in the streets of London or everybody would think his firm is going bankrupt: remember that if you ever go into business, Alec.'

'Thanks, I will.'

'Well, eighteen months after the Bentley's arrival in England, the father, instead of retiring from work in the ordinary way, makes a better job of it and dies, leaving the business to the two sons who are in it, in the proportion of two-thirds to John and one-third to William, the second son. To the third son, Alfred, he left most of the residue of his estate, which amounted in value to much the same as William's share of the business. John, then, who seems to have been the old man's favourite, came off very decidedly the best of the three. John therefore picked up the reins of the business and for the next three years all went well. Not quite so well as it had done, because John wasn't the man his father had been; still, well enough. So much, I think, for the family history. Got all that?'

Alec nodded. 'Yes, I knew most of that before, I think.'

'So now we come from the general to the particular. In other words, to the Bentley *ménage*. Now, have you formed any estimate of the characters of these two, *Monsieur* and *Madame*? Could you give me a short character-sketch of Bentley himself, for instance?'

'No, I'm blessed if I could. I was concentrating on the facts, not the characters.'

Roger shook his head reprovingly. 'A great mistake, Alexander; a great mistake. What do you think it is that makes any great murder case so absorbingly interesting? Not the sordid facts in themselves. No, it's the psychology of the people concerned; the character of the criminal, the character of the victim, their reactions to violence, what they felt and thought and suffered over it all. The circumstances of the case, the methods of the murderer, the reasons for the murder, the steps he takes to elude detection—all these arise directly out of character; in themselves they're only secondary. Facts, you might say, depend on psychology. What was it that made the Thompson-Bywaters case so extraordinarily interesting? Not the mere facts. It was the characters of the three protagonists. Take away the psychology of that case and you get just a sordid triangle of the most trite and uninteresting description. Add it, and you get what the film-producers call a drama packed with human interest. Just the same with the Seddon case, Crippen, or, to become criminologically classical, William Palmer. A grave error, my Alexander; a very grave error indeed.'

'Sorry; I seem to have said the wrong thing. All right. What about the psychology of the Bentleys, then?'

'Well, John Bentley seems to emerge to me as a fussy, rather irritating little man, very pleased with himself and continually worrying about his health; probably a bit of a hypochondriac. Reading between the lines, I don't think brother William got on at all well with him—no doubt because he was much the same sort of fellow himself. It doesn't need any reading between the lines to see that his wife didn't. She appears as a happy, gay little creature, not overburdened with brains but certainly not deficient in them, always wanting to go out somewhere and enjoy herself, theatres, dance-clubs, car-rides, parties, any old thing. Well, just imagine the two of them together—and remember that she's sixteen years younger than her husband. She wants to go to a dance, he won't take her because it would interfere with his regular eight-hours' sleep; she wants to go to a race-meeting, he thinks standing about in the open air would give him a cold; she wants to go to the theatre, he thinks the man in the next seat might be carrying influenza germs. Of course the inevitable happens. She gets somebody else to take her.'

'Ah!' observed Alec wisely. 'Allen!'

'Exactly! Allen. Well, that's where the facts of the case proper seem to begin; with that weekend Mrs Bentley spent with Allen at the Bischroma Hotel.'

'Now we're getting to it.'

Roger paused to re-light his pipe, which had gone out under the flood of this eloquence.

'Now,' he agreed, 'we're getting to it. That was on the 27th of June; Mrs Bentley going home to Wychford again on the 29th and telling her husband that she'd been staying with a girl friend of hers from Paris. Bentley doesn't seem to have suspected anything: which is what one might expect with that complacent, self-centred little type. But he has got his doubts about Allen. Allen's name crops up in the conversation that same night, we learn from brother William, who was staying in the house for the whole summer, and Bentley forbids his wife to have anything more to do with the chap. Madame laughs at him and asks if he's jealous.'

'The nerve of her!'

'Oh, quite natural, in the circumstances. He says he's not jealous in the least, thank you, but he's just given her his instructions and will she be kind enough to see that they are carried out (can't you just *see* him at it!) Madame, ceasing to laugh, tells him not to be an ass. Bentley retorts suitably. Anyhow, the upshot is that they have a blazing row, all in front of brother William, and Madame flies upstairs, chattering with fury, to pack her bag for France that very minute.'

'Pity she didn't!'

'I agree. Brother William steps in, however, and persuades her to stay that night at any rate, and in the morning he gets in a Mrs Saunderson from down the same road, with whom Mrs Bentley has been getting very pally during the last couple of years, and she manages to pacify the lady to such an extent that there is a grand reconciliation scene that same evening, with John and Jacqueline in the centre surrounded by the triumphant beams of Brother William and Mrs Saunderson. That was on June the 29th. On July the 1st Mrs Bentley buys two dozen arsenical fly-papers from a chemist in Wychford.'

'Well, you must admit that's suspicious, at any rate.'

'Oh, I do. Suspicious isn't the word. The parlourmaid, Mary

Blower, and the housemaid, Nellie Green, both see these fly-papers soaking in three saucers during the next two days in Mrs Bentley's bedroom. There had never been fly-papers of that kind in the house before, and they were not a little intrigued about them; Mary Blower especially, as we shall see later. That same day Bentley, fussing as usual over his health, goes to see his doctor in Wychford, Dr James, and gets himself thoroughly over-hauled. Dr James tells him that he's a little run down (the stock comment for people of that kind), but that there's nothing constitutionally wrong with him; he gives the man a bottle of medicine to keep him quiet, a mild tonic, mostly iron. Four days later, on a Sunday, Bentley complains at breakfast that he's not feeling up to the mark. William tells us with a properly shocked air that Mrs Bentley received this information callously and told him straight out that there was nothing the matter with him; but really, the poor lady must have heard the same thing at so many breakfasts before that one can understand her not being exactly prostrated by it. In any case, he's not feeling so bad that he can't go out for a picnic that same afternoon with her and William, and Mr and Mrs Allen.'

'Having climbed down over the Allen business, apparently,' Alec commented.

'Yes. But of course he had to. With the possible exception of Mrs Saunderson, the Allens were their closest friends in Wychford. Unless he wanted to precipitate an open scandal, he couldn't maintain his stand about Allen. To do so would be tantamount to informing Mrs Allen that, in Bentley's opinion, her husband was in danger of becoming unfaithful to her. One's sympathies are certainly with Bentley there; the position was a very nasty one for him. And I can't imagine him liking the man much. They must have been complete opposites, mustn't they? Bentley, fussy, peevish, and on the small side; Allen, big, breezy, hearty, strong, and packed with self-confidence—or so I read him. Yes, I can quite understand Bentley's uneasiness about friend Allen just about that time.'

'And Mrs Allen didn't know her husband was taking Mrs Bentley out all this time?'

'So I should imagine. She probably guessed he was taking somebody out, but not that it was Mrs Bentley. I can't quite get Mrs Allen. She seemed perfectly calm, even icy, in the police-court; and probably her deliberate manner did Mrs Bentley actually more harm than Mrs Saunderson's hysteria. She is the wronged wife, you see, and she's certainly investing an igno-minious rôle with a good deal of quiet dignity. Mrs Saunderson's the person who appears to me to emerge worse than anybody else in the whole case; she seems really rancorous against her late best friend. What inhuman brutes some of these women can be to each other, when one of them's properly up against it! However. Well, Bentley comes back from the picnic complaining that he feels a good deal worse and goes straight to bed, where shortly afterwards he is very sick. He attributes his trouble to sitting about on damp grass at the picnic; the police say that it followed the first administration to him by his wife of the solution of arsenic obtained from the fly-papers.'

'Um!' said Alec thoughtfully.

'He passed a fairly good night, but stayed in bed during the next day though feeling decidedly better. Dr James called in during the morning and, after a thorough examination, came to the conclusion that the man was a chronic dyspeptic. He changed his medicine and gave instructions about his diet, and the next day, Tuesday, Bentley was well enough to go back to business. That same night Mrs Bentley went with Allen to the Four Arts Ball at Covent Garden, the last big public event of the season, going back with him afterwards to the Bischroma again. The evidence of the proprietor, Mr Nume, is quite conclu-sive on that point.'

'Bit risky, after the last row.'

'Oh, yes, risky enough. But as I see Madame Bentley at that time (leaving the question of her subsequent guilt or innocence out of it for the moment), she just didn't care a rap what happened. We don't know whether she was really in love with Allen or not, but we do know that her middle-aged husband not only bored her, but irritated her as well; and in these circumstances a woman is simply ripe for madness. The effects of the late reconciliation had probably quite worn off, and she simply didn't mind whether she were found out or not. Quite possibly she hoped she would be, so that Bentley would divorce her and give her her freedom. There were no children to complicate things, you see.'

'Might be something in that,' Alec admitted.

'Well, after that matters begin to move swiftly. There's a blazing row when she gets back the next day, and this time Bentley loses his head altogether, knocks her down and gives her a black eye. Again Madame flies upstairs to pack for France, again brother William and Mrs Saunderson intervene in the rôle of good angels, and again the quarrel is patched up somehow or other. Madame Bentley stays at home. That is Wednesday. Bentley has been to his office that day, and he goes on Thursday too, this time taking in a thermos flask some food specially prepared for him by Mrs Bentley herself. He left the flask there, as you know; the residue inside was subsequently analysed and it was found to contain arsenic.'

'How is she going to get over that?'

'How, indeed? That's just what I'm wondering. On this day, Thursday, Bentley's younger brother, Alfred, calls in during the morning and Bentley tells him that, in consequence of his wife's behaviour, he is altering his will, leaving her only a bare pittance; nearly the whole of his estate, which consisted chiefly of his holding in the business, he is dividing between his two brothers—not much to William, because he and William don't get on very well, by far the greater share to Alfred himself. On his death, therefore, Alfred will own the larger holding in the business, although he has never been in it and William has been there all his life.'

'Yes, I saw that. Why on earth did he do that?'

'Well, it's obvious enough. Bentley, though a big enough fool in private life, wasn't so in business at all. William, on the other hand, was, and Bentley knew it. Once let the business get into William's full control, and in no time it would go pop. Alfred, on the contrary, is a very different sort of fellow—very different from both his brothers. His character strikes me as more like that of a Scotch elder than a member of the Bentley family—dour, stern, uncompromising, hard and not far removed from cruel; also a bit, if I'm not wrong, on the avaricious side. An amazing contrast. Anyhow, there can't be a better way of throwing light on his character than by reminding you that as soon as he heard this news, prudent brother Alfred took his brother off to a solicitor there and then that very morning and stood over him while the new will was drawn up! Oh, a very canny man, brother Alfred.'

'I think I prefer him to Bentley himself though, for all that.'

'That's the Scotch strain in you coming out, Alec; you recognise a fellow-feeling for brother Alfred, no doubt. Well, and so we come to Bentley's last illness and death. Do you want to break off here and go on tickling the trout?'

'No!' said Alec surprisingly. 'It's rather interesting to hear the whole thing like this in one connected whole instead of in snippets; though what you're getting at I'm hanged if I can see. Carry on!'

'Alec,' said Roger with emotion, 'this is the most remarkable tribute I have ever had in the course of a long and successful career.'

CHAPTER III

MR SHERINGHAM ASKS WHY

'THE next day,' Roger continued after a short pause, 'Friday, the 10th of July, Bentley felt too ill in the morning to go to work. He complained of pains in the leg, and was vomiting. Dr James was called in and prescribed for him. The next day the pains had disappeared, but the vomiting continued, which Dr James attributed to the morphia he had given him on the previous day. On the Sunday he was a little better; on the Monday a little better still. On the next day Dr James expected him to be almost recovered, but instead of this a slight relapse set in and, on Mrs Bentley's suggestion, another doctor was called in, Dr Peters. Dr Peters also diagnosed acute dyspepsia, and gave the patient a sedative. On the Wednesday he was no better.

'Now this day, the 15th of July, is a very important one indeed, and we must examine it in some detail. It was in the course of this day that the idea was first mooted that all was not as it should be.

'All this time Mrs Allen and Mrs Saunderson had been continually in and out of the house, while Mrs Bentley was nursing her husband—doing the household shopping for her, running errands, giving advice and generally fussing round. On this evening Mary Blower (who seems to have a grudge of some sort against her mistress) told Mrs Saunderson of the fly-papers she had seen soaking a fortnight before. Mrs Saunderson, twittering with excitement, tells Mrs Allen, and in three minutes these two excellent ladies have decided that Mrs Bentley is poisoning her husband. And since that time not a single person seems to have had the least doubt of it. Off goes Mrs Saunderson to telephone brother William at the office and tell him to come

15

back to Wychford at once, while Mrs Allen runs round to the post-office to send a mysterious telegram to brother Alfred. Of all this Mrs Bentley, of course, remains in complete ignorance. Late in the morning the brothers arrive, and you can imagine the seething excitement.

'In the meantime, Mrs Bentley has decided that she can't go on nursing her husband alone and has telegraphed for a nurse, who arrived just after lunch. Brother Alfred, who already seems to have assumed entire control of the household, takes the nurse aside at once and tells her that nobody but herself is to administer anything to the patient, as they have reason to believe that something mysterious is going on. With the consequence that we now have a twittering nurse as well as twittering friends and twittering brothers. In fact, the only person in the house just at that time who does not seem to have been twittering is Mrs Bentley herself.

'But there's more excitement to come. During the afternoon Mrs Bentley handed a letter to Mary Blower and asked her to run out to the post with it. Mary Blower looks at the address and sees that it is to Mr Allen, who was at this time away from Wychford on business in Bristol. Instead of posting it, she hands it over to Mrs Allen, who promptly opens it. And then the fat was in the fire with a vengeance, for Mrs Bentley had not only been idiot enough to make reference to their weekend at the Bischroma, but she had mentioned her husband's illness in terms that certainly weren't very sympathetic—though it's more than possible that she didn't then realise the serious state he was in.

'Anyhow, coming after the fly-papers revelation, that was enough for the four. Where there had been any possibility of doubt before, there was none now. Brother Alfred put on his hat at once, went round to the two doctors and told them both the whole story. The three of them held a council of war, and decided that Mrs Bentley must be watched continuously.

'Well, that was bad enough, but there was still another piece of news waiting for brother Alfred when he got back, and that certainly is the most damning thing of all. The nurse had come down a short time ago with a bottle of Bovril in her hand and explained that she had seen Mrs Bentley pick it up in a surreptitious way and convey it out of the bedroom, hiding it in the folds of her frock; a few minutes later she brought it back and replaced it, when she thought the nurse's back was turned, in the exact spot from which she had taken it. That bottle was handed over to the doctors next day and was subsequently found to contain arsenic.'

'Well, that I *am* dashed if you can get over!' Alec observed.

'It isn't for me to get over it,' pointed out Roger mildly. 'I'm not saying the woman *is* innocent. All I say is that we ought to bear the possibility of her innocence in mind, and not assume her guilt as a matter of course. In any case I am most uncommonly interested to hear what she's got to say about that particular incident. Well, up to this time, you've got to remember, Bentley's condition, though serious, wasn't considered to be in any way dangerous (which does go a long way to explain the somewhat flippant tone of Mrs Bentley's letter to Allen that has helped to create so much prejudice against her); but that same night things took a very rapid turn for the worse. Both doctors were hurriedly summoned, and they were with him all night. By the next morning Mrs Bentley and the others were warned that there could be very little hope for him, at midday he became unconscious and at seven o'clock in the evening he died.

'But that wasn't all. Mrs Bentley had been removed at once, by brother Alfred's orders, to her own bedroom, where she was kept practically a prisoner, and the other four immediately began a systematic search of the whole place. Their efforts were not unrewarded. In Bentley's dressing-room there stood a trunk belonging to his wife. In the tray of this was a medicine bottle containing, as shown later, a very strong solution of arsenic in lemonade, together with a handkerchief belonging to Mrs Bentley which was also impregnated with arsenic. In a medicine-chest were the remains of the bottles of medicine prescribed by Dr James (two) and Dr Peters (one). None of these prescriptions contained arsenic, but arsenic was subsequently discovered in each bottle in appreciable quantities. And lastly, in a locked drawer in Mrs Bentley's own bedroom there was found a small packet containing no less than two whole ounces of pure arsenic—actually enough to kill more than a couple of hundred people! And that was that.'

'I should say it was!' Alec agreed.

'Of course the doctors refused a death-certificate. The police were called in, and Mrs Bentley was promptly arrested. Two days later a post-mortem was held. There was no doubt about the cause of death. The stomach and the rest of it were badly inflamed. Death due to inflammation of the stomach and intestines set up by an irritant poison—which in this case was the medical way of saying death from arsenical poisoning. The usual parts of the body were removed and placed in sealed jars for examination by the Government analyst. You read the result this morning in his evidence before the magistrates—at least three grains of arsenic in the body at the time of death, or half a grain more than the ordinary fatal dose, meaning that shortly before death there must have been a good deal more still; arsenic in the stomach, intestines, liver, kidneys, everywhere! And also, significant in another way, arsenic in the skin, nails and hair; and that means that arsenic must have been administered some considerable time ago—a fortnight, for instance, or about the time of that picnic. Is it any wonder that the coroner's jury brought in a verdict tantamount to wilful murder against Mrs Bentley, or that the magistrates have committed her for trial?'

'It is not!' said Alec with decision. 'They'd have been imbeciles if they hadn't.'

'Quite so,' said Roger. 'Exactly.' And he began to smoke very thoughtfully indeed.

There was a little pause.

'Come on,' said Alec. 'You know you've got something up your sleeve.'

'Oh, no. I've got nothing up my sleeve.'

'Well, there's something in your mind, then. Let's have it!'

Roger took his pipe out of his mouth and pointed the short stem at his companion as if to drive his next remark home with it. 'There *is* a question that I can't find an answer to,' he said slowly, 'and it's this—why the devil so much arsenic?'

'So much?'

'Yes. Why enough to kill a couple of hundred people when there's only one to be killed? *Why*? It isn't natural.'

Alec pondered. 'Well, surely there might be two or three explanations of that. She wanted to make sure of the job. She didn't know what the fatal dose was. She—'

'Oh, yes; there are two or three explanations. But not one of them is the least bit convincing. You don't think people go in for poisoning without finding out what the fatal dose is, do you? Poisoning is a deliberate, cold-blooded job. Such a simple measure as looking up the fatal dose in any encyclopædia or medical reference book would be the very first step.'

'Um?' said Alec, not particularly impressed.

'And then there's another thing. Why in the name of all that's holy buy fly-papers when there's all that amount of arsenic in the house already?'

'But perhaps there wasn't,' Alec retorted quickly. 'Perhaps she got the other arsenic after the fly-papers.'

'Well, suppose she did. The same objection applies just as well. Why buy all that amount of arsenic when she'd already got half a dozen fatal doses out of the fly-papers? And once more, I haven't seen any police evidence offered to prove that Mrs Bentley did buy that arsenic. It's proved to have been in her possession, but it hasn't been shown how it came there. The police seem to be taking it completely for granted that as she had it, it must have been she who bought it.'

'Is that very important?'

'I should have said, vitally! No, look at it how you like, the question of this superabundance of arsenic does *not* simplify the case, as everybody seems to have assumed; in my opinion it infernally complicates it.'

'It is interesting,' Alec admitted. 'I'd never looked on it like that before. What do you make of it, then?'

'Well, there seem to me only two possible deductions. Either Mrs Bentley is the most imbecile criminal who ever existed and simply went out of her way to manufacture the most damning evidence against herself—which, having formed my own opinion of her character, I am most unwilling to believe. Or else—!' He paused and rammed down a few straggling ends of tobacco into the bowl of his pipe.

'Yes?' Alec asked with interest. 'Or else what?'

Roger looked up suddenly. 'Why, or else that she didn't murder her husband at all!' he said equably.

'But my dear chap!' Alec was compelled to protest. 'How on earth do you make that out?'

Roger folded his arms and fixed an unseeing gaze on the meadow on the other side of the little stream.

'There's too much evidence!' he began in an argumentative voice. 'A jolly sight too much. It's all too cut and dried. Now somebody manufactured that evidence, didn't they? Do you mean to tell me that Mrs Bentley deliberately manufactured it herself?'

'Well,' said Alec doubtfully. 'that's all very well, but who else could have done.'

'The real criminal.'

'But Mrs Bentley being the real criminal—!'

'Now, look here, Alec, do try and clear your mind of prejudice for the moment. Let's take it that we're not sure whether Mrs Bentley is guilty or innocent. No, let's go a step further and assume for the moment her complete innocence, and argue on that basis. What do we get? That somebody else poisoned Bentley; that this somebody else wished Mrs Bentley not only to be accused of the crime but also, apparently, to suffer for it; and that this somebody therefore laid a careful train of the most convincing and damning evidence to lead to the speedy and complete undoing of Mrs Bentley. Now that gives us something to think about, doesn't it? And take into consideration at the same time the fact that not only was Mrs Bentley to be disposed of in this way, but Bentley himself as well. In other words, this mysterious unknown had a motive for getting rid of Mr just as much as Mrs Bentley; whether one more than the other we can't yet say, but certainly both. And the plot was an ingenious one; the very fact of getting rid of the second clears the perpetrator of all suspicion of getting rid of the first, you see. Oh, yes, there's a lot to think about here.'

'You're going too fast,' Alec complained. 'What about the evidence?'

'Yes, the evidence. Well, assuming still that Mrs Bentley is innocent, she'll have an explanation of some sort for the evidence. But unless I'm very much mistaken, it's going to be a not particularly convincing one and quite incapable of proof— the mysterious unknown, we know, has quite enough cunning to have made sure of that. In fact we now arrive at a positively delightful anomaly—if Mrs Bentley's explanations by any chance do carry conviction, I should say she is probably guilty; if they're feeble and childish, I shall be morally sure of her innocence!'

'Good Lord, what an extraordinary chap you are!' Alec groaned. 'How in the world do you get that?'

'I should have thought it was quite clear. If they're feeble and childish, it'll probably be because they're true (you've no idea how frightfully unconvincing the truth can very often be, my dear Alexander); whereas, if they're glib and pat, it'll certainly point to their having been prepared beforehand. Once more I repeat—poisoning is a deliberate and cold-blooded business. The criminal doesn't leave his explanations to the spur of the moment when the police tap him on the shoulder and ask him what about it; he has it all very carefully worked out in advance, with chapter and verse to support it too. That's why poisoning trials are always twice as long as those for murder by violence; because there's so much more difficulty in bringing his guilt home to the criminal. And that, in turn, is not because poison in itself is a more subtle means of murder, but because the kind of person who has recourse to it is, in seven cases out of ten, a careful, painstaking and clever individual. Of course you do get plenty of mentally unbalanced people using it too, like Pritchard or Lamson, but they're rather the exceptions than the rule. The cold, hard, calculating type, Seddon, Armstrong, that kind of man, is the real natural poisoner. Crippen, by the way, was a poisoner by force of circumstances; but then he's an exception to every rule that you could possibly formulate. I'm always very sorry for Crippen. If ever a woman deserved murdering, Cora Crippen did, and it's my opinion that Crippen killed her because he was a coward; she had established a complete tyranny over him, and he simply hadn't got the moral courage to run away from her. That, and the fact that she had got control of all his savings, of course, as Mr Filson Young has very interestingly pointed out. An extraordinarily absorbing case from the psychological standpoint, Alexander. One day I must go into it with you at the length it deserves.'

'Lord!' was Alec's comment on this first lesson in criminology. 'How you do gas!'

'That's as may be,' said Roger, and betook himself to his pipe again.

'Well, what about it all?' Alec asked a minute or two later. 'What do you want to do about it?'

Roger paused for a moment. 'It's a nice little puzzle, isn't it?' he said, more as if speaking his thoughts aloud than answering the other question. 'It'd be nice to unearth the truth and prove everybody else in the whole blessed country wrong—always providing that there is any more truth to unearth. In any case, it's a pretty little whetstone to sharpen one's wits on. Yes.'

'What do you want to do?' Alec repeated patiently.

'Take it up, Alexander!' Roger replied this time, with an air of briskness. 'Take it up and pull it about and scrabble into it and generally turn it upside down and shake it till something drops out; that's what I've a jolly good mind to do.'

'But there'll be people doing that for her in any case,' Alec objected. 'Solicitors and so on. They'll be looking after her defence, if that's what you mean.'

'Yes, that is so, of course. But supposing her solicitors and so on are just as convinced of her guilt as everybody else is. It's going to be a pretty half-hearted sort of defence in that case, isn't it? And supposing none of them has the gumption to realise that it's no good basing their defence just on explanations of the existing evidence—that their client is going to be hanged on that as sure as God made little apples—that if they want to save her they've got to dig and ferret out *new* evidence! Supposing all that, friend Alec.'

'Well? Supposing it?'

'Then in that case it seems to me that somebody like us is pretty badly needed. Dash it all, they have detectives to ferret out things for the prosecution, don't they? Well, why not for the defence? Of course, her solicitors may be clever men; they may be going to do all this and employ detectives off their own bat. But I doubt it, Alexander; I can't help doubting it very much indeed. Anyhow, that's what I'm going to be—honorary detective for the defence. I appoint myself on probation, pending confirmation in writing. Now then, Alec—what about coming in with me?'

'I'm game enough,' Alec replied without hesitation. 'When do we start?'

'Well, let's see; the assizes come on in about six weeks' time, I think the paper said. We shall want to get finished at least a fortnight before that. That gives us a month. I don't think we ought to waste any time. What about pushing off tomorrow morning?'

'Right-ho! But what I want to know is, what exactly are we going to *do*?'

'My dear chap, I haven't the least idea! Whatever happens to occur to us. We shall have to make a bee-line for Wychford, of course, and the first thing we shall want to know is what the defence is to be. That's going to take a bit of finding out too, by the way; but I don't see that we can take up any definite line until we've heard Mrs Bentley's story. I'll try and hammer out a plan of some kind in the meantime. And Alec!'

'Yes?'

'For heaven's sake do try and give me a little more encouragement over this affair than you did at Layton Court!'

CHAPTER IV

ARRIVAL AT WYCHFORD

'I've had one brain-wave at any rate, Alec,' Roger remarked, settling himself comfortably in the corner of the first-class smoker and hoisting his feet on to the seat opposite.

Alec had just brought the upper part of his body into the carriage after bidding goodbye to a frankly derisive Barbara, and was now lifting their suitcases on to the rack as the train gathered speed—that same half-past ten train, by the way, to which Roger's attention had been called on the previous morning.

'Oh?' he said. 'What's that?'

'Why, the editor of the *Daily Courier* is by way of being rather a pal of mine. I'm going to call round there on our way through London to ask him if he'll take me on as unofficial special correspondent.'

'Are you?' Alec asked, dropping into his seat. 'What's the idea of that?'

'Well, it occurred to me that we shall be in rather a more favourable position for ramming our way into the heart of things if we've got the weight of the *Courier* behind us than if we just show up as two independent and vulgarly curious gentlemen on their own. The *Courier*'s name ought to help loosen a hesitating tongue quite a lot. Oh, and by the way, here's something for you, a list of the important dates in the case that I typed out last night. I've got a copy for myself; you can keep that.'

Alec took the paper which Roger was holding out to him and examined it. It was inscribed as follows:

DATES IN THE CASE

June 27 Saturday	Mrs Bentley stays with Allen.
June 29 Monday	Mrs Bentley goes home again. Quarrel.
July 1 Wednesday	Mrs Bentley buys fly-papers.
July 5 Sunday	Picnic. Bentley first taken ill.
July 6 Monday	Bentley better, but stays in bed.
July 7 Tuesday	Bentley back to business. Mrs Bentley to Four Arts Ball, and stays with Allen.
July 8 Wednesday	Mrs Bentley goes home. Quarrel, and Mrs Bentley is knocked down.
July 9 Thursday	Bentley takes flask down to office, subsequently found to contain arsenic. Makes new will in Alfred's favour.
July 10 Friday	Bentley taken ill for a second time.
July 11 Saturday	Bentley much the same.
July 12 Sunday	Bentley slightly better.
July 13 Monday	Bentley better still.
July 14 Tuesday	Bentley has a slight relapse. Second doctor called in.
July 15 Wednesday	Bentley's condition unchanged. Mrs Bentley's letter to Allen intercepted. Nurse arrives. Episode of the Bovril. Bentley taken much worse in evening.
July 16 Thursday	Bentley dies. Search of Mrs Bentley's effects and large quantity of arsenic discovered. Doctors refuse death certificate.
July 17 Friday	Mrs Bentley arrested.

'Thanks,' said Alec, tucking the paper away in his pocket. 'Yes, that'll be useful. Now then, what are you going to do about finding out the lines of Mrs Bentley's defence, as you said?'

'Well, I shall take the bull by the horns; go straight to her solicitor, tell him who I am and simply ask him.'

'Humph!' said Alec doubtfully. 'Not likely to get much change there, are you? Not a solicitor who knows his job.'

'No, none at all. I don't expect him to tell me for a minute. But I do expect to be able to catch a glimpse of a word or two between the lines. Anyhow, my name ought to be enough to stop them kicking me point-blank out of the door; they will do it politely at any rate. If they ever have heard of me, that is—which I hope and pray!'

'Yes, there are advantages in being a best-seller, no doubt. How many editions has the latest run through now?'

'*Pamela Alive*? Seven, in five weeks. Thanking you kindly. Bought your copy yet?'

The conversation became personal. Very personal.

Arrived at Waterloo a couple of hours later, Roger gave brisk directions. 'You take the cases along to Charing Cross and put them in the cloakroom, look up a train for Wychford sometime about three o'clock, and then come along and pick me up at the *Courier* office in Fleet Street. I'm going to get through on the 'phone right away and stop Burgoyne going out to lunch till I've seen him, and I'll wait for you there. Then we can have a spot of lunch at Simpson's or the Cock, and go on to Charing Cross afterwards. So long!'

They separated on the platform and Roger hurried off to telephone. Burgoyne was in and he made an appointment with him for ten minutes' time. Jumping into a taxi, he was carried swiftly over Waterloo Bridge and down Fleet Street, arriving in the Great Man's office with exactly fifteen seconds to spare. Roger rather liked that sort of thing.

It was not Roger's intention to give any hint, either to Burgoyne himself or to anyone else, of his theory that Mrs Bentley might possibly be the victim of somebody else's plot rather than the contriver of one of her own making. For one thing it was more of a suspicion than a theory, and his arguments to Alec, interesting though he had made them sound, had been delivered more with the idea of clarifying his own mind on the matter than of stating an actual case. For another thing he preferred, should anything eventually come of this surprising notion, to keep himself the only one in the field. His words to Burgoyne were therefore chosen with some care.

'This Wychford case,' he said, when they had shaken hands. 'Interesting, isn't it?'

'It's been a God-send to us, I can tell you,' Burgoyne smiled. 'Carried us all through August, thank heaven. Interesting, is it? Well, I suppose it is in a way. Going to write a book about it, eh?'

'Well, I might,' Roger said seriously. 'At any rate, I want to have a look at it at close quarters. That's what I've come to see you about. You know I'm a keen criminologist, and on top of that the case is simply packed with human interest. Those Allens! There are half a dozen characters down there I'd like to study. Well, what I want to ask you is this. Can I use the *Courier*'s name as an inducement for them to open their mouths to me? Can you appoint me honorary special correspondent, or something like that? You know I won't abuse it, and I'd really be awfully grateful.'

But Burgoyne was not editor of the *Courier* for nothing. He was a wise man.

'You've got something up your sleeve, Sheringham,' he grinned. 'I can see that with half an eye. No—don't trouble to perjure yourself! I see you don't want to talk about it, so I'm not asking. Yes, you can use the *Courier*'s name all right. On one condition.'

'Yes?' Roger asked, not without apprehension.

'That if you find out anything (and that's what I take it you're really going down for: good lord, man, haven't I heard you expounding theories on detective-work and the rest of it by the half-mile at a time?)—if you *do* find out anything, you give us the first option on printing it. At your usual rates, needless to say.'

'Great Scott, yes—rather! Only too pleased. But don't expect anything, Burgoyne. I don't mind admitting that I *am* going to nose around a bit when I get there, but I'm really only going down out of sheer interest in the case. The psychology—'

'Write it to me, old man,' advised Burgoyne. 'Sorry, but I'm up to the eyes as usual, and you've had your two minutes. Don't mind, do you? That's all right, then. You chuck our name about as much as you like, and in return you give us first chance on any stuff you write about the case and so on. Good enough. So long, old man; so long.' And Roger found himself being warmly hand-shaken into the passage outside. There were few people who could deal with Roger, but the editor of the *Courier* was certainly one of them.

Alec was waiting in the vestibule downstairs, and together they left the building, Roger recounting the success of his mission with considerable jubilation.

'Yes, that's going to help us a lot,' he said, as they marched down Fleet Street. 'There's nothing like the hope of seeing your name in a paper like the *Courier* to make a certain type of person talk. And I have a pretty shrewd idea that both brother William and Mrs Saunderson are just that type, to say nothing of the unpleasant domestic, Mary Blower.'

'But won't the *Courier* have had their own man down there all this time?'

'Oh, yes; but that doesn't matter in the least. He won't have asked the questions that I want to ask. Besides,' Roger added modestly, 'there's another factor in our favour for worming our way into people's good graces. I hate to keep on reminding you of it, Alexander, but you really are rather inclined to overlook it, you know.'

'Oh? What's that?'

'The fact that I'm Roger Sheringham,' said that unblushing novelist simply.

Alec's reply verged regrettably upon crudity. One gathered that Alec was lamentably lacking in a proper respect for his distinguished companion.

'That's the worst of making oneself so cheap,' sighed Roger, as they turned into their destination. 'If a man is never a hero to his valet, what is he to his fat-headed friends?'

After a thick slab of red steak and a pint of old beer apiece they hailed a taxi and were driven to Charing Cross.

'Do you know Wychford at all?' Alec asked when they were seated in the train once again, with a carriage to themselves.

'Just vaguely. I've motored through it, you know.'

'Um!'

'Why, do you?'

'Yes, pretty well. I stayed there for a week once when I was a kid.'

'Good Lord, why didn't you tell me that before? You don't know anybody there, do you?'

'Yes, I've got a cousin living there.'

'Really, Alec!' Roger exclaimed with not unjustifiable exasperation. 'You are the most reticent devil I've ever struck. I have to dig things out of you with a pin. Don't you see how important this is?'

'No,' said Alec frankly.

'Why, your cousin may be able to give us all sorts of useful introductions, besides being able to tell us the local gossip and all sorts of things like that. For goodness' sake open your mouth and tell me all about it. What sort of a place is Wychford? Does your cousin live in the town itself, or outside it? What can you remember about Wychford?'

Alec considered. 'Well, it's a pretty big place, you know. I suppose it's much the same as any other pretty big place. Lots of sets and cliques and all that sort of thing. My cousin lives pretty well in the middle, in the High Street. She married a doctor there. Nice old house they've got, red brick and gables and all that. Just before you get to the pond on the right, coming from London. You remember that pond, at the top of the High Street?'

'Yes, I think so. Married a doctor, did she? That's great. We'll be able to have a look at the medical evidence from the inside, you see, if we want to. What's the doctor's name, by the way?'

'Purefoy. Dr Purefoy. She's Mrs Purefoy,' he added helpfully.

'Yes, I gathered something like that. Not one of the doctors in the case. All right; go on.'

'Well, that's about all, isn't it?'

'It's all I shall be able to get out of *you*, Alec,' Roger grumbled. 'That's quite evident. What taciturn devils you semi-Scotch people are! You're worse than the real thing.'

'You ought to be thankful,' Alec grinned. 'There's not much room for the chatty sort when you're anywhere around, is there?'

'I disdain to reply to your crude witticisms, Alexander,' replied Roger with dignity, and went on to reply to them at considerable length.

His harangue was still in full swing when the train stopped at Wychford, and the poorly disguised relief with which Alec hailed their arrival at that station very nearly set him off again. Suppressing with an effort the expression of his feelings, he joined Alec in following the porter with their belongings. They mounted an elderly taxi of almost terrifying instability, and were driven, for a perfectly exorbitant consideration, to the Man of Kent, a hotel which the driver of the elderly taxi was able to recommend with confidence as the best in the town; certainly it was the farthest from the station.

The business of engaging rooms and unpacking their belongings occupied some little time, and Roger ordered tea in the lounge before setting out. Over the meal he expounded the opening of his plan of campaign.

'There's nothing like going straight to the fountain-head,' he said. 'Nobody in Wychford can tell us so much of what we want to know as Mrs Bentley's solicitors, so to Mrs Bentley's solicitors I'm going first of all.'

'How are you going to find out who they are? Bound to be several solicitors in a place this size.'

'That simple point,' Roger said not without pride, 'I have already attended to. Three minutes' conversation with the chambermaid gave me the information I wanted.'

'I see. What do you want me to do? Come with you, or stay here?'

'Neither. I want you to go and call on your admirable cousin and see if you can wangle an invitation to some meal in the very near future for both of us. Not tea, because I want the husband to be present as well and doctors' hours for tea are a little uncertain. Don't say why we've come; just tell her that we expect to be here for a few days. You can say that I've come to inspect the local Roman remains, if you like.'

'Are there any Roman remains here?'

'Not that I know of. But it's a pretty safe remark. Every town of any size must have Roman remains: its a sort of guarantee of respectability. And use the cunning of the serpent and the guilelessness of a dove. Can I rely on you for that?'

'I'll do my best.'

'Spoken like a Briton!' approved Roger warmly. 'And after all, who can do more than that? Answer, almost anybody. But don't ask me to explain that because—'

'I won't!' said Alec hastily.

Roger looked at his friend with reproach. 'I think,' he said in a voice of gentle suffering, 'that I'll be getting along now.'

'So long, then!' said Alec very heartily.

Roger went.

He was back again in less than half an hour, but it was after six before Alec returned. Roger, smoking his pipe in the lounge with growing impatience, jumped up eagerly as the other's burly form appeared in the doorway (Alec had got a rugger blue at Oxford for leading the scrum, and he looked it) and waved him over to the corner-table he had secured. The lounge was fairly full by this time, and Roger had been at some pains to keep a table as far away from any other as possible.

'Well?' he asked in a low voice as Alec joined him. 'Any luck?'

'Yes. Molly wants us to go to dinner there tonight. Just pot-luck, you know.'

'Good! Well done, Alec.'

'She seemed quite impressed to hear I was down with you,' Alec went on with pretended astonishment. 'In fact, she seems quite keen about meeting you. Extraordinary! I can't imagine why, can you?'

But Roger was too excited for the moment even to wax facetious. He leaned across the little table with sparkling eyes, making no attempt to conceal his elation.

'I've seen her solicitor!' he said.

'Have you? Good. Surely you didn't get anything out of him, did you?'

'Didn't I just! Roger exclaimed softly. 'I got everything.'

'Everything?' repeated Alec startled. 'Great Scott, how did you manage that?'

'Oh, no details. Nothing like that. I was only with him for a couple of minutes. He was a dry, precise little man, typical stage solicitor; and he wasn't giving away if he knew it. Oh, nothing at all. But he didn't know it, you see, Alexander. He didn't know it!'

'What happened, then?'

'Oh, I told him the same sort of yarn as I told Burgoyne, and asked him point-blank if he could see his way to giving me any information as to whether Mrs Bentley had a complete answer to the charges against her, or not. Of course I had him a bit off his guard, you must remember. It'd be the last thing any solicitor would expect, wouldn't it? A chap to blow into his office and ask him questions about another client like that. He was a good deal taken aback. In fact he probably thought I was quite mad. In any case, he shut up like a little black oyster, said he regretted he had no information to give me and had me shown out. That's all that *happened*.'

'What do you mean, then? You haven't found anything out!'

'Oh, yes, I have,' Roger returned happily. 'I've found out that we haven't come down to Wychford in vain. Alec, in spite of his care, that little man gave himself away to me ten times over. There isn't a shadow of doubt about it—he's quite sure that Mrs Bentley is guilty!'

CHAPTER V

ALL ABOUT ARSENIC

FOR a moment Alec looked bewildered. Then he nodded.

'I see what you're driving at,' he said slowly. 'You mean, if Mrs Bentley's own solicitor thinks she's guilty, then her explanation of the evidence can't be a particularly convincing one?'

'Exactly.'

'And according to what you were saying yesterday morning, that makes you yourself still more convinced of her innocence?'

'Well, don't put it as strongly as all that. Say that it makes me still more inclined to think she may be innocent.'

'Contrary to the opinion of everyone else who is most competent to judge. Humph!' Alec smoked in silence for a minute. 'Roger, that Layton Court affair hasn't gone to your head, has it?'

'How do you mean?'

'Well, just because you hit on the truth there and nobody else did, you're not looking on yourself as infallible, are you?'

'Hit on the truth!' exclaimed Roger with much pain. 'After I'd reasoned out every single step in the case and drawn the most brilliant deductions from the most inadequate data! *Hit* on the truth, indeed!'

'Well, arrived at the truth, then,' Alec said patiently. 'I'm not a word-fancier like you. Anyhow, you haven't answered my question. You're not beginning to look on yourself as a story-book detective, and all the rest of the world as the Scotland Yard specimen to match, are you?'

'No, Alec, I am not,' Roger replied coldly. 'The point I made about the unnaturalness of that large quantity of arsenic was a perfectly legitimate one, and I'm only surprised that nobody else seems to have noticed it, instead of promptly drawing the diametrically opposite conclusion. As to whether I'm right or wrong in the explanation I gave you, that remains to be seen; but you'll kindly remember that I only put it forward as an interesting possibility, not a cast-iron fact, and I merely pointed out that it *was* just enough to cast a small doubt on the absolute certainty of Mrs Bentley's guilt.'

'All right,' Alec said soothingly. 'Keep your wool on. What about all that chit-chat about mysterious unknowns?'

Roger affected a slight re-arrangement of his ruffled plumes. 'There I'm quite ready to admit that I was using my imagination, and plenty of it too. But it was plausible enough for all that. And if Mrs Bentley by any weird chance *is* innocent it must be true. In any case, isn't that just what we're supposed to have come down here to find out?'

'I suppose it is,' Alec admitted.

Roger regarded his stolid companion for a moment with a lukewarm eye. Then he broke into a sudden laugh and the plumage was smoothly preened once more.

'You're really a bit of an old ass at times, you know, Alec!'

'So you seem to think,' Alec agreed, unmoved.

'Well, aren't you? Still, never mind that for the moment. The story-book detective has another point to bring forward. It occurred to me while I was thinking over things before you arrived just now. You remember that Mrs Bentley bought those fly-papers they're making all this fuss about at a local chemist's here?'

'Yes?'

'Well, now, I ask you again—is that natural? Is it natural, if one wants to buy fly-papers for the purpose of extracting the arsenic in order to poison one's husband, to walk into the local chemist's where one is perfectly well known and ask for them there? A certain amount of fuss always follows a murder, you know; and nobody realises that better than the would-be murderer. Is it likely that she'd do that, when she could have bought them equally well in London and never have been traced?'

'That's a point, certainly. Then you think that she didn't get them with any—what's the phrase?—ulterior motive?'

'To poison her husband with them? Naturally, if she didn't poison him.'

'Then what did she get them for?'

'I don't know—yet. Would it be too much to suggest that she got them with the idea of killing flies? Anyhow, we must leave that till we've discovered her own explanation.'

'You're determined to assume her innocence, then?'

'That, my excellent Alexander,' said Roger with much patience, 'is exactly what we have to do. It's no good even keeping an open mind. If we're to make any real attempt to do what we've come down here for, we've *got* to be prejudiced in favour of Mrs Bentley's innocence. We've got to work on the assumption that she's being wrongly accused and that somebody else is guilty, and we've got to work to bring home the crime to that somebody else. Otherwise our efforts as detectives for the defence are bound to be only half-hearted. You've got to lash yourself into a fury of excitement and indignation at the idea of this poor woman, a foreigner and absolutely alone in the country, being unanimously convicted even before her trial when in reality she's perfectly innocent. That is, if you ever could work up the faintest flicker of excitement about anything, you great fish!'

'Right-ho!' Alec returned equably. 'I'm mad with excitement. I'm bursting with indignation. Let's go out and kill a policeman.'

'I admit that it's a curious position in many ways,' Roger went on more calmly, 'but you must agree that it's a damned interesting one.'

'I do. That's why I'm here.'

'Good. Then we understand each other.'

'But look here, Roger, ragging aside, there's one point about the purchase of those fly-papers that I think you've overlooked.'

'Oh? What?'

'Well—assuming for the moment that she is guilty, did she

know that it *was* going to be recognised as murder? I seem to remember that arsenic poisoning can't be detected as poisoning, even at a post-mortem, without analysis and all that sort of thing. Wouldn't she be hoping that the doctors and everybody would think that it was natural death?'

'Alec,' Roger said thoughtfully, 'that's a jolly cute remark of yours.'

'Just happened to occur to me,' said Alec modestly.

'Well, whether it just happened to occur to you or whether you thought of it, it's still jolly cute. Yes, you're perfectly right. Each criminal does think his or her particular crime can't ever be found out—each deliberate criminal, I mean; and the poisoner is the deliberate criminal *par excellence*. It's a very remarkable point in criminal psychology that, and I'm only sorry we haven't got time now to go into it at the length it deserves—the real *conceit* (there's no other word) of the deliberate murderer. One realises it time and time again. Other people have been found out, yes; but he—he's far too clever! They'll never bring it home to *him*. But however conceited they may be, they very seldom behave like complete lunatics before the deed; and that's what Mrs Bentley certainly would be in this case.'

'You've got to remember that there wasn't any suspicion of murder raised at all till Mary Blower told Mrs Saunderson about the fly-papers.'

'Alec,' said Roger with warm approval, 'you're showing a most commendable grasp of this case. Yes, that is so. And what a tremendous lot depended on that chance communication! If Mary Blower had never said a word, it's my opinion that we should never have heard of the Wychford Poisoning Case at all. Just think! Mary Blower herself wouldn't have handed that letter to Mrs Allen and that particular complication would never have come out; brother Alfred wouldn't have been telegraphed for and taken control of the whole business; the doctors wouldn't have been put on the *qui vive*; the bottle of Bovril wouldn't have been analysed; there would have been no search made after the death. You're right—there wouldn't even have been a doubt about the death at all. If Mary Blower hadn't been smitten by fortuitous desire for self-importance, the doctors would almost certainly have given a certificate for death from gastroenteritis!'

'Gastroenteritis?'

'Yes, acute dyspepsia; which they'd already diagnosed, you remember.'

'They might have done that even if the man had been poisoned by arsenic?'

Roger took a pull at the tankard which, together with another for Alec, he had prudently ordered before that gentleman's arrival.

'I see,' he said, 'that if you're to get a proper understanding of this case I shall have to give you a short lecture upon arsenical poisoning. What you've got to realise is, to put it loosely, that death from poisoning by arsenic *is* death by gastroenteritis. The poison arsenic kills by setting up gastroenteritis, just as any other violent irritant might—ground-glass, to take a particularly vigorous example. Without being too technical, it ploughs up the coating of the stomach. That is gastroenteritis.'

'Then if they're the same thing, arsenical poisoning and gastroenteritis can't be told apart? At a post-mortem, I mean, and without analysing the various organs.'

'Well, to a certain extent they can. It would be more true to say that arsenic sets up a special form of gastroenteritis; the symptoms *are* a little different from the ordinary form of it. There are distinctive ones in arsenical poisoning (I believe the number recognised is twenty), such as the violent and prolonged vomiting and the acute pains in the legs mentioned in Bentley's case, which aren't usually found in ordinary gastroenteritis, but the whole thing is very anomalous and the dividing line extraordinarily fine.'

'Then that's why so many poisoners use arsenic? Because

unless suspicion does happen to be raised, it's so jolly easy to get away with?'

'Without a doubt. And also because it's so easy to obtain. The ordinary doctor isn't on the look out for arsenical poisoning, you see. Probably not one in a hundred ever meets a case in his whole life. When he has to treat a perfectly legitimate case of gastroenteritis, as he thinks, and the patient just happens to die instead of recovering, he doesn't hesitate to give a certificate. It never occurs to him not to. Why should it? But I'd bet a very large amount of money that a positively staggering number of those cases of innocent gastroenteritis would have turned out to be arsenical poisoning if only they'd been followed up.'

'Horrid thought! A staggering percentage?

'Well, half of half of one per cent, would be staggering enough in the aggregate, you know. Why, just look at some of the cases that have been brought to light recently by the merest possible chance. Seddon! It was the nearest thing imaginable that he was never found out. The certificate had been given and the body even buried. Armstrong again. One could go on for hours.'

'What a devil of a lot you seem to know about all this!' Alec observed, with as near an approach to admiration as he had yet shown.

'I do,' Roger agreed. 'Since we stayed at Layton Court together a couple of years ago, as you may remember, Alexander, what I haven't read up on this subject hasn't only not been worth reading, it hasn't even been written. In fact,' he added candidly, 'I shouldn't be at all surprised if I don't know a trifle more about criminology than any man living.'

'You'll be able to write a detective story then,' Alec suggested brightly. 'In the meantime, what about going up and getting ready for dinner? It's nearly seven o'clock.'

CHAPTER VI

INTRODUCING MISS PUREFOY

MRS PUREFOY was a pleasant little person with hair just beginning to go grey and a jolly smile. Roger took a liking to her at first sight, while she was at no pains to hide her gratification in welcoming so distinguished a guest.

'I've read all your books, Mr Sheringham,' she said at once as she shook hands with him. 'Every single one!'

Roger was never in the least embarrassed by this sort of thing. 'Well, I hope you enjoyed reading them more than I did the writing of them, Mrs Purefoy,' he said easily.

'Does that mean you didn't enjoy writing them? I thought you novelists were only really happy when you'd got a pen in your hands.'

'Somebody's been misinforming you,' Roger replied with a grave face. 'If I can speak for the tribe, we're only really happy when we've got a pen out of our hands.' As far as Roger was concerned, this was perfectly untrue; he had to write, or explode. But he had an intense dislike for the glib talk about self-expression indulged in by so many second-rate writers who take themselves and their work a good deal too seriously, and put it down to posing of the most insufferable description. That his own anxiety not to emulate these gentry had driven him into no less of a pose of his own, in the precisely opposite direction, had curiously enough never occurred to him.

'But this is most devastating! You're shattering all my most cherished illusions. Don't you write for the joy of writing, then?'

'Alas, Mrs Purefoy, I see I can hide nothing from you. I don't!

I write for a living. There may be people who do the other thing (I have heard rumours about them), but believe me, they're very rare and delicate birds.'

'Well, you're candid at any rate,' Mrs Purefoy smiled.

'Roger's got a hobby all right, Molly,' Alec put in, 'and it's got plenty to do with words; but it isn't writing.'

'Oh? What is it, then, Alec?'

'You'll have found out before dinner's over,' Alec replied cryptically.

'What he means is that I won't let him monopolise the conversation all the time, Mrs Purefoy.'

Mrs Purefoy looked from one to the other. 'I suppose I'm very dense, but this is beyond me.'

'I think Alec is hinting that I talk too much,' Roger explained.

'Oh, is that all? Well, I'm very glad to hear it. I like listening to somebody who can talk.'

'You hear that, Alec?' Roger grinned. 'I'm going to be appreciated at last.'

The conversation was interrupted by the entrance of a dark, shingled maiden, in a pale green dinner-frock.

'My eldest daughter,' Mrs Purefoy announced with maternal pride. 'Sheila, dear, this is Mr Sheringham.'

'How de do?' said the dark, shingled maiden languidly. 'You're the great Roger Sheringham? Read some of your books. Topping. Hallo, Alec, old hoss. Dinner nearly ready, mum?'

'In a few minutes, dear. We're waiting for father.'

'Well, need we wait for him on our feet? What about sitting down to it?' And she collapsed wearily into the largest chair in the room.

Alec pulled one up beside it, and they embarked immediately on a discussion of the Gentlemen and Players match then in progress at Lord's. Roger sat down beside his hostess on a chesterfield couch.

'Alec didn't mention that you have a daughter, Mrs Purefoy,' he remarked.

'Didn't he? I have two. And a son. The other two are away from home just at present.'

'I—I suppose you're not making any mistake, are you?' Roger asked warily. 'The lady at present telling Alec things he doesn't know about cricket really *is* your daughter?'

'She is, Mr Sheringham. Why?'

'Oh, nothing. I was just wondering whether you weren't getting a little mixed in the relationship. I should have said off-hand that you were the daughter and she the mother.'

Mrs Purefoy laughed. 'Yes, Sheila is a little overpowering in her sophistication, isn't she? But it's only a pose, you know. All her friends are just the same. I've never seen her quite like this before though; I think this must be a pose for your special benefit. She'd do anything rather than admit to the slightest respect for any person living, you see. I'm afraid she's dreadfully typical.'

'The modern girl, *vide* Sunday papers *passim*, eh? Well, scratch her and you'll find much the same sort of girl there always has been underneath her powder, I suppose.'

'A very good idea,' Mrs Purefoy smiled. 'Scratch Sheila by all means, Mr Sheringham, if you want to pursue any investigations into the modern girl; it would do her all the good in the world. Aren't I an inhuman mother? But really, I simply ache at times to turn Sheila over my knee and give her a good old-fashioned spanking! And most of her silly precocious friends as well!'

'You're quite right,' Roger laughed. 'That's the only cure. There ought to be a new set of sumptuary laws passed and a public spanker appointed in every town, with a thumping salary out of the rates, to deal with the breaches of them (no joke intended). Ration 'em down to one lipstick a month, one ounce of powder ditto, twenty cigarettes a week, and four damns a day, and we might—Ah, here's your husband.'

Dr Purefoy, in contrast to his wife, was long and cadaverous. His face was lean, but from time to time a twinkling of almost unexpected humour lit his eyes. He looked tired, but shook hands with Roger warmly enough.

'So sorry to have kept you waiting like this,' he said, 'but there was a tremendously big surgery tonight. There always is when I particularly want to finish early.'

'Very busy just now?' Roger asked.

'Very. Autumn just setting in, you see; that always means a busy time for us. Well, shall we go in at once? Molly, you don't want us to form a procession and link arms, do you?'

'Of course not, dear. This isn't a dinner-party. Sheila, dear, will you show Mr Sheringham the way?'

The little party made their way informally to the dining-room and took their seats. For a few minutes, while the maid was in the room, the conversation turned upon the usual topics; but it was a very short time before the subject cropped up which was uppermost in all their minds.

It was Sheila Purefoy who introduced it. 'Well, Mr Sheringham,' she said, 'what do you think of our local thrill?'

'Meaning, of course, the Bentley case?' said Roger, who was sitting next to her. 'I think it's rather a remarkable business.'

'Is that all? I was hoping that you'd think something rather more original than that about it.'

'I'm most stereotyped about murders,' Roger assured her. 'Always have been, from a child. What do you think about it?'

'Oh, I d'no. I think the Bentley woman's innocent.'

'You do?' cried Roger, genuinely startled.

'Sheila, dear!' exclaimed Mrs Purefoy. 'Whatever makes you think that?'

'Don't get alarmed, mum. I was only trying to be original.'

'Oh, I see,' said Roger, not a little disappointed. 'A hint for me, eh?'

'For all that, I shouldn't be so ghastly surprised if she was,' observed Sheila languidly. 'Everyone's quite made up their minds that she's guilty, you see.'

'Mass suggestion, you mean. Well, somebody's being very cunning indeed if that is the case.'

'I don't know anything about mass suggestion, but it's a fact that most people spend their lives being wrong about everything. Most people think she's guilty. Therefore, she isn't. Shove the gravy over, please, Alec. Ta.'

'It's an ingenious defence,' Roger said gravely. 'Do you agree, Dr Purefoy?'

'That she's innocent? No, I'm afraid not. I wish I could say that I did, but I can't see the faintest possibility of it.'

'Now, I'm *quite* sure she's innocent,' Sheila murmured.

'Sheila, Sheila!' said her mother.

'Sorry, mum; but you know perfectly well that father's never been known in all his life to grasp any stick except by the wrong end. To my mind, that proves it. I'd better write to the woman's solicitor.'

'You see the respect with which we parents are treated nowadays,' smiled Dr Purefoy.

'Sheila,' said Alec suddenly, 'I think I'll scrag you after dinner. Like I used to when we were kids.'

'Why this harshness?' inquired Miss Purefoy.

'Because you jolly well deserve it,' said Alec, and relapsed into silence again.

'Thank you, Alec,' Dr Purefoy said pathetically. 'You're a brave man. I wish I had your courage.'

'I like that, father,' said his daughter indignantly. 'When you absolutely *ruined* my best evening frock only last week.'

But Roger had no intention of allowing the conversation to wander off into the paths of family badinage. 'Do you know the Bentleys or any of the people mixed up in the case personally?' he asked the girl at his side.

'Not the Bentleys. I know the Saundersons more or less, and I believe I've met Allen. Of course I know Dr James and Dr Peters.'

'You know Mrs Saunderson, do you?' Roger said with interest. 'What sort of woman is she?'

'A damned little cat,' said Miss Purefoy frankly.

'*Sheila!*' This from her mother.

'Well, she is, mum, as jolly well you know; so why on earth not say so? Isn't she, father?'

'If my information is correct, your remark was a laudable under-statement, my dear,' Dr Purefoy said with a perfectly grave face.

'I'd rather gathered that, from the newspaper reports,' Roger murmured. 'In what way, Miss Purefoy?'

'Well, look at what she did! That's enough, isn't it? Of course she hasn't got a husband to teach her decent behaviour (she's a widow, you know), but there are some things that simply aren't done. After all, she was supposed to be the Bentley's friend, wasn't she? But that's just like her; double-faced little beast. She'd give her soul to be talked about. Of course she's in the seventh heaven now. I shouldn't be a bit surprised if it turned out that she'd poisoned the man herself just to get her name in the papers. That's the sort of daisy she is.'

'Is she, though?' Roger said softly. 'That's very interesting. And what about Mrs Allen?'

'Oh, she's a good bit older. Older than her husband, too. Always happens, doesn't it?' went on this sophisticated damsel. 'Any woman who marries a man younger than herself deserves all that's coming to her, in my opinion. But of course Mr Allen *is* a bit of a lad, you know. I heard about him before I was out of my teens. You know, whispers in dark corners and breath well bated. Well, it's a matter of common knowledge that he—'

'That will do, Sheila!' said Mrs Purefoy, whose expression had during the last minute been growing more and more appre-hensive.

'Mother always shuts me up before I can get on to the really spicy bits,' confided Miss Purefoy to the world at large.

The entry of the parlourmaid cut short any further attempts on the part of her daughter to add to the grey in Mrs Purefoy's lustrous dark hair. The conversation which ensued would have satisfied a Sunday school teacher.

It was not until the three men were left alone together after dinner that Roger re-introduced the subject. He did not wish, for the present at any rate, to advertise the reason for his visit to Wychford, even to the Purefoys; and too great an interest in the murder, unless its cause were to be more fully explained, would only appear to spring from a curiosity unbridled to the point of indecency. When the two women had retired, however, and the doctor's excellent port was circulating for the second time, he did feel at liberty to raise the matter.

'About this Bentley case, doctor,' he remarked. 'Of course you know the two doctors concerned. Is there any point of particular interest, do you think, in the medical evidence?'

Dr Purefoy stroked his lean jaw with the palm of his hand. 'No, I don't think so, Sheringham. It all seems perfectly straightforward. Do you mean about the cause of death?'

'Well, yes. That or anything else.'

'Because that, of course, isn't in doubt for a minute. As clear a case of arsenical poisoning as there could possibly be. Actually more than a fatal dose found in the man's body after death, and that's very rare indeed; a great deal is always eliminated between the time of swallowing the dose and death.'

'How much would you say he had been given, then?'

'Well, it's impossible to say. Might have been as little as five grains; might have been as much as twenty. Making a pure guess at it, I should say about eight to ten grains. He didn't vomit nearly as much as one might expect, James told me, which points to a comparatively small dose.'

'A fatal dose being about three grains?'

'Yes, two and a half to three. Two and a half is reckoned an average small fatal dose, but it would have been ample for Bentley, I imagine.'

'Why for him particularly?'

'Well, he was rather a poor creature. Undersized, delicate, poor physique; a bit of a little rat, to our way of thinking.'

'And very fussy about his health, I gather?'

'Exactly. One of those maddening patients (we all have 'em) who think they know a sight more about their ailments and the right drugs to cure them than their doctor does. Oh, quite impossible people; and I understand from James that Bentley was as bad a specimen of the tribe as you'd hope to see.'

'Oh? In what way?'

'Well, you prescribe for 'em and all that, and then find that the prescription can't be used because the fellow's already been prescribing for himself before he came to you at all, and the two prescriptions clash; and then you prescribe something else, and the fellow goes and takes something perfectly different that he thinks is going to suit his case better. Oh, hopeless! That's just the lunatic Bentley was. Always dosing himself from morning to night: never happy unless he was stuffing some drug or other inside his skin.'

'Do you mean that he drugged? Morphia, or anything like that?'

'Oh, dear me, no. I was using the word in its correct sense, not the particular meaning with which the public seem to invest it. No, I don't mean that he took any *harmful* drugs; just that his chief joy in life seemed to lie in turning his long-suffering stomach into a fair imitation of the inside of a chemist's shop.'

'So that it wouldn't take a big dose of arsenic to finish him off?'

'Just so. His stomach must have been in a very delicate state. You might say that he had already a predisposition to gastro-enteritis. That's why James hadn't the least hesitation in diagnosing it when he was called in to see him the morning after the picnic, if you remember. Of course there hadn't been any talk of arsenic then.'

'Oh, yes; that was another thing I meant to ask you about. Two things, in fact. One of them is—why did Dr James diagnose acute dyspepsia on that occasion? You've answered it partially, but was there anything else to make him think so? Had Bentley eaten anything to disagree with him at the picnic, so far as you know?'

'Dear me,' Dr Purefoy smiled, 'this is a regular cross-examination!'

'Am I being frightfully rude?' Roger asked in concern. 'I am, aren't I, Alec?'

'Not more than usual,' grunted that gentleman.

'Not a bit!' the doctor protested. 'I was only joking.'

'I'm afraid I am, for all that,' Roger laughed. 'But I must plead an overwhelming interest in this case, as you've no doubt gathered.'

'I don't blame you. It's a most interesting case, in spite of the lack of any element of doubt about it. And if I can tell you anything you want to know, I shall be only too pleased. James and I are very old friends, and I know almost as much about his share in it as he does.'

'Well, I must say I'd be most awfully obliged. About this picnic business, now?'

'Oh, yes. Well, it wasn't so much what he'd had to eat that prompted James's diagnosis, as the climatic conditions. It wasn't by any means a warm day and Bentley had gone off in the car without his overcoat. Added to which he undoubtedly sat on the damp grass. Those facts would have been quite enough to give a man in his state of health an internal chill, which would perfectly well have accounted for that particular set of symptoms.'

'But you think now that Dr James was wrong?'

'There's no doubt about it. James says so himself. That attack was certainly the result of a first administration of arsenic.'

'Yes, that's the second question I had in mind. *Why* is the medical evidence so firm that this attack was due to arsenic?'

'Well, you see, it's like this. Arsenical poisoning can be of two kinds, chronic or acute. Chronic arsenical poisoning consists of a number of small doses spread over a period of time, the poison then acting cumulatively; acute arsenical poisoning is the result of one large fatal dose. Now this case has been proved to have been a mixture of both methods.'

'The traces of arsenic found in the hair, nails and skin showing that the administration must have begun at the very least a fortnight before death,' Roger put in promptly.

'But you know as much about it as I do!' exclaimed the doctor.

'I have studied it a bit,' Roger admitted, with childish enjoyment of his triumph. 'Yes, I thought that was the reason, but I just wanted to verify it. And now another thing. I've often noticed, reading the trials of these poisoning cases, that the defence is nearly always based on the plea that the dead person did not die from the effects of poison but that death was due to natural causes—in spite of the inconvenient presence of poison in the body. And what's more, they nearly always seem able to call experts in support of the contention. Now do you think that is likely to happen in this case? Of course we don't know yet what the defence is to be; but supposing it does run on those lines, do you think that any expert will be found to give it as his opinion that Bentley did, in fact, die of natural gastroenteritis (I know that's a medical contradiction in terms, but let it pass; you see what I mean) and not from arsenical poisoning?'

'No!' Dr Purefoy said with emphasis. 'I do not. If there had been less arsenic found, then perhaps they might have got hold of somebody with pet theories about the symptoms of arsenical poisoning to come and say that all the symptoms he would have expected to see weren't present and therefore death couldn't possibly be due to arsenic. But nobody can get over those three grains.'

'I see. Then in that case the defence will have to rest on some other basis, won't it? And there's only one other possible basis it can rest on, and that is that Mrs Bentley did not herself administer the poison but that someone else did.'

'It'll be interesting to see what they fake up,' agreed Dr Purefoy pleasantly. 'Alec, help yourself to some more port and pass the decanter along.'

'No more for me, thanks,' Alec said, jumping suddenly to his feet. 'If you two'll excuse me, I'm going along to the drawing-room.'

'Why the hurry, Alexander?' asked Roger. 'Am I boring you so much?'

'Oh, no. It's not that. But I promised to scrag Sheila, and I'd better get it done before you two've finished gassing. So long!'

'Alec,' observed Dr Purefoy as the door closed, 'is one of those rare and refreshing people who have nothing to say and therefore don't say it. I've only met one before in my life, and that, it may surprise you to learn, was a woman. Well, help yourself to the port, Sheringham, and then push it along to me, will you? Now then, any more questions?'

'Thanks,' Roger said, re-filling his glass. 'Yes, there is one other thing. What is the usual sort of period to elapse between the administration of a fatal dose of arsenic and death?'

'Well, it's really impossible to say. It may be anything between a couple of hours and several days.'

'Oh!' said Roger.

'Twenty-four hours is usually reckoned the average, but death in three to eight hours is quite common.'

'And when do the symptoms begin to show themselves after the dose has been swallowed?'

'In half an hour to an hour.'

'Ah!' said Roger.

There was a short pause, while Dr Purefoy sipped his port appreciatively. It was good port, but for the moment Roger appeared to have forgotten all about it.

'Then in a disputed case, one might say that anybody was under suspicion who came into contact with the dead man during the penultimate half-hour before the symptoms appeared?'

'Certainly.'

'And anybody who did *not* do so would be automatically cleared?'

'Within reasonable limits, yes. But it's all rather anomalous.'

'Um!' said Roger, and finished his port off at a gulp.

Dr Purefoy looked a trifle pained. It was good port, and undoubtedly it merited a little more consideration than that.

CHAPTER VII

MOSTLY IRRELEVANT

'ALEC, you're not to! Alec, you *beast*! Mother, tell him he's not to. Alec, you'll ruin this frock! Alec, I will not have it! You'll have to buy me a new frock, you know. Oh, hell, there's one of my suspenders gone. Mum, do for goodness' sake tell him he's not to! Are you going to sit there and see your daughter murdered? *Alec*! Alec, I swear I'll—ALEC! I'll kick your shins with my heels—I swear I will! Alec, I will *not* be treated like this. Alec, stop it! A joke's a joke, but—*Alec*!—Oh, thank God, here's father! Father, will you tell Alec—Alec, no! Not with Mr Sheringham here. No, this is too much of a good thing. I'll get cross in a minute—I mean it! ALEC! Oh, father, do say something to the damned man, for Heaven's sake.'

Dr Purefoy said something. He said: 'Don't mind me, Alec.'

'Father, I loathe you!' observed Miss Sheila Purefoy with intense feeling.

It must be admitted that Miss Purefoy had reason for her emotion. She was standing in a curious position, bent like a hair-pin over the end of the big couch, her face, very red and unpowdered, burrowed upside-down among the loose cushions in the corner of the seat. She could not regain an erect position because Alec's large hand was planted firmly on the nape of her neck. Every now and then she heaved violently in an effort to follow her head on to the seat of the couch; on these occasions Alec's other hand would grab her hastily by the scruff of the back and pull her back again. Frequently too she would lash out with a vicious jab of her high-heeled shoe, and then Alec would either jump nimbly out of the way, or else be caught off his guard and suffer intense discomfort. Nor had Alec himself

52

escaped all signs of conflict. His hair was decidedly ruffled, his tie unfastened and a button missing from his dinner-jacket.

'Well, will you keep still while I smack you?' he demanded reasonably.

'No, I'm damned if I will? Let me up this minute, you hulking great bully.'

'You're not coming up till you've been smacked.'

'But why not?' cried Miss Purefoy plaintively. 'I've never done anything to you. Why are you going on like this, curse you?'

'Because it's good for you, Sheila. You're getting too jolly big for your shoes. Now then, stand still!' He removed his hand from her back, and Miss Purefoy instantly dived forward on to her head. He was only just in time to grab her frock at the back and drag her back again. A rending sound arose.

'Now, you've done it!' wailed Miss Purefoy. 'Alec, you hound of hell, let me up. Didn't you hear me split then? I don't feel as if I'd got one whole garment left on me.'

'Look here, Roger,' Alec said, quite unperturbed, 'I wish you'd come and whack her for me, will you? You see, whenever I take my hand off her back, she nearly gets away.'

'Alec,' Roger said with considerable emotion, 'there are few things I wouldn't do for you, but whacking my hostess's daughter is most decidedly one of them.'

'Thank you, Roger Sheringham,' came a grateful if muffled voice from among the sofa cushions. 'You're a gent, you are. Alec, on the other hand, is a hound of hell.'

'Sheila, will you stand still while I do it, then?' demanded the hound of hell once more.

'No, blast you, I won't!'

'Alec, dear,' interposed Mrs Purefoy, 'I think you might let her up now, don't you?'

'Oh, thank heaven for miracles!' gasped Miss Purefoy in stifled tones. 'Mother's found her heart.'

'But she hasn't been whacked yet, Molly,' Alec protested.

'No, but I think you've dealt with her drastically enough even without that, haven't you?'

'All right,' Alec conceded reluctantly. 'I'll take pot-luck and whack her on the run. Now then, Sheila!'

He whisked his hand away from Miss Purefoy's back and applied it heavily three or four times to another portion of that young lady's anatomy as she promptly hurled herself, with yet more rending sounds and a flourishing of green silk stockings, head over heels on to the couch.

'And now,' panted Miss Purefoy, picking herself up and smoothing down her dishevelled person, 'somebody tell me a fairy-story. It's more restful.'

'I think you'll find her a bit more like a human being for the next day or two now, Jim,' observed Alec, dropping into a chair and applying a handkerchief to his brow.

'Thank you, Alec,' replied Dr Purefoy simply.

His wife felt that it was time to impart a somewhat more conventional note to the proceedings. 'Alec tells me that you and he may be staying some days here, Mr Sheringham,' she remarked.

'Yes,' Roger said. 'It's quite possible. I don't know how long, but three or four days, I expect, at least.'

'Well, wouldn't you rather come and stay here than at the Man of Kent, both of you? We should be very pleased to have you if you cared to come.'

'That's most extraordinarily kind of you, Mrs Purefoy,' Roger said warmly. 'But surely we should be most terribly in the way?'

'Not a bit. I should leave you to amuse yourselves; I always do leave my visitors alone, I'm sure they much prefer it. You wouldn't be any trouble at all.'

'This is really quite overwhelming,' Roger murmured. 'Of course we should like to come most awfully. If you're absolutely certain it would be all right.'

'Good. Then that's settled,' Dr Purefoy said briskly. 'You'd better get your things round tomorrow morning.'

'Need Alec come, mum?' queried Sheila in some concern. 'Couldn't Mr Sheringham come alone?'

'Do you want to be scragged again, Sheila?' Alec asked with a grin.

'Shut up, Alec!' retorted his cousin. 'I'm not on speaking terms with you at present.'

'Because the next time I have to take action,' continued Alec weightily, 'the next time, Sheila—I'm going to drop you into a bath of cold water. So look out!'

'The bathroom, Alec,' remarked Dr Purefoy airily, his eyes fixed innocently upon the ceiling, 'is the second door on the left at the top of the stairs.'

An excellent evening then ensued.

A few minutes before eleven Roger and Alec, reiterating for the fourteenth time their decision that they really *must* go now, really went.

'Alexander,' said Roger with his usual frankness as they turned down the High Street, 'I like your cousins most tremendously. Two more charming people than Dr and Mrs Purefoy I've never met.'

'Yes, they're a topping couple. Awfully decent to me when I was a kid. Sheila used to be a jolly kid too, but she's grown up pretty ghastly.'

'Oh, she's all right. Just the usual pose of nineteen or twenty or whatever she is. She'll grow out of that sort of thing.'

'I certainly did her a bit of good tonight,' said Alec, with a reminiscent grin. 'I didn't notice any more of that dam' silly languidness about her after I'd finished with her.'

Roger stopped dead on the pavement and solemnly lifted his hat. 'Heads uncovered to Mr Alexander Grierson, Strong Silent Man and Tamer of Women,' he said reverently.

'Don't be an ass,' said the Woman-tamer tolerantly.

'And also,' Roger added, 'as I was nearly forgetting, Hound, I understand, of Hell. I say, Alec, it really was most awfully good of them to invite us to stay there.'

'Yes; they're jolly hospitable.'

'And mark my words, that young lady is going to be a great help to us. She can give us an introduction to the Saunderson, as she calls her, off her own bat, and she could certainly wangle any others we might want. I think we shall have seriously to consider taking her into our confidence.'

And then Alec said a very unexpected thing. 'We might do a jolly sight worse,' said Alec.

Roger looked at him with considerable surprise. It was the last advice he would have expected Alec to put forward.

'Alexander,' he remarked, 'if ever I've called you a darned and blithering old fool, I herewith take it back. I really don't think you are.'

'Thanks,' said Alec without exuberant gratitude.

They reached the Man of Kent and ordered the night-caps to which their position as residents entitled them, in defiance of the dictates of a maternal government, pussyfootism and all the other futilities which order our lives for us in these days.

'Well, you didn't get much forrarder tonight with the business in hand, I noticed,' Alec observed, when a sleepy provincial waiter had set their glasses in front of them. 'Cheerio!'

'Good luck. Didn't I, though! But most decidedly I did; after you'd gone to interview Sheila. Alec, my friend, this case looks as if it's going to turn out to be uncommonly simple after all.'

'How do you make that out?'

Roger told him what he had learned regarding the appearance of the symptoms in arsenical poisoning. 'So you see,' he pointed out, 'this narrows everything down to a very fine point indeed. We've only got to find out who came into contact with Bentley during that penultimate half-hour before the symptoms appeared, and among those very few people is your murderer. At any rate we shall know after that whom *not* to waste time over.'

'And Mrs Bentley?' Alec asked. 'How does this affect her?'

'Well, that's going to be rather interesting. If by any chance she didn't come into contact with her husband during that time

(how the deuce are we going to find all this out, by the way?),
one can't say that she's cleared completely. The rule isn't a
hard-and-fast one, you see. But as far as all practical probabilities go, I think we might say that she would be.'

'And if on the other hand,' Alec said slowly, 'she was the only
one to do so, then the case against her appears to be clinched?'

Roger nodded. 'Exactly. That's what I meant. In either alter-
native the case may turn out comparatively simple.'

There was a short silence.

'Lord, I wish I'd *known* the woman,' Roger remarked rest-
lessly. 'We haven't got anything to go on, you see, as to whether
she's capable of murder or not. No personal knowledge.
Poisoning, as I said before, isn't a thing you do in a hurry, like
shooting someone in a temper or whacking somebody else over
the head with a crowbar on the spur of the moment. It's a
deliberate, cold-blooded business, and you've got to be a "pure"
murderer, as they call it, to carry it through. You've got to be
capable of murder—which nine hundred and ninety-eight
people out of a thousand aren't!'

'I can see that,' Alec murmured, almost to himself. 'Anybody
might shoot a chap; but I'd sooner be shot myself than poison
one.'

'It's all a question of the personal factor,' Roger continued.
'The dear old Law doesn't recognise the personal factor in the
slightest (that is, not consciously; though it was the personal
factor which hanged Seddon for all that), but it's a devilish
important factor in any case where the murder is a deliberate
one. Anybody's capable of murder on the spur of the moment
and with sufficient provocation; precious few people are
capable of deliberately planning and carrying out the elimination of an unwanted fellow-creature. It does take a bit of nerve,
you know. The French recognise the importance of the
personal factor, of course; but then their legal procedure is
based on the science of criminology, you might say, whereas
ours is based on precedent.'

'But I thought the French legal system was so harsh. Don't they consider a person guilty till he's proved innocent, while we do just the opposite?'

'And isn't that exactly what a detective unravelling a mystery does? Not that I'm defending the entire French legal system by any means. It *is* much harsher than ours and much more cruel, but there are plenty of points where it has the advantage of ours. All the French are concerned with is getting at the truth, and they don't care a cuss how they get there; we're mostly concerned with protecting the interests of every person or thing connected with the case, from the prisoner himself down through the barristers to the usher's cat. The French confront an accused person with the corpse of his supposed victim and watch him with a magnifying-glass to see what his reactions are; we spend a couple of hours arguing whether a certain piece of evidence, about which the jury perfectly well know already, is to be admitted formally as evidence or not. The French go about it like a business; we go about it like a game—with the prisoner's life as the prize for the cleverer side.'

'But this is eloquence!' murmured Alec. 'Go on, though; it's damned interesting all the same.'

'Thanks; I will. You mentioned that the French treat a prisoner as guilty till he's proved innocent, and we treat him as the reverse. That's the old parrot-cry of the difference between the two systems, and there's about as much sense in it as there is in most parrot-cries. If I wanted to be startling I might say that precisely the opposite is true—that the French treat a prisoner as innocent and we treat him as guilty; and there'd be just about as much sense in that as in the other. The real truth lies between the two, and you might say that the only way of expressing it is negatively. The French do *not* necessarily require a prisoner prove his innocence, and we certainly do not consider him innocent until he's proved guilty. I could give you plenty of instances of that if you doubt what I'm saying, but I'll confine myself to two. Seddon was certainly never *proved* guilty of poisoning Miss Barrow; Mrs Thompson was still more certainly never proved guilty of instigating the murder of her husband. Yet they were both hanged. Why? Because they couldn't prove their innocence. Mind you, I'm not saying that either of these two convictions was necessarily unjust; that's a very different thing. What I do say is that, if our law is administered as we suppose it to be administered, neither of these two persons should have been convicted; that they were, shows that the administration of the law does not, in fact, sing in tune with our parrot-cry about the benefit of the doubt. Of course I know that's only one side of the question. If you knew of them, you could produce plenty of instances in which the accused person *has* been given that benefit and found not guilty because some vital link in the chain wouldn't stand the test of proof. But that's not the point. The point is that the other side of the case ought not to have examples in support of it at all.'

'The point is conceded,' Alec said with due solemnity. 'So what about a spot of bed?'

Roger broke into a laugh. 'Quite right, Alexander. I'm afraid all this is getting rather a hobby-horse of mine. Tip me gently off when I've ridden it long enough.'

'I will,' Alec promised, as they rose from their chairs.

'So now to bed. Well, *dormez bien, Alexandre*. We've got a strenuous day before us tomorrow—I hope!'

CHAPTER VIII

TRIPLE ALLIANCE

At eleven o'clock the next morning Sheila Purefoy arrived at the Man of Kent with a little two-seater car. Roger and Alec were packed in with their belongings, Alec overflowing into the dickey at the back, and Sheila conveyed them to the house. Mrs Purefoy welcomed them herself and took them up to their rooms.

'And now I must leave you to your own devices 'til lunch time,' she smiled. 'We busy housewives, you know. Please do anything you like. I'll leave Sheila to look after you.'

'Or us to look after Sheila?' Alec grinned. 'That's more like it. All right, Molly, we'll look after her for you.'

Roger wandered into Alec's room.

'Ready, Alec?' he said. 'Then come on down. I want to tackle that young lady right away. It's a good opportunity, and the sooner the better.'

'Right-ho, I'll come and hold her down for you,' Alec volunteered.

Sheila was waiting for them in the drawing-room. 'Hallo, unpacked your little bibs and tuckers?' she asked kindly. It was noticeable that Miss Purefoy retained no traces whatever of that air of life-long weariness which she had worn on their arrival the evening before. Alec's methods were evidently sound.

'Yes,' said Roger briskly. 'Look here, Sheila, I want a word with you.'

Miss Purefoy's eyebrows rose, perhaps, one thirty-second of an inch. 'Chat away then—Roger,' she replied.

The snub bounded off Roger's back like a ping-pong ball off the table. 'That's right,' he approved heartily. 'Now we all know each other. Well, it's like this, Sheila. We're not here in

Wychford aimlessly, Alec and I; we've come for a very set and definite purpose. We're anxious to look into this Bentley case a little more thoroughly than we can do from a distance!'

'Oho!' observed Miss Purefoy. 'Going to write a book about it?'

'That's what I'm saying to anybody outside the family, so to speak. But no. I'm not going to write a book about it; at least, not so far as I know. Alec and I have come down here because we're of the opinion that there may be very much more in this case than meets the eye. In fact, not to put too fine a point on it, that Mrs Bentley may just possibly be innocent!'

Miss Purefoy whistled. 'How in the name of all that's holy do you make that out?' she asked frankly.

Roger told her.

As he enumerated the doubtful points in the case, the suspicions to which these had given rise in his own mind and the deductions from them which it was quite possible to draw, Miss Sheila's face became a study in more and more conflicting expressions. When Roger had finished (and it took him some considerable time to state his case) she looked at him eagerly.

'I'm going to have a hand in this,' said Miss Purefoy.

'That's precisely why I decided to tell you,' Roger agreed.

'It's jolly interesting. There *is* a lot in what you say. I wonder it never occurred to me before, now you've pointed it out. But mind you, you won't get a single person down here to listen to you. Everybody made their minds up ages ago.'

'I know. And not only here, but all over the country as well. That's what makes it all the more interesting. Supposing we turned out to be right, you see!'

'And put it across the whole blinking lot of them?' said Miss Purefoy excitedly. 'Meredith, I'm in! I'd jolly well like to see Mrs Bentley get away with it too. She sounds as if she's worth fifty editions of that little rat of a husband. I'm all in favour of her.' Her face dropped suddenly. 'Oh, Lor'! But how on earth are you going to get over that evidence? The Bovril and all that, I mean?'

'Well, before we can attempt to do that, we've got to find out by hook or by crook what her explanations of that is. It may have come out before her solicitor got hold of her and told her not to say anything, you see. That's the first thing we've got to tackle. And at the same time, find out who were with Bentley during that crucial half-hour, as I explained.'

'Umps! All this isn't half going to take a bit of doing, is it? Anyhow, count on me. How are you going about it, and what do you want me to do?'

'Well, this is the rough plan of campaign I've worked out. The first thing to do, obviously, is to interview every single person who is mixed up in the case; the prosecution's witnesses, that is to say. And the only one of those we can approach on a personal basis, so to speak, is Mrs Saunderson, on your introduction. Well, I want you to fix up a meeting for me with Mrs Saunderson this afternoon, if you can.'

Sheila nodded. 'That ought to be pie. If I know the woman, she'll jump at you with both feet.'

'Good. Then I see her as Roger Sheringham. To people who don't seem as if they'd be interested in Roger Sheringham I appear, by a swift and miraculous transition, as the special correspondent of the *Daily Courier*. So that's two cards we've got to play for getting at our information. Now, I think I'd better see this Saunderson woman alone, so while I'm doing that there's a little job I want you to do and that is to run round and see if you can pick up any information about Mrs Bentley's character—little incidents, other people's impressions, anything to help us form a rather clearer idea of the lady, And a photograph of her I shall want too.'

'But why all this?'

Sitting astride the arm of the couch, Roger told her, at some length. He was still talking when Alec, tip-toeing up behind him, decanted him neatly upside-down on to the seat.

'Alec!' exclaimed Mr Sheringham in tones of pained reproach. 'Why this exhibition of kittenishness?'

Alec contemplated his inverted friend with a happy grin. 'Tipping you off your hobby-horse,' he said laconically. 'Thought you told me to.'

'*Touché!*' acknowledged Roger a little ruefully, regaining an upright position. 'Anyhow, you see the idea, Sheila.'

'Detective Purefoy, please, to you,' rejoined that young lady tartly. 'Detective-for-the-defence Purefoy. Yes, I like that notion of yours, Roger. Right-ho, yes, I see the idea. Your orders shall be attended to, Superintendent Sheringham.'

'What about me?' asked Alec. 'Haven't you got any job for me to do?'

'*You?*' queried his cousin with much scorn. 'What use do you think you'd be at this sort of thing? This is work for bright, intelligent people; not mutts and goops and boneheads.'

'Very well, Sheila,' Alec said grimly, and advanced full of purpose.

'No!' squeaked Miss Purefoy, retreating precipitately. 'I didn't mean you, Alec. Honour bright, I didn't! And if I did I take it back. You're not a mutt or a goop, Alec. You're simply bursting with bright intelligence. Darling Alec, you're not a bit of a bonehead!'

'That's better,' Alec commented, abandoning the chase.

'At least, not *always*,' added Miss Purefoy, just not *sotto voce*.

'Peace, little children,' Roger interposed, as Alec showed signs of renewed grimness. 'We've got to find a job for Baby Alexander this afternoon. You might have tried your hand at discovering something about that half-hour, Alec, but I think it'd be easier if Sheila exercised her wiles on Dr James for that. What a help it's going to be, by the way, to have a lady detective attached to us with such a prepossessing exterior.'

'For these kind words,' murmured Sheila, sweeping him a curtsey, 'this person's thanks. Oh, Hades, how does one curtsey in short skirts? Shall I go and vamp the man this afternoon, then, Roger?'

'Yes, I think you might, if you can spare time from your other duties. It's a thing we've got to find out as soon as we can. Quite possibly James won't know at all, but he's obviously the person to try first. As for Alec, I think you'd better take him with you; he might be useful to see after one thing while you're doing another. He could take over some of the inquiries about Mrs Bentley's character for you; Alec can splash the name of the *Courier* about, you see, which you can't very well do, Constable Grierson, you will take your orders this afternoon from Detective-Inspector Purefoy.'

'Ay, ay, sir; and may the best girl win.'

'We will now,' said Roger firmly, 'discuss the case once more in all its bearings. We can't do that too much, so don't leave all the talking to me this time.'

'Roger doesn't like talking too much, you know,' Alec confided behind his hand to Sheila.

'Wait a minute, Roger. I'll get on the telephone to the Saunderson first and ask her if she's going to be in this afternoon. Don't start till I come back.'

The discussion lasted them without difficulty till lunch time, and though no new fact or theory of any importance emerged in the course of it, all three felt by the time Mrs Purefoy interrupted them an hour later, that their grasp of essential dates and facts was a good deal clearer. Roger had made careful newspaper cuttings of the case, and these were brought down and studied. Mrs Saunderson was out, but Sheila rang her up again shortly before lunch and returned with the information that she would be *delighted* to make Mr Sheringham's acquaintance.

'It's a pity I haven't got time to stick a few hundred drawing-pins on your suit for you,' observed Miss Purefoy as she delivered this message. 'I'm afraid you'll find her a bit of a human burr.'

'Please don't bother,' Roger returned politely. Roger was beginning rather to look forward to his interview with the human burr.

Lunch passed off to a pleasant running accompaniment of badinage between father and daughter (gentle) and cousin and cousin (extremely violent), with Mrs Purefoy smiling gently on all of them and Roger talking volubly upon any subject on which he could find anyone to listen to him. After lunch, when her father had set out once more on the never-ending business of a general practitioner, Sheila took matters into her own extremely capable small hands.

'I'm taking the two children out this afternoon, mum,' she announced. 'I don't suppose we'll be back for tea.'

'I say, you don't mind us running off like this, Mrs Purefoy, do you?' Roger asked, feeling that this treatment of their hostess was really a little cavalier.

'Good gracious, no! I want you to do just whatever you like, both of you. But are you sure Sheila won't be in your way?'

'Really, mum!' protested that indignant young lady.

'Well, as a matter of fact, Molly, she *will*,' Alec explained earnestly; 'but we feel we owe you something for asking us here, so we're going to—'

'Alec, stop trying to be funny; it doesn't suit you. I'm going up to get ready now, Roger. Won't be five minutes.'

One of the most surprising things about the young woman of today is her sense of time. With a previous generation a feminine five minutes, where the question of putting on a hat was concerned, was an invariable euphemism for fifteen or twenty, and in those days, it might be noted, neither lipstick nor powder was an essential part of one's attire. Yet in only a second or two over her stipulated time behold Sheila running downstairs, powdered, lipsticked, gloved, coated and with a little grey felt hat pulled well down over her dark shingled hair. The fact of the matter, as any of the penny Sunday papers will tell you, is that the young woman of today has no *reverence*—not even for the most important things of life.

'Afraid we shall have to trudge it,' Sheila remarked, as they turned into the street and headed up past the pond. 'Father's rather busy just now, so no hope of the car.'

'Now, I want you to come in and introduce me to the lady,' Roger said, 'stay about three minutes talking about the weather, and then buzz off and leave the heavy work to me. Is that clear?'

'Perfectly, thank you, sir. And what shall I do with my poodle while I'm inside?'

'Better tie him up to the front gate, I should say. Is he safe with strangers?'

'With strangers, yes. It's me that he's not safe with. Oh, dear, and I never brought his muzzle!'

'You could fasten his jaws together with a bit of string if he begins to snap,' Roger suggested.

'So I could,' Sheila agreed gratefully. 'Oh, and here's a golf-ball in my pocket. I could throw that along the road for him, couldn't I? He's very playful, you know. I often—'

'You are funny, you two, aren't you?' said Alec wearily. 'Sheila, stop trying to be; it doesn't suit you. Anyhow, if you yap any more I'll drop you in this pond. I'm about ready for another scrap with you.'

Miss Purefoy prudently hastened to interpose Roger between herself and the object of her playful humour.

Beyond the pond the High Street ended in crossroads. Sheila led the way straight ahead, down a road which still bore traces of having once been open country, for nearly half a mile; then took a turning to the right. Before a large house, comparatively new like all the others in the neighbourhood and standing in its own grounds of perhaps two acres, she came to a halt.

'This is the Bentley's place,' she explained. 'The next one is Mrs Saunderson's, and the Allens live about a hundred yards down on the other side.'

Roger and Alec scrutinised the house with interest. It looked exactly the same as any other important house in a quiet road; there was nothing to distinguish it from the hundreds and thousands of others of exactly the same appearance. Yet about it there hung, in the imagination of all three of them, an air of sinister mystery; indefinable enough in all conscience, yet so real as to cause three perfectly respectable citizens to glue their eyes on it in mildly horrified fascination as if they could hope to read in its bricks and tiles the riddle of the secret that it shrouded.

What is this attraction which invests a house in which a particularly horrible crime has been committed—an attraction that induces even the least imaginative or morbid of us to go a few yards out of our way in order to stare in passing at its unresponsive front? Is it simply, as we tell ourselves with an uneasy little smile, that we just wish to see for ourselves the exact circumstances in which they lived, these unfortunate people whose names have become so ominously familiar to us, and the most intimate details of whose lives have been quiveringly exposed to our avid gaze by the ruthless knife of the law? Is it that we feel we know them so well that we want to see with our own eyes the sort of place they lived in, the sort of front gate they pushed open every morning, the sort of people they looked like and the sort of neighbours they had? Is it just that, or does there really brood over the place, as the spiritualists would have us believe, some dark uneasy cloud born of violent human emotions, the fringes of which touch our spirit with some of that same horror which brought it into being?

'To the Saunderson, then!' said Roger, turning away with a little shiver.

CHAPTER IX

INTERVIEW WITH A HUMAN BURR

MRS SAUNDERSON proved to be a fragile, tiny little person, twenty-six-or-seven years old, with black hair and huge brown eyes and a general air of helplessness and appeal. Roger recognised her type the instant she opened her drawing-room door and came forward to greet them, and his soul rejoiced; he was quite sure that he knew the way to go about charming out of Mrs Saunderson any information which she might have to impart.

'Miss Purefoy,' she said in a soft little voice. 'How do you do? So good of you to come round.'

'Awfully kind of you to let us, Mrs Saunderson,' Sheila said briskly. 'May I introduce Mr Sheringham?'

'Mr Roger Sheringham!' murmured the lady, fixing her big eyes on Roger's face with a rapt expression. 'This *is* an unexpected treat.'

'Very kind of you to say so, Mrs Saunderson,' returned Roger cheerfully, as he shook hands. Very, very gently he pressed the small fingers; very, *very* gently the pressure was returned. Roger smiled to himself; he was certain of his ground now.

'Do please sit down, won't you?' Mrs Saunderson implored.

'Well, I've got to be pushing along, unfortunately,' Sheila explained. 'Mr Sheringham wants to stay and have a chat with you, if you'll let him, so I won't interrupt.'

'If you would be so exceedingly kind—!' Roger murmured, fixing a look of admiration on the little lady almost indecent in its sheer blatancy.

'Kind?' she said softly, dropping her eyes modestly beneath Roger's ardent gaze. 'The kindness is all on your side, Mr Sheringham.'

'Then I'll be getting along,' said Sheila, who had been watching this exchange with the liveliest interest; she spoke with some reluctance.

Roger gave her no encouragement to stay. 'Very well, Sheila!' he said, and held open the door for her. As she passed he favoured her with a slight wink. The wink was intended to say, 'How about this for a bit of acting?'

Sheila returned the wink, but it is doubtful whether she quite understood its purport. Her first words to Alec when she met him outside were blank enough. 'Well, what's going to happen in there God alone knows,' said Miss Purefoy with startling frankness. 'The ghastly woman's started holding hands with him already, and Roger's sitting there with a face like a sick cat about to produce kittens!' A remarkable tribute to Roger's powers of dissimulation, no doubt, but one that it would certainly have filled him with pain and sorrow to overhear.

Roger was a cunning man. He knew that it would not be the least use with a lady of Mrs Saunderson's brand to approach his objective with any degree of directness. The most important thing in Mrs Saunderson's life was clearly Mrs Saunderson; anything else was only of purely relative interest in so far as it reacted upon the main theme. If Mrs Saunderson was required to divulge her knowledge of the inner history of the Bentley case, then the first requisite was to suggest delicately that the one and only real interest in that case, as far as Roger was concerned, was the part which she herself had played in it, the feelings it had caused her to experience and the way in which her personality had influenced the whole course of events. And to work up to that state of things a good deal of preliminary ground-work was necessary. If you're going to do a thing at all do it heartily, was Roger's motto.

He proceeded to manœuvre himself and his temporary hostess on to the same deep couch which stood out from the wall on one side of the fireplace. Not very much manœuvring was required.

'It's extraordinarily good of you to let me come and see you, Mrs Saunderson,' Roger opened the ball.

The lady's eyes swam at him. She was wearing a soft clinging frock of black georgette, and she certainly did look undeniably attractive. It was equally certain that she had had every intention of looking attractive.

'Oh, Mr Sheringham!' she said. 'If you only knew how I *adore* your books!'

Good, thought Roger to himself. Wonder if she's ever read any of 'em! Aloud he replied earnestly, 'Do you really like them? I am so glad.' His tone conveyed the impression that, whatever he might have thought before, now at any rate he knew that his books had not been written in vain.

'Pamela, in your new one—I thought that was a *wonderful* character. How miraculously you understand women, Mr Sheringham! You seem to see right into our very *souls*!'

I do, Roger agreed complacently; and nasty, shallow, smudgy little souls some of 'em are. He said, 'What a delightfully appreciative reader you are. Yes, I must admit that women do have a very strong attraction for me—*some* women.' And his expression added clearly, 'Of which number you, madam, are most indubitably one.'

'And how beautifully you write about love!' continued the lady in a rapt voice. 'Really, the love passages in your books make me simply *thrill*. I seem actually to be *living* them with the girl herself. You must have been a very great lover, Mr Sheringham!'

Good Lord, ran Roger's thoughts, she's making the pace all right. Well, it's no good me being slow on my cues. 'At any rate I always know at very first sight whether a woman is going to attract me or not,' he replied softly.

Mrs Saunderson dropped her eyes. 'Always?'

'Always!' said Roger firmly. And that was the first round.

'Of course you've heard about our terrible affair in Wychford, Mr Sheringham?' said the lady, changing the subject with a little flutter of discretion.

Roger had been waiting for this. 'Yes, I have; and that's why I'm here, Mrs Saunderson—not only in Wychford, but in your drawing-room. I've read, of course, of the exceedingly plucky way in which you did your duty about—about those fly-papers after the servant had told you of them.'

'I only did what I thought to be right,' murmured the lady modestly.

'Exactly!' cried Roger with much warmth. 'But how extraordinarily difficult it is at times to do what is right. And nobody could have been in a more awkward predicament than you. With remarkable intuition you realised even then (correct me if I'm wrong) that all was not as it should be; but instead of sitting on your suspicion, as an ordinary person might have done, you acted with energy and initiative. In fact one would hardly be wrong in saying that the whole subsequent course of events was entirely due to your care and foresight on that occasion. It was admirable—really admirable.' For I judge, Roger thought to himself, that this small person prefers it on a trowel; on a trowel, therefore, she shall certainly have it.

Mrs Saunderson bridled charmingly. 'Oh, Mr Sheringham, I think you—surely you exaggerate just a little bit, don't you?'

'Not the tiniest bit in the world!' Roger assured her untruthfully. 'It was a most remarkable piece of work. And the fact of the matter is,' he added with calculated candour, 'that I felt I simply couldn't rest until I'd made your acquaintance and seen for myself what sort of a woman we all have to thank for having brought this dreadful crime to light.' For, if a trowel, why not a shovel? A shovel, after all, is the more capacious instrument.

'Oh, Mr Sheringham! This is really quite overwhelming. And—and now you have seen her, is it permitted to ask what you think of her?'

'That reality for once actually surpasses anticipation,' Roger replied promptly, discarding the shovel and employing a pail. And that was Round Two.

Once again the lady led off. 'Are you—oh, are you going to

put us all into a book, Mr Sheringham?' she asked ecstatically. 'Is *that* why you've come to see me?'

'I'm certainly going to put you into a book, Mrs Saunderson, if you'll let me. Or should I say, write a book round you!—May I?'

'Do you really find me as—as interesting as all that?' Mrs Saunderson turned her head modestly away but allowed her hand to drop from her lap on to the couch between them. Roger promptly closed his own over it.

'It isn't so much what I find you; it's what you *are*. Do you mean to say you don't *know* how interesting you are? Yes, and fascinating too! Do you mind if I put you into a book?'

'N-no,' faltered the little lady artistically. 'If—if you really want to.' And again her slender fingers tightened in an almost imperceptible squeeze.

Roger thanked her with gratitude; he had every intention of putting her into a book. End of Round Three.

It was Roger's turn to open the sparring. 'I wonder if you'd do me a very great favour, Mrs Saunderson—tell me the whole story in your own words. Would you?'

'Certainly,' purred his victim, gently withdrawing her hand. 'Right from the very beginning?'

'From the time that *you* came into it,' Roger amended gallantly. He knew the beginning.

By no means loath, Mrs Saunderson complied. She told him how her hair stood on end, how the marrow froze in her bones, how she could hardly bring herself to believe the conclusions she had leaped to, how she never got a wink of sleep for three whole nights, how she had cried and *cried* when she thought of that poor Mrs Allen (of course she *is* a lot older than her husband, one must admit that; and not very good-looking now; and her temper isn't all that it might be— one must be *fair*; but that's no excuse for a man, is it? But then, Mrs Bentley was *French*, you see), and how she had known—oh, *ages* ago that Jacqueline had something *queer* about her—a sort of look, you know, when she didn't know anybody was watching her; oh, it was difficult to describe, but Mrs Saunderson had felt right from the beginning that she wasn't the sort of person you could, well, *trust* exactly. All these things she told him, and many, many more; but now and then, by accident, a fact did manage to leak out as well. Roger let her talk, listening with an expression of almost painful sympathy and looking (had he but known it—that is, if we are to take Sheila's word for it) like a sick cat in an interesting condition.

'How extraordinarily vivid you make it all!' he declared when the lady had killed off Mr Bentley, post-mortemed him, arrested his wife and shed tears into his grave. 'I almost feel that I've actually lived through the scenes you've been describing. What an extraordinary character Mrs Bentley must be!'

'Oh, she's a monster, Mr Sheringham! There's simply no other word for it, I'm afraid. A *monster*!'

'A monster!' Roger repeated with admiration. 'Absolutely *le mot juste*. But tell me, Mrs Saunderson, what is her explanation of all these things? She must have had some excuses for them, surely. She doesn't sound to me as if she were a stupid woman.'

'Stupid? No, indeed she isn't. Anything but! She's full of most dreadful deceit and cunning.'

'Yes, that's just what I should have said. But these things she did—they don't sound cunning at all; they sound really stupid. So I suppose she must have some very clever explanation up her sleeve?'

'Oh, she's got plenty of explanations, no doubt,' Mrs Saunderson sniffed. 'Jacqueline would have. But you can take it from me that there's nothing in them, Mr Sheringham. They're just lies. Silly, stupid, vulgar lies.'

'Oh, quite,' Roger said soothingly. 'They—they must be, mustn't they? But do you happen to know what they are? It would be so interesting to me, as a student of psychology, to know what a person like that would say to try and explain away the inexplicable. Did you ever hear her make any attempt to do so?'

'Oh, dear, yes! Plenty of times. But she didn't take *me* in, I can assure you.'

'That I can quite believe,' Roger said, trying hard to prevent the excitement he was feeling from showing on his face; he had hit the right trail with a vengeance! 'But what sort of thing could she say? About the Bovril, for instance. How on earth could she give any reasonable excuse for that?'

But here came an unexpected check. Perhaps Roger had been indiscreetly eager; but whether it was that the lady felt the centre of interest to be in danger of shifting too far from herself or whether she didn't, she certainly proceeded to pull it back again with a jerk.

'Oh, you mustn't ask me anything about that, Mr Sheringham,' she said demurely. 'That's part of my evidence, you know, and I've been specially warned that I mustn't say a single word about that to anybody.'

'Quite right,' Roger approved warmly, concealing his disappointment. 'Oh, quite right, of course.'

He decided swiftly on his next move. That this was only a temporary set-back he felt sure; Roger had too good an opinion of himself to doubt that, with sufficient time and patience, he could cozen out of this ridiculous little person anything on which he had really set his heart. But in the meantime he must walk warily; a false move might delay matters very badly. He would administer a little stimulant in the way of studied indifference and see whether that would precipitate matters.

Withdrawing into his own corner of the couch he proceeded to talk firmly upon such matters of impersonal interest as entered his head, to the lady's patent bewilderment and concern.

He was just completing a wordy examination into the causes of unrest among the native population of Southern Nigeria, when the expected result of his diplomacy came to pass.

'Have you met Mrs Allen yet, Mr Sheringham?' his companion asked irrelevantly.

'Mrs Allen?' Roger repeated with a careless air. 'No, I haven't. I was thinking of going to call on her tomorrow afternoon. Now, about this question of totem-worship, Mrs Saunderson, has it ever struck you how very short-sighted the authorities are in not permitting the natives to—'

'Oh, just excuse me one minute, Mr Sheringham! You will stay and have some tea, won't you?'

'May I really? I should simply love to, of course. But I'm afraid I've been boring you dreadfully for the last half-hour.'

'Oh, not at all. I'm—I'm most interested in the poor natives of Southern Iberia. So—so quaint. If you wouldn't mind just ringing the bell on the other side of the fireplace! Oh, thank you *so* much.'

'Why did you ask if I'd met Mrs Allen?' Roger remarked as he resumed his seat.

'Oh, well, I just *wondered*, you see. Of course she doesn't know nearly so much about this terrible affair as I do, you know.'

'No?'

'Oh, no. You see, after she found out that dreadful news about her husband, she hardly went there any more. She couldn't bear to see Jacqueline again, naturally.'

'That was just about twenty-four hours before Mr Bentley died, wasn't it?'

'Yes, less. No, Mrs Allen wasn't there at all when the nurse gave us the bottle of Bovril. It wasn't till we'd had to shut Jacqueline in the spare room after Mr Bentley's death that his brother sent for her to come and make another witness when we decided to make that search.'

'I see,' Roger said with a little smile. A point to Mrs Saunderson certainly.

There was a discreet knock at the door.

'Come in!' said the lady. 'Oh, Mary, will you bring tea, please. And I'm not at home if anybody calls.'

They talked on indifferent subjects till the tea had been served. Then Roger reverted to a point which his companion's last remark had raised in his mind.

'Mrs Allen wasn't in the house after dinner that evening at all, then?' he asked. 'The evening before Mr Bentley died, I mean.'

'Oh, yes. I was forgetting. She did come in once for a few minutes, while the nurse was having her dinner downstairs. She came to see Mr Bentley.'

Roger pricked up his ears. 'To see Mr Bentley, did she? Now I wonder why she did that.'

'I think it must have been about something to do with Mrs Bentley and her husband, because she wanted to see him alone. Do have one of those little cakes, won't you? They're really quite nice. Yes, I was sitting with him at the time while the nurse was downstairs, and Mr Alfred Bentley brought her up and asked me to leave her alone with him.'

Roger took two of the little cakes in his excitement. 'Would that have been about—about an hour before he was taken so ill that evening?' he asked as calmly as he could.

Mrs Saunderson wrinkled her white forehead rather delightfully. 'Yes, it would have been; just about. Let me see, the nurse must have come downstairs at eight o'clock or so, because I remember that Mr Alfred Bentley and I had just finished our dinner as the clock struck on the dining-room mantelpiece.'

'And she asked you to take her place upstairs?'

'Yes, you see, after what we'd found out that day, Mrs Bentley wasn't allowed to be alone with him for a single minute.'

'But Mrs Bentley was alone with him while the nurse was going downstairs?'

'Oh, no; she wasn't in the room then. Besides, Mr William Bentley was there. He came down when I went up.'

'I see. And then Mr Alfred Bentley brought up Mrs Allen and you and he went down again?'

'Yes. Oh, Mr Sheringham, even then I *knew* something was

going to happen! Quite plainly. I'm supposed to be psychic, you know. It's from my mother's family; they're Scotch. Quite often I *feel* something dreadful is going to happen, long before it does. It's so terribly uncanny. You can't understand, if you're not psychic yourself, how—'

'But I am!' Roger told her with perfect gravity.

'Oh—oh, are you?' said the lady, somewhat dashed. 'How—how interesting!'

'Yes, isn't it? But I don't know that I've ever felt anything so strongly as this. You felt even then that something was going to happen, did you? That's very notable indeed. But why do you say "even then"? Weren't you all expecting anything to happen?'

'Oh, no!' cried Mrs Saunderson, much heartened. 'That's just the extraordinary thing. We weren't expecting anything. Right up to nine o'clock that evening Mr Bentley seemed to be quite a lot better. We all thought he was going to recover. And then that last awful attack came on quite suddenly, and he never got over it.'

'And that started at about nine o'clock?'

'Just about nine, yes.'

'Was Mrs Allen still with him?'

'Oh, no; she'd gone ages ago. She was only with him about five minutes. She was crying dreadfully, poor thing, so I had to take her into the drawing-room and try to comfort her. So horrible for her; and being so much older than her husband and not nearly so pretty as Jacqueline and everything. *Horrible!*'

'Horrible!' Roger repeated mechanically. 'But wasn't Mrs Bentley alone with her husband then, while you were with Mrs Allen in the drawing-room?'

'Oh, no. Mr Alfred Bentley had gone up to bring Mrs Allen down, and he stayed with him for a few minutes till the nurse came.'

'The devil he did!' observed Roger under his breath, totting up in his mind the number of people who might perfectly well have fed arsenic to the unfortunate man during that critical half-hour. 'And what time did the nurse go up again?'

'Oh, soon after half-past eight, as far as I know,' returned Mrs Saunderson in a voice which was unmistakably verging on boredom. 'Another cup of tea?'

'Thank you. Then as far as you know, Mr Bentley wasn't left alone for a single minute between eight o'clock and half-past?'

'As far as I know. But he may have been, mayn't he? So many people running in and out. Anybody might have left him for a minute or two, just like I did to run down to the library and get a book.'

Roger very nearly jumped in his seat. 'You went down to the library to get a book?' he repeated with commendable mildness. 'How long did that take you?'

'Really, I haven't the least idea. Three or four minutes, I suppose. It couldn't matter, leaving him just that little time!'

'Oh, of course not. I was meaning—was Mrs Bentley with him then?'

'No,' said the lady petulantly. 'I told you she wasn't. She was having her dinner downstairs with the nurse, if you really want to know.'

Roger knew he was driving her hard, but he had to ask one more question. 'And when you got back, Mr Bentley was still alone?'

'No, he wasn't! The servant, Mary Blower, was with him. As a matter of fact, she was giving him a drink of lemonade; though what that matters to anybody, goodness knows. You seem very interested in all these silly details, Mr Sheringham.'

'They're only incidental,' Roger replied unctuously, hastily disguising himself as a sick cat again and reaching for his shovel. 'What really interests me is the part *you* played in this appalling tragedy, and the magnificent way you played it!' Two minutes later he was lighting the lady's cigarette for her, while she lightly rested the tip of her little finger on his hand to keep it steady.

And quite possibly Roger's hand did need steadying just then; let us be fair.

Less than a quarter of an hour afterwards he rose, despite warm protests, to go. He knew perfectly well that no more information would be volunteered that afternoon, and he did not wish to force matters. But before departing he angled for and very promptly received an invitation to tea on the following afternoon; the two words 'Mrs Allen,' ensured that.

'Personally,' observed Mr Sheringham to himself, as he turned out of the drive gates into the road and wondered which ever way he had to go, to make his way back to the High Street. 'Personally, I think there's the very devil of a lot to be said for the modern girl. I shall write an article for a Sunday paper about it.'

CHAPTER X

SHOCKING TREATMENT OF A LADY

It was nearly half-past five when Roger got back to the big house in the High Street. Mrs Purefoy was alone in the drawing-room.

'No,' she said in answer to his first question. 'They came in to tea, but they went out again immediately afterwards. Sheila gave me a message for you if you came in first.'

'Oh?' Roger asked eagerly. 'What was that?'

'"Not much luck." She was very mysterious about it, and wouldn't tell me a word of what she is doing or why she was looking so important and pleased with herself.'

'In other words,' Roger laughed, 'you know perfectly well that there's something going on, and please, what is it?'

'Well, not quite so bluntly as all that,' Mrs Purefoy smiled.

'Yes, we are up to something, the three of us,' Roger had to admit. 'But would you mind very much if I asked you not to ask me what it is? I'm responsible; it's just a little bee in my bonnet. But I can promise you that it's nothing that a perfectly respectable mother wouldn't like her perfectly respectable daughter to be mixed up in.'

'Then I suppose I shall have to be content with that, shan't I?' returned Mrs Purefoy serenely.

'I say, do you mind frightfully? I'll tell you like a shot if you really want me to.'

'Of course I don't! I was only teasing you. Now then, sit down and talk interestingly to me about the weather 'til the other two babies come back.'

'I like you, Mrs Purefoy,' said Roger frankly.

It was not 'til an hour later that Alec and Sheila returned.

They marched in single file into the drawing-room, halted and right-turned.

'All present and correct, Superintendent,' announced Miss Purefoy, saluting briskly. 'But I have to report Constable Grierson for a grave derewhatd'youcallit of duty, to wit and namely viz. that at half-past six on the twenty-first inst. prox. he did commit a grievous assault against the peace of our sovereign lord the King and of Superintendent Sheringham by endeavouring to shove his superior officer into the pond. I demand his immediate execution without bail.'

'Not guilty, m'lud,' said Alec promptly. 'The woman tempted me and she fell. I didn't shove her. I just blew at her.'

'Gentlemen of the jury,' Roger summed up, addressing the chair in which Mrs Purefoy was sitting, 'you have now heard the evidence on both sides. The plaintiff's case is that she paid for the pork-pie and obtained a receipt, which she has subsequently mislaid, while the defendant contends that the words uttered were true both in substance and in fact; it is for you to say which of them is speaking the truth. You will take the law from me. In order that the charge of arson can lie, you must first be satisfied in your own minds that the goods found on the plaintiff were not only in intention but also *de jure* the goods missed from the defendant's shop on the date in question. I will now ask you to deliver yourselves of a verdict.'

'M'lud,' replied the jury, gathering up its knitting, 'I must ask permission to retire—and leave you three silly children alone together which I know you're wanting to be. No, don't bother to be polite! In any case I've got to go and have a word or two with my cook.'

'It's rather nice, having a mother with a sense of humour, isn't it?' observed Sheila, as Alec closed the door behind the retiring jury. 'It's a thing so many mothers seem to lose, poor dears. Now then, Roger, tell us all about it! Did you kiss the Saunderson?'

'Miss Purefoy!'

'Well, did she kiss you, then? Perhaps that's more like it—though I'm not a bit too sure.'

Roger turned pointedly to Alec. 'Have you anything to report, Constable Grierson?' he asked coldly.

'He's huffy, 'cos I spoke disrespectably about the Saunderson and he's smitten with her,' Miss Purefoy confided to that gentleman in a loud aside.

'Not me,' Alec replied. 'I spent most of the afternoon shivering outside different places, waiting for Sheila to come out.'

'Men always fall for the Saunderson,' Miss Purefoy continued with much scorn. 'She just makes a couple of goo-goo eyes at 'em, and down they go like blinking nine-pins.'

'Alexander,' Roger said with energy, 'last night I believe you made a request of me. I refused. I'm sorry I refused, Alec. Is it too late to accept now?'

'Not a bit! Three times a day, before or after meals, is the prescription. Wait while I fix her!'

'*No*!' squealed Miss Purefoy, repenting too late. 'I'm sorry, Roger. I take it back. You never fell for her at all. You just kissed her without falling. No, Alec! What's it got to do with you, anyway? Stop it, you brute! Let me *go*! Mother! *Mother*!'

With some difficulty Miss Purefoy was persuaded to arrive at the end of the couch and assume a position suitable for chastisement, her agonised appeals to the deity meeting with no response. With a rolled-up magazine Roger dealt with this first breach of discipline in his force.

'Roger Sheringham,' exclaimed the indignant recipient of his attentions when, very red in the face, she was allowed at last to regain her erect position. 'I hate you worse than boiled beef. I won't play detectives with you any more, and I think your books are *tripe*!'

'There, my child,' Roger returned equably, 'I am more than disposed to agree with you; still, they sell well enough, and that's the main thing, isn't it? So now to business. It may interest you both to learn that I, at any rate, have had a most successful afternoon.'

'Then you *did*—' Sheila began, caught Alec's eye and thought better of it. 'Have you found out anything, dear Roger?' she cooed in a voice of honey.

'I have. A devil of a lot. And I'm going to find out a good deal more before very long. Seriously, you two, I've struck oil. Listen!'

He went on to give a condensed version of the conversation he had had with Mrs Saunderson, picking the facts like plums out of the dough of their surrounding emotion. Sheila, by a swift transition perfectly serious, listened as attentively and as gravely as Alec himself.

'Half a minute!' she interrupted, as Roger was nearing his conclusion. 'Just say that again, will you? I want to get that quite clear. How many people were alone with him during that half-hour?'

'For varying periods, no less than six—Mrs Saunderson, Mrs Allen, Brother William, Brother Alfred, Mary Blower and the nurse. Six for certain.'

'Then, Mrs Bentley herself wasn't?' Alec asked.

'So far as we know, that is so,' Roger assented.

'Then that clears her!' Sheila cried.

'Oh, no. Not in a court of law, it wouldn't. The defence could make a point of it, no doubt, and a big point too; perhaps they intend to in any case. But the prosecution could tear it to shreds with the greatest ease.'

'How?'

'Well, for one thing we don't *know* that she didn't nip into his room. She had at least one opportunity, while that fool woman was in the library; probably others. So for that matter had anybody else—a point, by the way, which we mustn't forget to remember! But the chief thing is that this question of the time before the symptoms of poisoning appear, is, as your father said, somewhat anomalous; that is to say, you can't lay down a really hard and fast rule about it. In ninety-seven cases out of a hundred, perhaps, they would begin to show themselves in from an hour to half an hour after administration of the arsenic; in the remaining three they wouldn't. Going by probabilities, Mrs Bentley is certainly cleared. But it's only probability. One can't say that there's the least certainty about it. And "probability" as a defence in a court of law isn't worth two pence, I fear.'

'How do you mean?' Alec asked.

'Oh, it's this futile attitude towards things known as "the legal mind". To the legal mind a thing either is or it isn't; there's no half-way house, no "pretty nearly, but not quite," no "rather less than more," no "not *exactly*"; everything is either fact or not fact. Any more absurd way to approach just the very problems that the courts are there to tackle I defy anybody to imagine. To put it in a nut-shell, the legal mind is absolutely lacking in any sense of proportion.'

'This is too deep for me,' said Sheila.

'Well, I'll try and give you a simple example of what I mean. Suppose there was some question about these quack electric belts that you see advertised everywhere and whose proprietors ought one and all to be shoved away in prison as common charlatans and thieves. (Would you believe it, but I know of a real case in which some wretched woman was taken in by the glibness of the advertisements and actually persuaded into parting with twenty pounds for one of the rotten things. Twenty pounds—for a thing not worth half a crown!) Well, supposing it was a question of the validity of one of these abominations, and a doctor was in the witness-box. This is the way the legal mind would go to work. He'd be asked, you see, whether this belt did or did not, as it claims to do, generate electricity when worn on the body; and he'd have to say "Yes!" Couldn't help himself. It does, you see—just as drawing the tip of your finger across the tablecloth does; and just about the same amount. Any friction whatever generates electricity. 'Aha!' says the legal mind. 'It does, does it? Then that's all right. The thing is not a fraud. It says it generates electricity, and it does generate electricity. Fine anybody who says it's a fraud a couple of hundred pounds, and whatever you do, make a precedent of it!' Not a bit of use for the doctor to try to explain (if he ever gets the chance, which he certainly wouldn't) that the belt doesn't generate enough electricity to make a fly's wings quiver. The legal mind doesn't care a hang about that. It does generate electricity, and there's an end of it.'

'He's getting all worked up,' observed Alec to his fellow-listener.

'Shut up, Alec! It's jolly interesting. Go on, Roger.'

'Well, take another example. Supposing a man had had nothing to eat for a whole day but a slice of bread. You'd say he had had something to eat, wouldn't you?'

Sheila nodded. 'Yes.'

'Well, now suppose it wasn't a slice, but one single crumb, Would you still say he'd had something to eat?'

'I—I don't know. In a way, I suppose, but—!'

'Well, finally suppose that it wasn't even a crumb, but just a speck of bread, almost invisible to the naked eye. Would you still say that man had had something to eat that day, or not?'

'No, I'm hanged if I would!'

'Exactly; you wouldn't. And nor would anyone else—who happened not to be afflicted with a legal mind! Nevertheless, on a strictly accurate statement of fact, that man had something to eat during that day; and that's what the legal mind would tell you. Now then, what chance has Mrs Bentley got of being acquitted on a question of "probability"?'

'Dam' little,' Sheila agreed.

'And over and above all, don't forget what I told you about her own solicitor. If he thinks her guilty, as I'm quite convinced he does, that means that he's got precious little hope of an acquittal. And if anybody ought to be in a position to know how much her defence is going to be worth, certainly he should.'

'And you say you're going to be able to get at that, you think?' Alec asked. 'What her defence is going to be and her own explanations of all this business?'

'Mrs Saunderson certainly knows what Mrs Bentley said about it all,' Roger said, 'and I imagine the defence is bound to be based on that. Whether I shall be able to worm it out of her remains to be seen. But in common fairness I ought to tell you,' he added modestly, 'that time and patience, when allied with Roger Sheringham, ought to work wonders.'

'Roger,' Sheila put in, 'do tell me! Honestly, not ragging—*did* you kiss her?'

'Miss Purefoy, you have a singularly prurient mind,' Roger said coldly. 'No, honestly, not ragging—I did *not* kiss her!'

'Oh!' said Miss Purefoy in frank disappointment. 'You dud!'

'Look here!' Alec exclaimed suddenly. 'Dash it all, Roger, we've been overlooking something tremendously important. Don't you see? If Mrs Bentley didn't do it, and always assuming she didn't, then the person who did must have been one of those six!'

'I've been wondering when one of my two bright subordinates was going to draw that rather shrieking deduction,' Roger remarked tolerantly.

'Oo!' cried Sheila. 'Who do you think did, Roger? I believe the nurse did.'

'The nurse, my infant? Why the deuce do you think that?'

'Because she's the most unlikely person, of course. Don't you know that it's *always* the most unlikely person who committed the crime? Superintendent Sheringham, I'm surprised at you. What sort of a detective do you think you are?'

'Talking about that, by the way, what sort of detectives are you between you? I've told you all my discoveries. I don't seem to have heard anything from you at all.'

'Oh, we didn't find out much. We tried three times to get hold of Dr James, but he was out each time.'

'Well, it doesn't matter about him now; I found all that out myself. Did you manage to collect any evidence about character? Not that that's wildly important, in view of what we know about that crucial half-hour. Still, did you?'

'Well, I saw a lot of her friends and people who knew her, and faked up a different excuse each time to bring the conversation round to her, but what's the use? They're all perfectly convinced she's guilty, and I don't think a single one of them had a good word to say for her.'

'God save us from our friends indeed! Yes, that was the same with my lady. Not the least earthly use trying to get any information as to character out of her. In fact, by her description, Mrs Bentley was a monster. And I told her it was *le mot juste*, Heaven forgive me! So not to put too fine a point on it, you didn't find out anything at all?'

'Well,' said Alec, 'we did—'

'Oh, let me tell him, Alec, there's an angel! Yes, Roger, we did find out one thing that I've never seen mentioned anywhere before, though whether it's the least importance or not I don't know. Probably not, as we discovered it and not you. It's this. Did you know that the servant who told them about the fly-papers, Mary Blower, was under notice to go?'

'The devil she was!' Roger exclaimed. 'That's interesting.'

'Sheila!' Mrs Purefoy's voice reached them faintly. 'Sheila! Time you were getting ready for dinner, dear!'

CHAPTER XI

AFTER breakfast the next morning Alec and Roger strolled out
to smoke their pipes in the delightful old garden at the back of
the house, with its two mulberry trees, its medlar tree, its green
fig tree, its peach border, quaintly shaped flower-beds and thick,
springy lawn to whose making a couple of centuries of assiduous
rolling and mowing had gone.

'Well, what's the programme today?' Alec asked.

'As far as you're concerned, nothing. We can't get on a step
now 'til I've tackled this Saunderson woman successfully, And
the dismissal of that servant; I shall have to include that in my
pumping operations too.'

'How are you going about it? Getting her to talk, I mean?'

Roger looked at his friend a little quizzically. 'I'm going to
make love to her, Alexander,' he said frankly.

'Humph!' Alec grunted with patent disapproval.

'Rather a curious reversal of the ordinary procedure in this
kind of circumstances, isn't it?' Roger mused. 'The best detectives, I understand, the pukka article, make love to the servant
in order to find out things about the mistress. I with my usual
contempt for convention make love to a mistress to find out
about a servant. And of the two, I must say that I think my
method is vastly to be preferred.'

They paced up and down the lawn for a few moments in
silence.

'Look here,' Alec said suddenly. 'I don't like this.'

'I knew it, I knew it,' Roger sighed. 'I've been expecting some
such remark as that, my excellent Alexander. I haven't forgotten
the enormous trouble you gave me at Layton Court over this

very same thing, or something very like it. Though I did hope that marriage might have at least modified your views. All right, go on; get it off your chest.'

'Oh, it's all very well for you to laugh,' Alec growled. 'You make fun of everything. But I'm hanged if it's playing the game, making a cat's-paw of a woman like this just to get information out of her.'

'It isn't you who'd be hanged, Alec,' Roger retorted crudely. 'It'd be Mrs Bentley. Is that what you're driving at—that it would be better to let Mrs Bentley be hanged than trifle with the other lady's innocent affections?'

'Don't be such an ass! You know very well it isn't. But what I do say is that there's no need to go about getting your information in that particular way. Why don't you go to her and tell her the whole story just as you told Sheila?'

'Because, my well-meaning but completely dunderheaded friend, the only result of that would be to shut the lady up tighter than seven clams. I tell you there's one way and one way only to get what I want out of her, and that is to make love to her.'

'Now how the deuce do you make that out?'

'Oh, well, I'll try and explain, though I quite despair of ever making you see it. The only thing on Mrs Saunderson's horizon is Mrs Saunderson; the only way of getting Mrs Saunderson to talk about anything is by keeping continually in the foreground of the conversation that thing's particular relation to Mrs Saunderson; the only way of getting into Mrs Saunderson's head the idea that one is not more interested in any other thing than her and thereby loosening her tongue upon matters is to make love to Mrs Saunderson. Good Lord, you talk as if the woman didn't want love made to her! Holy smoke, that's the only thing in the world she does want. Not to make love to Mrs Saunderson is, in Mrs Saunderson's opinion, an open insult to Mrs Saunderson; it would mean that one didn't find her attractive. Can you understand that?'

'You're not going to tell me,' Alec said obstinately, 'that any woman in this world is going to want love made to her by any chance man who happens to come along.'

Roger groaned. 'Alec, you're hopeless! Hasn't even marriage taught you that women do *not* live on the top of pedestals, leading good, pure, blameless little lives in a white cloud of superhumanity? Women, dear Alec, were sent upon this earth for just one purpose, the bearing of children; that's their job in life, and a damned big job too, and for that end solely and entirely have they been designed. I don't want to have to give you a lecture about women, but I do think you ought to know as much about them as an ordinary child of ten does. Nearly all women, then, Alexander, are idiots—mentally a trifle deficient, if you like; charming idiots, delightful idiots, adorable idiots, if you like, but always idiots, and mostly damnable idiots at that. Frequently devilish idiots as well; most women are potential devils, you know. They live entirely by their emotions, both in thought and deed, they are fundamentally incapable of reason and their one idea in life is to appear attractive to men. That's about all there is to women.

'Here and there, of course, one does meet with exceptions— thank Heaven! And invariably these exceptions make themselves felt, either in their own immediate circle or in business, if they happen to have no artistic abilities; or else as novelists (mostly), painters (occasionally) or musicians (very rarely)—strange about the last, by the way, music being decidedly the most emotional form of self-expression. And stranger still that music should so often go with mathematics; it does, you know. Strange thing altogether, music; the scale, for instance ... But I'm wandering; I'll lecture to you about music another time. Meanwhile, about women, just one thing more. There's a terrible lot of poppycock talked about the impossibility of understanding women, the eternal mystery of woman and all that junk (would you believe it—I once saw an article in one of the dear old Sunday papers which began like this, "Whenever two or three men are gathered together, the conversation always turns before long upon the eternal mystery of woman." Would you *believe* it? I've never forgotten that. Written by a woman, of course). Where was I? Oh, yes.

'Well, that idea was put about by woman herself, of course; they like to make their dear little silly empty-headed selves out as mysterious and deep and sphinx-like and all the rest of it; makes 'em important, you see, and Heaven knows they need all the importance they can fake up. Whereas the real truth of the matter is that any man with more than half a brain, combined with a modicum of sympathy and emotion and an understanding mind, can understand any woman backwards, from the heels of her fatuous little shoes to the crown of her artificially waved head; there's nothing to understand. But the woman was never yet born of woman who has really understood one single man. And that will be all about women.'

'My Lord!' sighed Alec, but not without a touch of admiration. 'How you can yap! And do you mean to tell me that you really believe all that stuff?'

Roger laughed. 'Candidly, Alexander, no! It's the kind of cheap and easy cynical drivel that a fourth-rate writer stuffs his books with in the hope that the undiscerning may mistake him for a third-rate one. But you go too far in the direction of the penny novelette, you know, so I thought it might be a little tonic. Nobody knows better than I that a man without his woman is only half an entity and that a woman (the right woman for him, needless to say) can not only make her man twice the fellow he was before, but she can turn his life, however drab, into something really rather staggeringly wonderful—too wonderful sometimes for a determined bachelor like me to contemplate with equanimity. And now I'm talking like a penny novelette myself.'

'Then if nobody knows that better than you,' remarked Alec curiously, 'why are you still a determined bachelor?'

'Because the right woman in my case, Alexander,' Roger

replied lightly enough, 'happens unfortunately to be married to someone else.'

Alec coughed gruffly. With the Englishman's almost morbid aversion from sentiment in the presence of his own sex, he was unable to frame a suitable reply; but under his silence he was deeply touched. It was the first time that Roger had ever even hinted at any such tragedy in his life, and that it was by way of being a tragedy Alec instinctively knew. In its light a good many things became plain to him which had been before obscure.

'Still,' Roger was continuing thoughtfully, 'there is a modicum of truth at the bottom of that diatribe I treated you to just now. The average woman is not over-burdened with brains, and she does consider herself a bit of a mystery, which of course she isn't. Anyhow there's quite enough truth in it to show you why I've got to make love to the excellent Saunderson; as no doubt you now quite understand?'

'No, I'm damned if I do.'

'I thought you wouldn't,' Roger replied, quite cheerfully.

'Still, apparently you think you've got to, so it's no use me saying anything one way or the other.'

'Ah, now that's more like it,' Roger approved.

They left it, and women, at that.

Before lunch Sheila sought out Roger where he was reading by the fire in the drawing-room.

'I say, you asked me to get you a photograph of Mrs Bentley yesterday, Roger, and I forgot clean about it. I've just been down the town and bought one. Here you are.'

'Thanks, Sheila,' Roger said, unwrapping the paper. 'Are they on sale in the shops, then?'

'Lord, yes! Everywhere. I only wonder they haven't got *A Present from Wychford* printed across the bottom.'

'Local industries, vamping respectable novelists and murdering husbands. Ah, well! So this is the lady, is she? Let's study her for a minute.'

With the frank *camaraderie* of the sexless young animal she still was, Sheila perched herself on the arm of Roger's chair and leaned on his shoulder, the brim of her little felt hat brushing his cheek as she peered down at the photograph on his knees. They gazed at it in silence. The face was an attractive one, round and full-cheeked in the characteristic Latin fashion, with big, laughing eyes, a mouth full-lipped but not sensual, tilted nose, delicately drawn brows, a high forehead and very dark, almost certainly black hair; she looked, perhaps twenty-two or three when the photograph was taken, and she was smiling merrily.

'Southern stock, I should say, from the look of her,' Roger murmured. 'Up towards Paris you get the Frankish type; this is pure Latin.'

'She might be Italian almost, mightn't she?'

'Not almost, but quite; it's the same race. Well, Sheila, what do you think? Can you imagine that woman poisoning her husband, or can't you?'

'No!' Sheila said without hesitation. 'Not for a minute. She's got too jolly a smile.'

'Don't be deceived by her smile; try and visualise her face in repose, or in anger for that matter. She'd have a wicked temper, I'll promise you that. And she's as passionate as they make 'em. Imagine her wildly, overpoweringly in love with this Allen man and tied to that little middle-aged rat of a husband of hers—longing with all her passionate heart to break free from him! Can't you imagine her killing him?'

'Oh, yes; easily. But that isn't what you said. I can imagine her killing him in a blind temper. But she'd stick a knife into him or shoot him—not poison him!'

Roger twisted round in his chair and looked up into her face. 'Miss Purefoy,' he said, and the usual mocking tone was a little faint in his voice, 'do you know you're a young woman of really rather remarkable acuteness?'

'I'm not a perfect fool,' returned Miss Purefoy equably, 'if that's what you mean. I never thought I was.'

'How old are you? Eighteen, is it?'

'Nineteen. Getting on for twenty.'

'Nineteen. It's amazing! And you've got as much sense in your little finger as five editions of the average boy of nineteen can muster between them—to say nothing of that irritating property of your own sex known as feminine intuition.'

Sheila leaned back against the back of the chair and crossed her knees. That the little tweed skirt she was wearing only projected stiffly an inch or two beyond the upper one, thereby displaying the full length of two slim calves, she either did not know or else was not in the least concerned about; one is inclined to suspect the latter.

'Go on, Roger,' she said comfortably 'I like talking about me. So I've got more sense in my little finger than five boys, have I?'

'You have,' Roger agreed, 'at present. And in a year or two you'll have completely lost every grain of it.'

'Oh! How do you make that out.'

'The process is known technically, I believe, as the development of sex-consciousness. But we won't go into that.'

'I know a hell of a lot about sex,' observed Miss Purefoy with candour.

'I've no doubt about that,' Roger said mildly. 'And when I want a little instruction in the subject, it's probably you or somebody like you I should go to. Still, as I said, we won't go into that for the moment. We were talking about sense. Yes, you're going to lose every atom you've got. But don't let that distress you. You'll get it all back again. Possibly after you've turned thirty, certainly by the time you're forty.'

'Fat lot of use that's going to be,' commented Miss Purefoy.

'Not much, certainly,' Roger admitted; 'considering that it's precisely during the time you want it most that you won't have it. Still, console yourself, my dear; every other member of your sex passes through the same process. Except perhaps the vast majority.'

'Now, what are you driving at? Why not the vast majority?'

'Because they haven't got any sense at all. Never had, poor dears, and never will have. For further remarks on this subject, apply to Cousin Alexander.'

'Now then,' said Miss Purefoy, swinging an unhampered leg, 'if you've finished being clever about women, shall I tell you something about men?'

'No, please don't. I know all about them. Let me tell you instead something about Miss Sheila Purefoy.'

'Rather! Go ahead!'

Roger twisted still further round in his chair. The photograph fell to the floor unheeded.

'Well, Miss Sheila Purefoy is sitting on the arm of my chair in an attitude which, in any other member of her sex, I should be inclined to call deliberately provocative. In fact, if I were not a person of admirable self-restraint and ascetic disposition, I should probably have been tempted to put my arm round her waist.'

'Well, carry on if you want to,' said Miss Purefoy kindly.

Roger closed his hand over the small brown one that was lying in Sheila's lap. 'I might even have been tempted to kiss her!'

'Roger!' exclaimed Miss Purefoy in high delight. 'I do believe you're trying to flirt with me!'

Roger withdrew his hand from Sheila's. 'Of course I was!' he said in pained tones. 'But that's not what you ought to have said. Run away and play with your dolls, Sheila. I'll come back and flirt with you when you're a big girl.'

'Oh, no, Roger!' implored Miss Purefoy pathetically. 'Do flirt with me now. I'll be good; I will really. I'll make goo-goo eyes at you like anything. Please flirt with me, Roger!'

'Go away, woman!' returned Roger with dignity. He turned round in his chair again, picked up and opened his book, and began to read with considerable ostentation.

'Roger!' said a small voice behind his left shoulder.

'Go away, woman!' Roger repeated sternly.

There was a moment's stillness; then Sheila slowly uncrossed her legs and sat up. 'All right, Roger,' she said in a curiously sober voice. 'I'll go.' She bent forward swiftly, kissed his cheek and ran to the door.

Roger's book fell off his knees and he did not pick it up. He stared at the door through which Sheila had vanished.

'Oh, *hell*!' he said softly.

A few minutes later Alec came in. He had been keeping Dr Purefoy company in the car on his morning round and he was cold.

'You frowsty blighter!' he observed pleasantly, pulling a chair up to the fire. 'Been reading in here all the morning?'

'Alec,' said Roger irrelevantly, 'we were talking about women this morning, weren't we?'

'Oh Lord! You're not going to start on that *again*, are you?'

'I think I mentioned, in passing, that they were idiots, didn't I?'

'You did!' agreed Alec with feeling.

'Well, so they are. Most consummate idiots, poor little devils; and the tragedy of it is, that they can't help it. But they're not such consummate idiots, such unutterable, thoughtless, careless, ineffable, altogether *damned* idiots as men are!'

'Good Lord!' Alec exclaimed, genuinely startled. 'Meaning me?'

'No, you ass!' Roger snapped. 'Meaning *me*!'

'Well, I'll be hanged!' gasped the astonished Alec. It was the first word of self-disparagement he had ever heard pass his distinguished friend's lips.

At lunch Mrs Purefoy was seriously perturbed about Sheila; that young lady's violent and hectic ragging of Alec not only passed all bounds of decorum, but almost those of decency as well. Roger, on the contrary, provided a pleasant contrast with his usual manner in the unwonted restraint and taciturnity of his behaviour.

After lunch he followed Alec upstairs and into his bedroom. 'Alec, come for a walk somewhere,' he said shortly.

Alec scrutinised his friend with exaggerated concern. 'I'm going to ask Jim to have a look at you, Roger,' he said. 'You must be ill. At lunch you sat there looking like a dead cow'— Roger's animal impersonations appeared to be singularly versatile—'and hardly opened your mouth, and now you want to go for a walk! Let me feel your pulse.'

'Don't try to be funnier than nature made you, Alec,' observed Roger wearily.

'Well, do cheer up!' Alec exhorted. 'Think of tea-time. That ought to buck you up.'

Roger rounded on him in sudden exasperation. 'Good Lord, you don't think I'm looking *forward* to it, do you? The thought of the wretched woman makes me feel ill. I tell you, Alec, I've a dam' good mind to go back with you to Dorsetshire and chuck the whole thing! In fact, if I weren't almost sure we're on the right tack, I certainly would.'

Alec stared at him with open mouth. 'Well I'll be jiggered!' he said blankly.

CHAPTER XII

THE HUMAN ELEMENT

THE end of the walk saw Roger restored to a somewhat more reasonable frame of mind. Severely as he was accustomed to castigate any claim on the part of others to an artistic temperament (holding as he did that this was even more of a palpable pose than to prate of writing for mere writing's sake), he was certainly to some extent himself the possessor of this inconvenient accessory. His infrequent reactions from his usual mood of frivolous complacency were, when they did occur, violent and murky.

His disposition was naturally buoyant, however, and it was not long on this occasion before the vehemence with which he had blamed himself for the palpable state of Sheila's feelings began to abate. His thoughtless pretence of a mock-flirtation had done nothing more after all than bring matters to a brief and fleeting climax; and though he was still distressed at the idea that the child might for the moment have imagined any hint of seriousness underlying his nonsense, his sense of proportion soon returned. Just as the flapper of the days before the war had vented her calf-love and her instinctive sense of hero-worship upon her favourite matinée idol, so must Sheila in nature have somebody to idolise in secret and spin dreams around in her small white bed at night. Roger was a trifle embarrassed that her choice should have fallen upon himself, for he liked Sheila and enjoyed the frank and easy *camaraderie* into which they had fallen so quickly. He made up his mind to treat her exactly as he had done for the last twenty-four hours and show not the faintest suspicion that everything might not be as it appeared on the surface.

Nevertheless, as Alec left him outside Mrs Saunderson's gates it was with distinct reluctance that he made his way up to the front door and rang the bell. The difference between Mrs Saunderson and Sheila Purefoy was the difference between black lingerie in a scented boudoir and small brogue shoes on an open moor; and Roger never had cared much about black lingerie.

It was nearly half-past seven before he got back to the house in the High Street. He looked into the empty drawing-room, then ran up the stairs to Alec's room, where he found that gentleman brushing his hair with a good deal of earnest attention in front of his dressing-table mirror.

'Hallo, Alec; I've found out one thing,' he began abruptly. 'Don't ask me how I did it, or I shall burst into tears; a detective's life must be a singularly hard one. But I've brought something back with me for my trouble.'

'You have? Good! What is it?'

Roger dropped into an armchair beside the dressing-table. 'Bentley had been carrying on an intrigue with Mary Blower!'

Alec whistled. 'Had he, by Jove! That looks nasty.'

'For us, you mean? But Mrs Bentley didn't know about it—or as far as the Saunderson's information is, she didn't.'

'She didn't, eh? Well, what do you make of that?'

'I'm not sure,' Roger confessed, lighting a cigarette. 'These are the facts, as far as I can make them out. Bentley (who, though a rat, appears to have been somewhat of an amorous rat; this wasn't his first affair by any means, according to the omniscient Saunderson)—Bentley had been playing about with the girl and then chucked her; Mrs Bentley had her suspicions, if nothing more, and gave her the sack; she demanded protection from Bentley, who told her quite plainly to go to the devil; in the correct way her love turned to loathing, but she didn't go to the devil; instead, she took some pains to send Mrs Bentley there. And that's the story. Mary Blower wept it all out on Mrs Saunderson's shoulder after Mrs Bentley's arrest. Nobody else knows a thing about it.'

'Humph! This seems to complicate matters.'

'It does; it throws discredit on all Mary Blower's evidence, you see. She hates both the Bentleys like poison, so we can't believe a word she tells us about them. And there's another thing. Mrs Bentley knew that her husband had been unfaithful to her before she herself embarked on this Allen affair. She told Mrs Saunderson so. Isn't it amazing—these women seem to have no decent reticence at all! They yap to their friends about the most intimate details of their married lives—things a man would sooner be burnt alive than tell to his very best lifelong pal. It does make me rather sick. Still, it has its uses for budding detectives, I must say.'

'Now don't go off the deep end about women again,' Alec admonished. 'Stick to the point. What does all this suggest to you? That Mary Blower poisoned Bentley herself?'

'Not necessarily. But it does give her a motive for doing so, doesn't it? Lord, this is getting difficult. Out of those six people on whom we're keeping a suspicious eye, no less than four have the most excellent motives for wishing friend Bentley under the turf—to say nothing of Mrs Bentley herself.'

'Four?' said Alec in some surprise.

'Why, surely. One, Mary Blower, for reasons mentioned; two, Brother William, to obtain full control of the business, out of which he considered himself to have been cheated by his father's will, you remember—and also remembering that he didn't know anything about Bentley's own new will; Brother Alfred, in consequence of that new will; and Mrs Allen.'

'Mrs Allen? How does she come into it?'

'Well, surely that's obvious. She's hating nothing more in the world than Mrs Bentley. What more satisfying revenge could she have than by causing her rival to be hanged as a murderess? It would be superb.'

'But dash it all, she couldn't go to the length of poisoning Bentley to ensure it?' Alec protested.

'Wouldn't she?' said Roger thoughtfully. 'I'm not too sure

about that. A woman can be a pretty dreadful devil in circumstances like those, you know. And how do we know that she hadn't got something against Bentley himself as well? Oh, yes, I think we can set her down as having a motive all right, and a strong one too. She goes down on our list of double suspects.'

'Double suspects?'

'Yes, opportunity and motive. There are six suspects under opportunity, and four of those crop up again under motive.'

Roger leaned back in his chair and expelled a cloud of smoke from his lungs. 'What's it going to turn out, Alec? Murder for gain, murder for revenge, murder for elimination, murder for jealousy, murder from lust of killing, or murder from conviction—according to a classification of motives in a most interesting book I read recently?* It seems to me that murder from conviction is the only one we can definitely rule out: nobody is likely to have come to a reasoned conviction that, for the sake of humanity, Mr John Bentley had better be wiped out of existence, and then have proceeded so efficiently to act upon it. That leaves us with five possible motives to put a possible criminal to.'

'I should think you might rule out murder from lust of killing too,' Alec suggested.

'Indeed and that's just what we can't do!' Roger retorted with energy. 'That's a possibility that can never be ruled out; and the more difficult a case is, the more must just that possibility be borne in mind. Supposing the nurse had homicidal tendencies!'

'Oh, come, I say! Be reasonable.'

'Curse you, Alexander,' Roger exclaimed, touched on the raw, 'that's precisely what I am being. You think a nurse could never suffer from homicidal tendencies or murder a patient? Then let me confound you with the case of one Catherine Wilson, who murdered no less than seven of her patients and

---

* *Murder and Its Motives*, by F. Tennyson Jesse.

attempted to murder several more and who was considered by the judge who tried her, as he stated privately afterwards, to be the greatest criminal that ever lived—his own words; with which, by the way, I don't altogether agree.'

'Humph!' said Alec.

'That was in 1862, and created no small stir at the time. I'm willing to grant you, if you wish to argue the point, that this wasn't entirely murder for lust of killing, because she always induced her victims to leave money to her in their wills or made sure in other ways of becoming a gainer by their deaths; though in my opinion she was certainly a homicidal maniac as well. Still, we must classify her under murder for gain. However, consider further the case of a lady named Van de Layden, also a nurse, who between 1869 and 1885 poisoned no less than twenty-seven people and did her best to poison seventy-five others. Consider also one Marie Jeanneret who had similar impulses and became a professional nurse in order to gratify them, which she did with considerable success. Am I still being unreasonable in suggesting that it is possible for a professional nurse to be a homicidal maniac?'

'No,' said Alec.

'I accept your apology,' Roger said with considerable dignity. 'Where were we when you disturbed the thread of my argument with your puking objections? Oh, yes. Well, murder for gain, Brother William or Brother Alfred; murder for revenge, though with complications, Mrs Allen or Mary Blower; murder for jealousy—well, I can't quite see anybody to fit that except Allen, and as far as we know he had no opportunity; murder for elimination, Mrs Bentley; murder for lust of killing, anybody. That's how the case stands at present.'

'Then you've still got Mrs Bentley under suspicion?'

'Oh, of course; it's no good losing sight of her.'

'Look here,' Alec said slowly, 'there's another point about her that's occurred to me and I don't think I've ever heard you mention it. The motive for murdering her husband, everybody says, is her affair with Allen, isn't it? So that she could be free. Well, it seems to me that a woman like that—a jolly sort of woman, as she looks in her photograph—wouldn't go to that extent to get her freedom; she'd just run away from him and have done with it.'

'But this is pure psychology, Alec!' cried Roger with warm admiration. 'And is Alexander also among the psychologists? Yes; but the answer to that (and you can be very sure that the prosecution will rub it well in) is that if she did that she'd lose his money, and she wanted not only her freedom but her husband's wealth as well.'

'Oh!' said Alec, somewhat dashed. 'Yes, I hadn't thought of that.'

'Still, for all that I think you're perfectly right. If my estimate of the lady is right, she wouldn't care a tinker's cuss about the money; she'd just pack up and leave him. She *was* on the verge of it twice, wasn't she? How most unfortunate for her that Brother William and Mrs Saunderson were able to restrain her, poor woman!'

'Mrs Saunderson seems to have had a finger in every one of those pies,' observed Alec, without malice.

'Her type *is* ubiquitous,' Roger agreed absently.

For a minute or two there was silence. Alec washed his hands, dried them, inspected his hair afresh and decided the parting would not do after all; he set about manufacturing another. Roger went on smoking with a thoughtful air.

'Aren't you going to get ready for dinner?' asked Alec.

'In a minute. Alec, I came across rather an illuminating sentence in a book I was reading the other day. It was this, or something like it; "Ordinary detective yarns bore me, because all they set out to do is to show who committed the crime; what I care about is *why* it was committed." See? In other words, the real interest in a murder case in actual life, the interest that keeps pages of newspaper columns filled and causes perfectly respectable citizens to let their eggs and bacon grow cold while they read and re-read them, is not the crime puzzle of the carefully manufactured detective story, but the human element which led the, quite possibly, very ordinary crime to be committed at all. There very seldom is a crime puzzle in real life, you know; yet the classical dramas of the Central Criminal Court are more absorbingly interesting than any detective story ever written. Why? Because of their psychological values. Crippen, for instance. Not a shadow of doubt as to who murdered Belle Elmore, or whether Crippen was guilty or not. But tell me the detective story that can compete with the story of that case for sheer, breathless interest.'

'This is a puzzle all right,' quoth Alec.

'Oh, yes; I'm not saying you never get a puzzle in real life. Take Steinie Morrison or Oscar Slater, for instance; or Seddon and Mrs Thompson, as I was quoting to you the other day in a different connection. All of those were puzzling enough, though personally I've quite made up my mind, after studying the trials of the last two, what the truth was in each case.' He paused.

'What was the truth, then?' Alec asked dutifully.

'That Seddon was guilty and Mrs Thompson innocent— innocent of the actual count on which she was tried, I mean. I'm quite sure that she and Bywaters had not arranged that encounter in advance, I'm quite sure that she didn't know murder was being done until it had been done, and I'm almost sure that Bywaters did not go out that evening with the intention of murdering; he lost first his temper and then his head, drew his knife and saw red. However, we can't go into that now; I could talk to you on that case till midnight. No, what I mean is—don't let's treat this case of ours just as a story-book crime puzzle; what we've got to do is to remember the human element, first, last, and all the time. It's the human element that makes the crime possible, and it's the human element which ought to lead us to the truth.'

'There's certainly no lack of the human element here,' Alec observed.

'There is not!' Roger agreed, with something like enthusiasm. 'Gay, jolly young wife and worrying, nagging, fussing middle-aged husband, getting on each other's nerves no doubt and driving each other half-crazy; wife consoling herself with the bluff, hearty husband of her acidulated best friend, husband ditto with one of his own servants, a calculating, crafty wench, as I see her, knowing very well not only which side her bread is buttered but how to butter it as well—and then finding that the butter, after all, was only margarine. And then that dangerish, tigerish (catty is altogether too feeble a word), purring little hypocrite of another best friend, always about the place, always with her finger, as you said, well in the middle of each and every pie, turning to bitter, implacable enmity at the very first breath of suspicion and now holding in those little hands of hers the clue to every riddle and probably the solution of the whole puzzle. To say nothing of those two Bentleys, one hard as iron and utterly relentless, and the other pliable as india rubber but just as stubborn, and both standing to benefit incalculably by the death of a brother for whom neither of them much cared. Oh, there's plenty of human interest here all right!'

'Well, the public are eating it all right.'

'Exactly. Because the circumstances are unusual as well, besides the characters of the people involved. The Bentleys are well-to do, for instance; and you very, very seldom get a murder among the well-to-do except in fiction. On the spur of the moment Constance Kent, the Ardlamont case and the various doctor-criminals are the only ones I can think of; the upper strata of society would appear to be either more civilised or more cunning. And lastly we've got here the pretty young wife and the husband far too old for her—the stock situation of every second penny-novelette ever published.'

'But the sympathy isn't with her. It's all against her.'

'Yes, and that's very interesting. I don't think it's entirely because people think she's guilty, you know, this tremendous feeling against Mrs Bentley; not entirely. It's partly because she's a foreigner, no doubt, but I think the root of it in the vast majority of cases is that curious streak of brutishness buried in the depths of practically everybody's soul—the brutishness that nobody dares give expression to individually, but which comes out so strongly in the mass; the lust for cruelty, if you like, that prompts the incredible inhumanity of mobs and leads to lynchings and clubbing helpless people to death and ghastly outrages on women in a revolution. As far as Mrs Bentley's concerned, the whole nation has formed itself into a mob. Mrs Bentley has been suggested to them as an object for execration, and without bothering to consider anything further the mob is clamouring that she be judicially lynched for them. The fact that she's a woman, and a young and pretty woman at that, actually puts an edge on their delight in their own blood-lust. Lord, I'm expressing this extraordinarily badly, but you may see—Hallo, there's the bell! I must hurry up. I've got to go out again after dinner.'

'Out?' Alec repeated in surprise.

'Yes, curse it,' Roger groaned. 'Back to that wretched woman. She wanted me to stay to dinner there, but I got out of that. I must say I have hopes for this evening, high hopes; but it's devilish hard work—and devilish ticklish work too. The least false step puts one back hours. Look here, take Sheila aside if you get the chance and see if you can wangle me a latch-key, Alec. I expect I'll be pretty late. And try and wait up a bit for me if you can.'

Alec was successful in obtaining the latch-key, and Roger made the best apologies he could to his host and hostess for his unseemly absence. To his relief Sheila was almost normal at dinner; she greeted him cheerfully and without embarrassment, and only the almost vicious note which characterised her unmerciful twitting of him with regard to his alleged infatuation for the Saunderson gave any inkling at all that anything might be out of the ordinary with her. For once Roger was almost glad to escape from the moors to the peaceful seclusion of the boudoir.

His prophecy had been a sound one. It was past one o'clock before he staggered into the drawing-room where Alec, by the remains of a moribund fire, was waiting for him alone.

Roger struck an attitude by the door. 'Alexander!' he proclaimed softly. 'I have succeeded! I have loosened the serpent's tongue, and lo! all the wisdom of the serpent is now mine. Roger Sheringham, serpent charmer. But oh! how I've had to labour for it! For God's sake give me a drink!'

CHAPTER XIII

WHAT MRS BENTLEY SAID

ROGER threw himself with exaggerated exhaustion on to the couch and Alec mixed a whisky and soda at a side table on which stood a decanter, syphon and glasses.

'That's good work, Roger,' he said with as great a display of enthusiasm as his cautious Scotch nature would permit. 'Have you got the explanations for everything?'

'Every single blessed thing.'

'How are they? Convincing?'

'To the man who's already made up his mind, no. To the man whose mind is still open, just as reasonable as the theories of the prosecution.'

'Good work! Here you are. I've made it a stiff one.'

'I need a stiff one,' said Roger simply, and applied himself to it.

'Hallo, Roger!' remarked a voice from the door. 'Any news?'

Sheila closed the door behind her with elaborate caution. She was wearing a black silk kimono patterned with silver storks, and little pink quilted bedroom slippers on her bare feet. As she moved one caught a glimpse of frivolous blue silk pyjamas. It was a costume in which many people might have betrayed signs of self-consciousness; Sheila evidently took it for the most ordinary thing in the world.

'You naughty little girl!' said Roger with severity. 'Go back to bed at once!'

'Try not to be an ass, Roger,' Miss Purefoy entreated. 'I've been lying awake for you for the last hour and a half. I was beginning to think you were going to stay the night there.' She dropped into a chair near the fire and crossed her knees, perfunctorily arranging the folds of the kimono over perhaps four inches of pyjama. 'Well, what's happened?'

'He's found out what Mrs Bentley says about things,' Alec informed her.

'Have you, Roger? I say, good for you! Let's hear all about it.'

Roger set his glass on the floor and cleared his throat importantly. 'Thus and thus and thus, my children. First, the fly-papers. Mrs Bentley says she got them to use as a cosmetic.'

'A cosmetic?' Sheila repeated in surprise.

'Yes. Didn't you know that arsenic is used as a cosmetic?'

'No, that I didn't.'

'Oh, yes, it is. There's an idea that it's good for the complexion (I don't know whether there's any truth in it or not), and it certainly functions as a depilatory. All this was thrashed out in the Madeleine Smith case, you won't remember; her explanation of buying arsenic was that she wanted it for use as a cosmetic. I think that's quite a feasible explanation as far as Mrs Bentley's concerned. She's a French woman, you must remember, and it's highly probable that she'd heard of this use of arsenic when she was a girl in Paris; probably actually used it. And in this country, of course, she wouldn't be able to buy arsenic without signing the poisons' book, except in the form of fly-papers or weed-killer. To clinch the matter, she was going to that ball with Allen two days later, wasn't she? Yes, the explanation sounds reasonable enough.'

'Pass fly-papers,' Sheila agreed. 'What about the Bovril? That's what I don't see how she could get over.'

'Well, now, what she says about the Bovril is really most uncommonly interesting. Her explanation of that is that her husband, a day or two after he took to his bed for the last time, produced a packet of white powder and told her a most extraordinary rigmarole about it. According to him, this powder was the only thing in the world that could do him any good, but it was something which the doctor would try and prevent him taking because it was a drug which no doctor properly under-stood (Bentley was always very sarcastic about doctors and drugs, I ought to tell you; he considered them far too timid in the use they make of them. So that all fits in). Well, he handed the packet over to her and asked her to put a tiny pinch or two into his food from time to time, but she wasn't to breathe a word about it to a soul, because if she did the doctor would be sure to hear of it and be down on him like a ton of bricks. Mrs Bentley didn't attach any particular importance to this. She knew her husband was always dosing himself, and she thought that the white powder was something like bicarbonate of soda or some other equally harmless ingredient. Besides, Bentley had particularly told her that it was absolutely innoc-uous.'

'And did she?' asked Alec.

'Yes, she put one or two pinches in his food just to humour him. Then there came that fuss about the letter, the nurse arrived, and she found herself debarred from administering anything to her husband direct. According to her story, Bentley also saw that he was going to have trouble in getting his doses of this white powder, so when the nurse was out of the room he asked his wife to put a pinch or two in the bottle of Bovril which, was standing on a table by his bed. At first Mrs Bentley refused, but he got so excited and worked up about it that just to keep him quiet she agreed to do so. The nurse came back, Mrs Bentley smuggled the bottle of Bovril out of the room and did as she'd promised. And that's how arsenic came to be found in that bottle of Bovril.'

'Sounds dam' fishy,' Sheila commented.

'So the police thought,' Roger said mildly.

'Then is that packet of white powder the same as the packet of arsenic which was found in the drawer in Mrs Bentley's room?' asked Alec.

'Presumably, yes.'

'Humph!'

'What about the other things, Roger?' said Sheila, 'Weren't there some other things found with arsenic in?'

'Yes; there was the medicine-bottle of arsenic and lemon-juice, and the handkerchief belonging to Mrs Bentley which was also impregnated with arsenic. These, she says, were the results of the fly-papers. The arsenic and lemon-juice was the cosmetic preparation, which she dabbed on her face to improve her complexion, and the handkerchief was what she dabbed it on with. She locked them away in her drawer with, later on, the packet of white powder, just for safety. Oh, and by the way, this statement of hers was corroborated to a certain extent by the analyst's evidence before the magistrates. The arsenic and lemon-juice certainly was the result of the fly-papers' decoction, because the analyst found paper fibres in it. Also, there were traces of lemon juice on this handkerchief, so that seems to be corroborated. As for the rest, the arsenic in Bentley's medicine-bottles and in the thermos, and all the rest of it, she says she doesn't know anything about at all, and the only thing she can think is that he put it there himself.'

'But, good Lord!' exclaimed Alec. 'A man wouldn't want to go and feed himself on arsenic.'

'That conclusion struck me too, Alexander,' Roger agreed. 'But if, as we decided to do, we are going to take Mrs Bentley's story as true, what's the obvious result that we get?'

'That he didn't know it was arsenic!' cried Sheila excitedly.

Roger beamed on her benignly. 'I *am* proud of my intelligent staff. Well done, Detective Purefoy. Precisely! He didn't know it was arsenic. And what in turn does that give us?' He paused inquiringly, but neither of them answered him. 'Why, that some-body had given him this arsenic and stuffed him up with some damned silly yarn about it, with the very neat consequence that he was induced to poison himself! Now then, what about that?'

'I say!' breathed Sheila. 'I wonder!'

'Putting aside Mrs Bentley,' Alec said slowly, 'that does seem the only other explanation.'

'But who would it be?' Sheila cried. 'It'd have to be somebody who knew him pretty well.'

Roger refreshed himself from his tumbler and lit a cigarette.

'One thing occurs to me,' he said thoughtfully, 'and that is that our net for suspects is considerably enlarged now, isn't it? I mean, we aren't limited any longer to those six people who were with Bentley during that half-hour. We imagine we know now how he got the arsenic into him; what we don't know is who gave it him in the first place. Well, that might have been anybody.'

'Still, you were taking a good deal of trouble just before dinner to show that a good many of those six had a motive for wanting Bentley out of the way,' Alec remarked. 'That still holds good, doesn't it?'

'Oh, yes; most decidedly. All I mean is that we're not *limited* to those. Supposing there was a business rival, for instance, whom Bentley was on the point of ruining. Our net's wide enough to take him in.'

'We mustn't go trying after too far-fetched ideas, though,' Alec observed with native caution. 'I can't quite see Bentley accepting white powders from the hand of a man who had every reason to be up against him.'

'Can't you, Alec?' Roger retorted. 'Well, I can. That's just that very point which makes our field so unpleasantly wide. With a hypochondriac and self-doser like Bentley one can see anything. You've no idea what blithering idiots people of that type can be where their own fads are concerned. Bentley might have been a sharp man of business and no fool in the ordinary things of life, but introduce the subject of drugs or propound some new theory of self-treatment, and he'll swallow absolutely anything, both metaphorically and literally!'

'By the way,' Alec remarked, 'all this rather does away with the idea that you had first of all, doesn't it? That the real murderer was working against Mrs Bentley just as much as Bentley himself, and deliberately laid all this train of evidence to lead to her.'

'Oh, yes. That was only a preliminary theory. It may still hold good, but more probably that conclusive train of evidence was sheer accident. How could the real murderer have insured that she would be making a cosmetic out of arsenical fly-papers so conveniently, for instance? Unless it was somebody in the house who just nipped in and took advantage of this very damning fact, I don't see how that could have happened.'

'And what about the arsenic in the medicine-bottles? I suppose that must have been carefully put there by the person interested.'

'Yes; and that does look rather like the deliberate manufacturing of evidence against Mrs Bentley, doesn't it? At least, I don't see for the moment what other reason there could be for it.'

'I say!' interposed Sheila excitedly. 'How do we know after all that the arsenic that killed him did come out of that white packet? We all jumped to the conclusion that it did, because it seemed so obvious. But we don't *know*, do we?'

'Alexander,' said Roger in awe-struck tones, 'do you know that we're in the presence of a genius? Sheer, screaming genius!'

'It was a bit of a brain-wave,' admitted Miss Purefoy modestly.

'It was indeed,' Roger agreed. 'Seriously, Sheila, that's a point, and I don't mind admitting that it hadn't occurred to me before. Yes, we must bear that in mind. Mind you, I don't think it's very probable, and if the drug had been hyoscin or aconite, or anything unusual like that, the chances would be a couple of million to one against there being anything in it. Still, you're quite right; we've got to bear every contingency in mind, and there's no doubt that if any second person *had* conceived the idea of using poison, arsenic is the one they would probably pick on; so the coincidence doesn't become as great as it might have been. What you mean, in other words, is that it might have been one of those six after all, even if he was given the packet by somebody totally different?'

'I suppose I did,' Sheila said a little vaguely.

'Yes,' Roger mused, 'and none of those people would have found any difficulty in getting him to take it, I should imagine. He knew all of them well enough to lap any new drug out of their hands. And here's another suggestion, to cap Sheila's brilliant effort—*was* the white powder administered to Bentley by his wife arsenic at all? We don't know. Supposing it was something perfectly innocuous, and that packet of arsenic was substituted for the other to be found in the search after Bentley's death! The person who substituted it having, of course, already poisoned Bentley in some other way. It's perfectly feasible. My hat, there are some weird possibilities in this case, to say nothing of complications!'

'And the biggest possibility of all,' said Alec, 'is—!'

'That Mrs Bentley did the whole thing herself,' Roger took him up. 'Yes, I know. But I do hope she didn't, because we're getting along so nicely.'

'Well, what's the next move, anyhow?' asked Sheila. 'What are you going to do about this new information?'

'The Lord knows!' Roger confessed. 'I shall have to digest it thoroughly first. And of course I shall have to interview each of my little band of suspects and collect a few personal impressions. Further than that for the moment I'm blessed if I can see.'

There was a moment's pause.

'I'm simply revelling in all this!' Sheila exclaimed suddenly. 'It's fun being a detective. I don't care what anybody says.'

Roger jumped to his feet. 'Well, you'd better go and revel in bed. You have a morbid and depraved mind, Miss Purefoy, and I'm not going to pander to it any longer. In any case there's nothing more we can do tonight. Run along, and take those fancy pyjamas with you. Isn't it a soul-stirring and pathetic sight, Alexander, when women adopt any of our garments for their own purposes? I used to think once that there was a certain dignity about a pair of pyjamas!'

CHAPTER XIV

INTERVIEW WITH A GREAT LADY

THE next morning Roger, fully dressed, sought Alec's bedroom before breakfast, while its occupant was still in process of shaving himself. 'Alec,' he said without preamble, 'I've decided what we must do first of all today.'

'Oh?' said Alec through soap. 'Well, it must be pretty urgent if it's got you up and dressed by this time.'

'It is. We must go and make the acquaintance of Mrs Allen. I ought to have done it before, but I haven't had time.'

'Yes, and talking of Mrs Allen,' Alec chimed in, lifting his chin to an acute angle, 'it occurred to me after I went to bed last night that this news of yours puts another person on our list of suspects.'

'Yes, it does,' Roger agreed instantly. 'Allen, you mean. I've been thinking about that too. He could just as easily have given that packet to Bentley and stuffed him up with a fool yarn about it being some wonderful secret medicine as anybody else.'

'Better,' said Alec laconically.

'How do you mean?'

'Well—dam' fishy, isn't it? I mean, he's in love with Mrs Bentley, and Mrs Bentley's in love with him.'

'Exactly. That's just the conclusion I've been arriving at. It never seems to have struck anybody before, but the motive imputed to Mrs Bentley (wanting to get rid of her husband) applies just as strongly to Allen. The husband's got to be got rid of somehow if these two are to come together, and one might have done it just as much as the other. Taking the case on its bare bones I should say that the chances in these circumstances are decidedly in favour of the man taking the law into his hands

115

in this way, not the woman. You can bet that Mrs Bentley had told him all about the sort of life she led with him and what a little blighter he was, and how he knocked her down and gave her a black eye. That's enough to make any man see red when he's fond of a woman.'

'But what about Mrs Allen?'

'Oh, yes, I'm not losing sight of her. But then there are bound to be all sorts of details that we don't know anything about. Absolutely bound to be! For instance, I shouldn't be at all surprised if Bentley had refused to let his wife have a divorce. In a case like this, that's simply asking to be murdered.'

'But if he'd been carrying on with Mary Blower?'

'But did Mrs Bentley know that? And in any case she couldn't divorce him without his consent, because of her affair with Allen.'

'But did Bentley know about *that*?'

Roger laughed. 'Goodness only knows! As I said, we're groping entirely in the dark. We don't know what they knew about each other, and we don't know all the little details of all these people's connections with each other. Mrs Saunderson, for instance. How do we know that she hadn't got some cause for furiously hating Mrs Bentley? She talks as if she hated her; but is that mere cattishness, or is there any deeper reason? And we don't know what other *amours* friend Bentley may have been indulging in. If a man plays about with his own servant, you can bet your last sixpence that he's had dozens of other affairs before he came down to that. You see the trouble is that we're outsiders. We haven't the intimate knowledge of these people that a personal acquaintance would give us, like we had at Layton Court; and we haven't got the authority to dig into their histories and cross-question them that the police have. For us, the whole thing is simply an exercise in deduction from fact to inference; we've hardly got an ounce of psychology to work on.'

'All the more credit to you if you get to the bottom of

it then, Mr Sheringham,' said Alec, sponging his face vigorously.

'True, Alexander. And that's why I'm so jolly keen to do so.'

Alec emerged from his basin and buried his face in a towel.

'I say,' he said suddenly, coming to the surface for a moment. 'Going back to the motives that we were discussing just now, what's the good of either Mrs Bentley or Allen going to this extreme to get rid of the fellow, when there's Mrs Allen still in the background? At that rate they'd have to polish her off too.'

'By no means, Alexander Grierson,' Roger objected. 'For one thing Mrs Allen might have been willing to divorce her husband. For another, a wife is in a very different category in those circumstances from a husband. A husband can pack up and leave his wife and it doesn't interfere with his livelihood in the least. A wife can't pack up and leave her husband without sacrificing her livelihood.'

'But Mrs Bentley was twice on the point of packing up and going,' Alec objected.

'She was on the *point* of packing up, yes. But did she really intend to go? And in any case, that was in the heat of the moment. She may have reconsidered. Lastly, if she *was* really intending to trot back to Paris, then that's the strongest possible argument in favour of her innocence. So now I'm going down to breakfast. Hurry up; we mustn't be late in starting out. I want to catch the lady before she goes into the town for her morning's shopping. These provincial dames always spend their mornings grinning like dogs and running about the city, don't they?'

'Do you want me to come with you, then?'

'Certainly I do. You look so blatantly honest. I emerge this morning as special correspondent for the *Courier*. You will be my cameraman.'

'But I haven't got a camera,' objected the practical Alec.

'Alec,' said Roger severely, 'you make me moan. For a detective, you've got about as much resource as a Welsh rarebit.

How does a person without a camera provide himself with a camera?'

'All right,' Alec grinned. 'I asked for it.'

'Yes,' said Roger gently, as he closed the door. 'And you'll pay for it, too.'

So punctually at half-past ten the new correspondent of the *Courier* presented himself at the front-door of Winsless Lodge, St Reginald's Road, accompanied by his cameraman, and demanded to see Mrs Allen.

'Are you a reporter, sir?' asked the maid immediately.

'Certainly not,' said Roger with dignity. 'I am a special correspondent to the *Daily Courier*.'

'I'm sorry, Mrs Allen isn't seeing any more reporters, sir,' said the maid, and promptly closed the door.

'Bother, drat and blow!' said Roger thoughtfully. 'We will now dismiss the special correspondent of the *Courier* and summon Mr Roger Sheringham to our aid.' And he rang the bell again.

On seeing the same couple, the servant made as if to shut the door in their faces without further conversation, but Roger deftly inserted a foot and blocked its passage. 'Will you kindly give Mrs Allen this card,' he said importantly. 'Perhaps I misled you just now. Mrs Allen knows my name.'

He did not add that Mrs Allen didn't know him, but fortunately the maid pursued no inquiries regarding this distinction. 'If you would wait a minute, I'll see Mrs Allen,' she said, and left them.

'You can't keep a good man down,' observed Roger to his cameraman. 'If Mrs Allen won't see me now I'll disguise myself as Santa Claus and plunge down the chimney at her.'

Luckily this course was unnecessary. The maid returned the next moment saying that Mrs Allen would see them and would they kindly come this way. They came, and were shown into a large, airy drawing-room, furnished with taste and restraint in a colour-scheme of light grey and mauve, with a fire burning brightly in the hearth.

Roger looked round him with interest. 'If this room was devised by its mistress,' he remarked, 'and not by a hireling from a furniture shop, the lady is one whom we shall not regret meeting. In fact, I shouldn't be at all surprised, Alexander, if the difference between Mrs Allen and black lingerie in an over-heated boudoir or little brogue shoes on an open moor is that of rustling silk on a ballroom floor.'

At that moment the lady in question entered the room, and Roger wheeled round to estimate his prognosis; for an instant he was so delighted with its accuracy that he quite forgot to burst into voluble and reassuring speech. Mrs Allen was between thirty-five and forty years old, tall and willowy, and with a charming dignity of presence from which even the little black morning frock she was wearing could not detract; her features were classical in their regularity, and her intensely blue eyes looked at Roger with a somewhat puzzled expression.

'Mr Sheringham?' she said. 'I don't think—'

'Oh, no,' said Roger quickly, 'I haven't the pleasure of knowing you personally, Mrs Allen. But I thought if I sent my card in you might be good enough to look on any book of mine you may have read (always providing that you have read one; it's surprising how many people haven't!) in the light of a formal introduction.'

Mrs Allen smiled very faintly, rather as if fulfilling her social duty to mere politeness than as if she found anything humorous in Roger's words. 'You are Mr Sheringham the novelist?' she asked in even tones.

'Yes.'

'I have read one or two of your books, of course. What is it you wish to see me about, Mr Sheringham?' She had not seated herself nor had she invited her two guests to do so. Her cool composure showed Roger clearly that he was going to have considerable difficulty in keeping the reins of the interview in his own hands.

'Well, as a matter of fact, you may think that I've gained an entrance here under false pretences,' he began with his most charming smile. 'The truth is that the *Daily Courier* has been good enough to ask me to act as their special correspondent for a few days down here in regard to this Bentley case and I want to ask you if you will be so good as to answer a few questions. Of course I wouldn't—'

'I'm sorry, Mr Sheringham,' Mrs Allen interrupted frostily, a touch of hardness that was in curious contrast with the essential repose of her bearing making its appearance in her voice. 'From the very beginning I have refused to grant an interview and I am afraid I cannot make an exception even in your case.' Without further beating about the bush she crossed to the fireplace and rang the bell.

'A charming day, isn't it?' said Mrs Allen tranquilly. 'I always think that some of these days in early autumn are really as delightful as anything else that the rest of the year can give us.'

'Yes, the evenings are drawing in now!' mumbled Roger with mechanical platitudinism.

Two minutes later Roger and Alec were walking down the short drive towards the road. The unnatural restraint of their manner suggested two small boys not yet out of range of the schoolmistress's eye. It appeared that something like this had occurred to Roger himself.

'That excellent lady made me feel exactly three years old,' he said with unwilling admiration. Roger was always fair; anybody who could make him feel three years old deserved admiration, and the highest admiration at that. Roger did not grudge it.

'She made me feel a blithering idiot,' observed the cameraman shortly.

'Not one of our successful interviews. Though I'd sooner have her than that ghastly little Saunderson woman any day of the year, even one of these early autumn ones. That really is one of the very few types of ladies to whom I remove my hat.

What a nerve! Poor old Roger Sheringham didn't cut much ice there. She got rid of us like a couple of rotten apples. I only wonder she didn't have us thrown in the dustbin.'

Alec gave vent to a sudden explosive sound. 'I like seeing you get it in the neck occasionally, I must say, Roger,' he observed with candour.

'You're a low and vengeful hound, Alexander,' said Roger mildly. 'You should try and curb your naughty passions.'

They passed in silence through the front-gate and turned automatically to the right.

'*Was* the interview a failure though?' Roger said suddenly. 'After all what went we out for to seek? A voice crying in the wilderness? Nay. A voice crying in Mrs Allen's drawing-room. And that's precisely what we heard. In other words, the great thing is not that we saw her for so short a time, but that we did see her at all. All we set out to do was to try and get a personal impression of the lady, wasn't it? Well, I'm jolly sure that I've got a personal impression all right, haven't you?'

'Two minutes was ample,' Alec agreed. 'What do you make of her?'

Roger considered. 'That Mrs Allen,' he said with some care, 'is a woman of singularly strong character and resolution. In my humble opinion, given enough provocation she would be *capable de tout*. I put that into French,' he added, 'because it sounds so much more refined than to say straight out that she would be capable of committing murder if the need arose—a thing I should simply hate to put into plain words.'

'I'm dashed if I can see a woman like that committing murder,' Alec disagreed.

'That,' Roger replied gently, 'is because you will continue to look only upon charming outside coverings and disregard entirely hidden and seething interiors. For purely routine work, Constable Grierson, you may be excellent at discovering who stole the bath-bun from the station waiting-room, but among us greater detectives of the higher psychology you're a washout!'

'Humph!' said Constable Grierson briefly.

'And now,' confided Roger, turning in at a gateway on the left of the road, 'for Miss Mary Blower. Let's hope for better luck in that quarter.'

CHAPTER XV

MISS BLOWER RECEIVES

MISS BLOWER turned out to be easy prey. William Bentley was still living in his late brother's house and, as Roger had surmised, most of the domestic staff were there with him. Certainly Mary Blower was, and admitted to her identity the moment she opened the door.

'That's fine,' Roger said with a bland smile. 'I'm representing the *Daily Courier,* Miss Blower, and I should be so grateful if you would let me have a few words with you.'

'Oh, you newspaper gentlemen!' observed Miss Blower, with a distinct toss of her head. 'You make life quite a trial, you do really. I did think you'd all finished with me by this time, to be sure.'

Roger had recognised his cue the moment the lady tossed her head. She was a finely-built girl, coarsely pretty in that high-cheekboned, wide-mouthed, slanting-eyed, oblong-faced way which generally betokens a complete lack of the moral sense—the type of face, peculiar to a certain Anglo-Saxon stratum, which seven out of ten of the women walking the London streets seem to possess. It was evident to Roger that Miss Blower had mistaken her obvious vocation in entering domestic service—though she had certainly taken steps since then partially to remedy her error.

He tried to put as much admiration into his eyes and voice as they could conveniently hold. 'Ah, but this is very extra-special, Miss Blower. To tell you the truth, we've come to the conclusion on the *Courier* that the most interesting person in the whole case emerges as yourself. It was you who had the initiative and foresight in the first place to speak of those fly-papers, and your conduct throughout has been in the highest degree exemplary and admirable.' Roger found this opening a singularly useful one.

'Lor'!' said Miss Blower.

'In fact,' he went on in hushed tones, 'we think on the *Courier* that if it hadn't been for you, there would never have been a Wychford Poisoning Case at all. We want to make a full-page feature of you for the interest of our readers.'

'I don't mind, I'm sure,' observed Miss Blower, pink with gratification.

'Well, then, could you take us somewhere where we can talk? Oh, by the way, let me introduce my friend and colleague, Mr Sebastian Sheepwash—one of the most brilliant of the younger generation of cameraman,' he added in a loud aside. 'A coming man, Miss Blower, believe me.'

Miss Blower scrutinised the blushing colleague with kindly interest; he might be a coming man, but she was an arrived woman. 'Well, if it's like that, Mr—?'

'Twobottles, my name is,' said Roger quickly. 'Percival Twobottles.'

'Well, if it's like that, Mr Twobottles, p'raps you'd come in. I dare say I can find some place where we can talk.'

Nothing loath, Roger followed her and Alec followed Roger. They crossed a wide hall and entered a big room, obviously a drawing-room, though it conveyed a very different message from that of the last one they had visited. In place of the latter's chaste severity, this room struck a note of frank frivolity. Deep chairs, upholstered in cheerful blue and orange coverings and stuffed with blue and white cushions, orange and blue curtains, blue and white paper, any number of small tables, pouffe cushions, knick-knacks and gay little trifles. Not that the room was exactly overcrowded, nor that the taste was not good, but in comparison with the simplicity of the other, the effect was certainly a little *outré*. Roger marked it with satisfaction. It was just such a room as he might have put to the credit of the original of that photograph which Sheila had brought him.

'We might as well sit in the drawing-room,' observed Miss Blower. 'Mr Alfred and Mr William's away at their business, so there's no harm done.' She seated herself with a slightly self-conscious air in one of the deep armchairs, an incongruous figure in her housemaid's cap and apron, and Roger took up his stand in front of the empty grate. The coming man set his camera down on one of the small tables and hovered without joy.

'So Mr Alfred is staying here as well, is he?' Roger remarked.

'Yes; been here nearly two months now, he has.'

'Oh, I didn't know that. Now let me see; where shall we start? About those fly-papers. Had you ever seen fly-papers soaking in Mrs Bentley's room before?'

'Oh, no. Never, I hadn't, that's what made me think it was funny-like, you see.'

'What did you think when you did see them, then, Miss Blower?'

'Why, that it was funny-like. I thought it was funny-like, you see.'

'And why did you think it was funny-like?'

'Why, because I'd never seen anything of the sort before. Besides, there wasn't no call for them. We always had the sticky sort before.'

'And how did you know what these were, and that they were dangerous?'

'It was written on them. "Fly-papers, dangerous, poison," Something like that, it said.'

'I see. Now, how long have you been here?'

'Two years next November.'

'Had Mr and Mrs Bentley seemed to you to be on pretty good terms, before these last quarrels?'

'No, that they hadn't! Always biting each other's heads off, they were, in a manner of speaking.'

'Did Mrs Bentley seem to you upset, when her husband was taken ill?'

'Not her! She pretended to be all right, but I could see through her play-acting.'

'Oh, she did pretend to be, then?'

'Yes, but she always was a cunning one. All those foreigners are.'

'No doubt,' Roger said mildly. 'Now, Miss Blower, I want you to tell me your own impressions of Mr and Mrs Bentley. For instance, did you, before this business began, like Mrs Bentley?'

Miss Blower snorted. 'That I didn't, Mr Twobottles!' she replied with emphasis. 'Not from the very first moment I ever set eyes on her, I didn't. She was a proper cat, Mrs Bentley was—a proper cat! I never could stand her.'

'What makes you feel so strongly about her? Wasn't she a good mistress?'

'A good Nosey Parker!' retorted Miss Blower with much scorn. 'That's what she was, a Nosey Parker. Dear me, you must think I'm dreadful to be talking like this, but I always was one for saying what I thought. And reelly—!'

'But that's exactly what I want you to say, Miss Blower; what you really thought.'

'Well, it does seem funny, don't it? Me sitting in here and talking to a gentleman like you.'

'But I'm not a gentleman!' Roger replied with energy. 'Don't think that for a minute. I'm just a reporter, and I want you to talk to me just as you do to the cook out in the kitchen.'

'Not if I did, you wouldn't,' giggled Miss Blower coyly. 'I'm a one for the rough side of my tongue, I am. Lor', the things I say to poor cook sometimes! You wouldn't believe!'

'I'm sure I wouldn't,' said Roger gallantly. 'But about Mrs Bentley, why do you call her a Nosey Parker?'

'Well, always interfering and messing about with things that didn't concern her, she was. Used to make me wild at times, I can tell you. It's a wonder to me I never give in my notice months ago.'

'But aren't you sorry for her now, with this terrible accusation hanging over her head?'

'Not me! She deserves all she's going to get *and* more, you mark my words.'

'Of course you have no doubt whether she's guilty or not?'

Miss Blower tossed her head. 'Whether she's guilty or not, there's them as 'ud be glad to see her swing,' she observed darkly.

Roger lit a cigarette with some care. He realised that Miss Blower might be on the verge of some really important revelation; but as things were, he doubted whether she could be induced to give voice to it to a person so far removed from her own sphere. Roger knew all about the intense class-feeling that a person of Miss Blower's type might be expected to possess; and he knew also that a thing of which she might talk freely to a person of her own standing, she would probably conceal instinctively from anybody belonging to the division of society known to herself as 'toffs' He determined swiftly, before proceeding with the matter in hand, to do something towards breaking down the barriers between them.

'I'm so sorry,' he said chattily, holding his cigarette case out to her. 'Do you smoke? Have a cigarette.'

'Well, I don't mind if I do,' said Miss Blower graciously.

Roger lit one for her, employing the tip of his finger in the orthodox way. 'You know, I'm rather surprised to see you in service, Miss Blower,' he remarked in tones of some earnestness.

'You are? Why?'

'Well, you seem to me to be rather wasted here. You ought to be on the stage, you know, with your looks and figure.'

'Well, I have thought of the stage meself,' Miss Blower admitted with a little giggle. 'But there! It's not reelly the sort of thing for a respectable girl, is it?'

Roger reassured her. He went on to invent a perfectly fictitious cousin of his own whom he asserted to be an ornament to the chorus of one of the big London revues. He was quite certain that this cousin could be persuaded to use her remarkable influence with London's theatrical managers on Miss Blower's behalf. He was equally certain that London's theatrical managers, once given the opportunity of inspecting Miss Blower's form and features, would vie eagerly with each other for the privilege of displaying them from their respective stages to an eager public.

Miss Blower bridled visibly. 'Me on the stage in a string of beads and a couple of doodahs!' wriggled Miss Blower delightedly. 'I'd be a scream, wouldn't I?'

'Well, I'll certainly speak to my cousin,' Roger affirmed, deciding that the ice was now sufficiently shattered. 'Oh, by the way, there was something I was intending to ask you. What did you mean, about Mrs Bentley, just now when you said "whether she's guilty or not"? Have you any reason to suppose that she mightn't be?—Our readers will naturally attach tremendous weight to your views, you know,' he added perfunctorily.

But Miss Blower was not to be drawn so easily as that. She leaned back in her big chair and puffed unskilfully at her cigarette.

'Oh, she's guilty all right,' she replied carelessly. 'They're going to try her, aren't they?'

'Yes, but that doesn't necessarily follow. Now just see how interesting it would be if I could tell our readers that you think she might be innocent,' Roger urged persuasively. 'Why, it would be the sensation of the hour! Everybody would be talking about you. Just think for a minute and see if you can't give me some fact that you haven't mentioned to anybody else.'

'No, I don't know anything like that,' replied Miss Blower evasively.

'Just think! the *Courier* would be ready to pay very handsomely for any information that might point to a sensation of that sort.'

'She's guilty all right,' retorted Miss Blower with a touch of sullenness. 'There's nothing I can tell you that I haven't told anyone else.'

Roger changed the subject; he had no wish to dam the stream of this lady's promising information. 'You never liked Mrs Bentley, then. Did you like Mr Bentley'?

'Oh, he was all right, as they go,' said Miss Blower, in a curiously flat voice.

Roger's eye gleamed, but he did not betray himself. 'That doesn't sound as if you thought much of him?'

'I didn't; not a fat lot.'

'You didn't like him at all?' Roger insinuated.

'Oh, he was—Oh, well, if you must know, I hated the sight of him, an' I don't care who knows it!'

'Quite right. Why should you? I can't say I have a very high opinion of him myself if it comes to that. And why particularly didn't you like him?'

Miss Blower shifted uneasily. 'He—he didn't treat me properly.'

'Oh? How was that?'

'He promised me—' An expression of intense malignance distorted Miss Blower's features. 'He was a dirty dog!' she exclaimed with sudden defiance. 'He was a dirty dog, an' I'm glad he's dead, see? I don't care who hears me say it—I'm *glad* he's dead!'

Roger paused for a moment, looking at her closely. Miss Blower's face was flushed and she was breathing heavily; her emotion was obvious.

'At about half-past eight on the evening before Mr Bentley died,' he went on deliberately, 'you gave him a drink of lemonade out of a glass, in spite of the fact that strict orders had been issued that nothing should be administered to him except by the nurse in charge. Now, why did you do that?'

Miss Blower's flushed face paled slowly to a dead-white. She swallowed convulsively and her small slits of eyes widened unnaturally as she stared at her visitor.

'I—I never did!' she cried a little stridently after a pause of nearly half a minute. 'I never did anything of the sort!'

'You were seen in the act,' Roger returned impassively.

'It's a lie! Who told you a filthy lie like that, I should like to know?'

Roger exchanged glances with his cameraman. 'But why deny it, Miss Blower?' he asked in a soothing voice. 'Surely it was a perfectly harmless thing to have done. We know it for a fact, but we didn't attach any importance to it. Why deny it?'

Miss Blower continued to stare at him. Suddenly she burst into noisy tears.

'I—I didn't see any harm in it,' she sobbed. 'He said he was thirsty, an' I didn't see any harm in it. I wouldn't have done it if I'd known, not if it was ever so. He was a swine to me, but I wouldn't have done that, honest to God I wouldn't!'

'You wouldn't have done what?' Roger asked quickly.

Miss Blower raised a tear-stained face and sniffed. 'I wouldn't—I wouldn't have gone against Mr Alfred's orders, sir. Not if it were ever so, I wouldn't. But I didn't see no harm in it, sir.' Her cringing demeanour was in marked contrast with the former familiarity of her manner.

Roger contemplated her for a moment. 'Where did you get the lemonade from?' he asked suddenly.

'From—from the top o' the chest-of-drawers, sir.'

'I see,' Roger nodded. 'There was a glass of lemonade standing on the top of the chest-of-drawers?'

A noticeably crafty look appeared in Miss Blower's eyes. 'Oh, no, sir. That there wasn't, if you'll pardon me, sir. It was a jug of lemonade on the top of the chest-of-drawers, an' I just poured some out of it, sir. An' it wasn't a glass either, sir; it was a cup.'

'I see.' Roger appeared to be pondering.

'But sir,' remarked Miss Blower with some anxiety, 'you won't put anything about this in your writing, will you, sir? There's no harm done and nobody any the wiser, but just as it happens, I haven't told anybody about it, an' it might get me into trouble in a manner of speaking, what with going against Mr Alfred's orders an' all, sir. So you won't put any of that into your writing, will you, sir?'

'Very well,' Roger agreed. 'Provided you answer truthfully the rest of my questions, I won't.'

'You see, it isn't as if there was any *harm* done, sir, is it, sir?' Miss Blower persisted. 'If there had been, then I'm not saying but what—but what things might have been different. But there isn't, you see, is there, sir?'

'Of course not,' Roger said absently. 'Now, about that packet of white powder which was found in the locked drawer in Mrs Bentley's bedroom. You were there when it was found?'

'Yes, sir; I was, sir.'

'And you'd never seen it before?'

'Oh, yes, sir. I'd seen it on the table by Mr Bentley's bed. On his bed-table, sir.'

'Had you, indeed? Just once, or several times? I mean, had it been there for some time?'

'Yes, sir, it had. A matter of two or three days, I should say, right up to when Nurse Watson came.'

'And then it disappeared?'

'Yes, sir. Clean disappeared.'

'Now, can you remember when you first noticed it? Which particular day?'

Miss Blower screwed up her face in a painful effort of memory. Miss Blower was very palpably anxious to please.

'Yes, sir; it was—it was—it'd be the Monday evening. Yes, that's right, sir, when I was helping madam fix him up for the night. I can tell you that, 'cos I cleared the table when I brought his supper-tray up, and it wasn't there then, an' when I moved the table out of the way later on, I saw it an' said to meself, "Lor'," I said, "here's another medicine for 'im to dose 'imself with," I said.'

'I see. And it stayed there 'til Nurse Watson arrived on the Wednesday. Now are you quite sure that this really was the same packet as was found in the drawer in Mrs Bentley's room?'

'Oh, yes, sir. Because of the label, you see.'

'The label?' Roger repeated eagerly. 'Was there a label on it? What did it say?'

'Well, there was a label on it in a manner of speaking, sir, an' yet there wasn't. It'd bin torn off. But there *had* bin a label.'

'Oh!' Roger said disappointedly. 'It had been torn off, had it? Ever since you first saw it?'

'Well, all but one corner, sir. There was still one corner left, you see, sir. That's how I knew it had bin a label.'

Roger brightened again. 'Ah! Now, was there anything written or printed on that corner? Any words, or a pattern, or anything like that?'

'Well, yes, sir, you might say there was. A sort of squiggle, if you see what I mean, sir, an' C.3 printed on it.'

'See three?' Roger repeated in puzzled tones.

'Yes; I could draw it for you, sir, the squiggle, just to give you an idea like.'

'That's a good notion. Yes do!'

Roger produced his notebook and pencil, and Miss Blower applied herself to her task. Her finished sketch was rough and ready, but the nature of the squiggle appeared to be more or less indicated.

'Oh, C.3!' Roger said, looking at it carefully before putting it away in his pocket. 'I understand. Some part of a chemical formula, I suppose. Thank you very much, Miss Blower. Now then, is there anything more I want to ask you? I don't think so. Oh, by the way, how are you able to say so certainly that it was Monday evening when the packet first made its appearance, and not, perhaps, Sunday evening, or Tuesday?'

'Oh, that's easy, sir. It was after I'd let that Mr Allen out, you see, sir; that's how I remember. Mr Allen, he'd bin spending the evening with Mr Bentley; though if you ask me, sir, it's more like it was madam he wanted to see. She an' her goings-on!—I say, sir, do you think they *will* hang her? Cook, she says, no, they won't, she says; but I'm not so sure myself. What do you think, sir?' Miss Blower was rapidly recovering her self-possession.

'I think, Miss Blower,' Roger said weightily, 'that you'll find that Mrs Bentley will *not* be hanged. And now we must be getting along.'

'Well, I can't say as how I hope she will be,' Miss Blower remarked frankly as she rose to her feet. 'A cat she was to me an' a cat she always will be, but I hope they don't hang her. Not but what she don't deserve it, though!' she added with stern morality.

She accompanied them to the front-door, and Roger made their joint farewells. Alec had not opened his mouth from the time they had entered the house. Miss Blower's manner became decidedly more cheerful.

'Here, wait!' she exclaimed indignantly, as they were on the point of turning down the drive. 'You've forgotten to take my photograph!'

'God bless my soul, so we have!' cried Roger. 'Here, Mr Sheepwash, unsling that camera of yours and look nippy.'

Miss Blower was duly posed on the front-door step, Roger taking a good deal of trouble to get her in exactly the right light and in the best possible position, and Alec gloomily clicked an empty camera at her. After that, they were allowed to depart.

'Well, Alexander,' Roger said, as they turned into the road, 'what did you make of all that? A distressing young person, wasn't she? Offensively familiar at first, then cringing, and then familiar again. A low type, about the lowest there is; no brains, plenty of cunning, and no morals. At the moment, also, absolutely eaten up with her own importance over this business. Rather a dangerous young animal, eh?'

'You didn't show that you knew she'd been Bentley's mistress?'

'No; I didn't want any hysterics this morning. I'm holding that, in case I ever want to frighten anything out of her later.'

'She knows something, you know,' Alec said. 'I'm positive

she's got something up her sleeve that she wouldn't tell us about.'

'Not so much knows something, I fancy, as fears something,' Roger amended. 'And she did tell me, as a matter of fact; though she certainly didn't intend to. Didn't you arrive at the same conclusion? I thought it was obvious enough.'

'No, what?'

'Why, that Mrs Bentley is innocent!'

'Oh! Yes, I did have vague suspicions about that. Jolly interesting. I thought you were meaning that she thought somebody else was guilty.'

'Yes, I did mean that, too.'

'Oh? Who, then?'

'Miss Mary Blower!' returned Roger happily.

CHAPTER XVI

CONFERENCE AT AN IRONING-BOARD

'THAT she did it herself?' Alec cried.

'Yes, that she did it herself—by accident! It was quite clear that when she said she poured the lemonade out of the jug on the chest-of-drawers into a tumbler she was lying; obviously there was a tumbler of lemonade standing on the chest-of-drawers. It's my opinion that Miss Mary Blower isn't at all sure that that lemonade isn't part of the stuff which was found in the tray of Mrs Bentley's trunk.'

Alec whistled. 'Oh—ho! That she fed him with Mrs Bentley's arsenical cosmetic, you mean?'

'Exactly. Didn't that occur to you?'

'No; but it's clear enough now that you point it out. Yes, I think you're right, Roger. And of course she hasn't said a word to anybody else.'

'Oh, no; she's not the sort to do that. Whoever was responsible for Bentley's death, Miss Mary Blower isn't putting herself into any unnecessary hot water over it.'

'What a little blighter! And you really think that she'd have let Mrs Bentley even hang without saying a word?'

'Not a doubt of it. She's got a very big grudge against her, and she's not going to worry herself for a small thing like that one little bit. No, not at all a pleasing young person, Miss Mary Blower.'

'But look here, do you think there's anything in the idea? Do you think she really did give that stuff to Bentley? And if so, *was* it a mistake?'

'I don't know. If she did, and if it *was* a mistake (and I don't think it was anything else), then really, all one can say is that

Mrs Bentley deserves all that's happened to her, because a more glaring instance of culpable negligence you could hardly imagine. Fancy leaving a tumbler of arsenic and lemonade in a sick man's bedroom! It's tantamount to murder. No, I must say that, if Mrs Bentley didn't leave it there deliberately, it's almost incredible.'

'That's an idea, though,' Alec said reflectively. 'You mean she might have left it there in the hope that Bentley would help himself to it? In other words, that she meant Bentley to die, but not exactly to murder him; the thing would be more or less of an accident.'

'Yes, that's the sort of thing a woman might do to salve her conscience, though of course it's no less murder than forcibly feeding a man with the stuff. But if she did, then we're up against the same old difficulty that I pointed out right at the beginning—why trouble about the decoction of fly-papers when there's that big packet of arsenic so handy?'

'But look here, she might not have known that packet *was* arsenic. Supposing you were right when you said that somebody might have given it to Bentley to dose himself with. You see what I mean; in that case Mrs Bentley wouldn't know that it was arsenic, would she?'

'But Alexander, this is brilliant! That leads us to a conclusion that I certainly never had contemplated before—that *two* people were trying to poison him; Mrs Bentley herself with fly-papers and somebody else with the packet of arsenic!'

'Well, we did rather touch on that idea last night, didn't we? You remember when Sheila said that it mightn't have been the arsenic out of the packet that killed him. You said something about it being a coincidence, but not so great as it would have been if the drug was aconite or something like that.'

'Yes, I remember; but that was rather different. What I meant was that some unknown person gave him the packet of arsenic, and some other unknown person fed him arsenic on his or her own initiative—not that Mrs Bentley was either of them. But Lord, the whole thing's getting so blessed complicated I really don't know what I did say or what I did think or what I think now! Only one thing is extraordinarily clear in my mind at the present moment.'

'And that is?'

'That if friend Allen was on our list of suspects before for reasons of pure motive, he's now there for other very concrete reasons indeed. And his name's written in capital letters and it's underlined three times with red ink.'

'Great Scott, yes!' exclaimed Alec, almost excitedly. 'I'd forgotten all about that. I was meaning to mention it as soon as we left the house. Because he'd been spending the evening with Bentley before that packet made its appearance?'

'That's the idea. It seems a reasonable inference that friend Allen might have something rather interesting to say about that packet, if he could only be induced to talk.'

'That's going to be a bit of a job,' Alec mused.

'Yes,' Roger agreed. 'But it's got to be tackled, and as soon as possible. In fact, it's obviously the next step in this train of interesting inquiries. "Our Representative Interviews Suspected Man."'

'How are you going about it?' Alec asked with interest.

'Well, I've been turning that over subconsciously in my mind ever since we left that house. I shall have to try and find out this afternoon as much as I can of Allen's habits and character, and then act accordingly. There are all sorts of different ways of getting all sorts of different people to talk, and I've got to try and get some idea in advance of the sort of methods to adopt with this particular gentleman. Let's hope Sheila's in; I shall have to consult her about it.'

They had reached the front door of Dr Purefoy's house, and Roger pressed the bell-push with a thoughtful air.

'I say,' Alec said, not without apprehension. 'will you want me for this interview with Allen?'

'No, thank you, Mr Sheepwash,' Roger replied a trifle absently. 'This is going to be a very delicate affair indeed, and blundering cameramen who forget to take photographs would be altogether out of place.'

It was now a few minutes past twelve o'clock. In answer to Roger's inquiries the maid who opened the door informed them that Mrs Purefoy was out and that Miss Purefoy was upstairs in her bedroom.

'I wish you'd tell her that we've come in, and would like to see her for a minute if she's not busy, would you?' Roger asked.

'Yes, certainly, sir.'

'No, don't bother, Jane,' Alec interposed, making his way to the foot of the stairs. 'I'll see to it.' He tilted his head back and opened his mouth; a noise not unlike the note of a fog-horn issued forth and travelled hurriedly to the upper regions. The noise might with difficulty be construed into the word 'Shee-*la*!'

'Great Scott!' observed Roger mildly.

Jane hastily clapped her hand to her mouth and retired to her own fastness, uttering stifled sounds. A door upstairs could be heard to open.

'Hal-*lo*!' floated down a shrill howl.

'Want you! Come downstairs!' enunciated the fog-horn.

'Can't! Busy! Come up here!' replied the howl.

'Right-*ho*!'

They bounded up the stairs.

'That's right,' said Sheila, meeting them at her door. 'Come on in. I couldn't go down. I'm ironing.'

'Domestic young woman,' observed Roger, following her inside.

'Oh, one always has to wash and iron one's own undies. I wouldn't trust anyone else with them.'

'I very seldom do mine,' Roger murmured. 'But then I have a very trusting nature.'

'What do you think of my room?' Sheila demanded. 'Pretty useful, isn't it? All my own idea. Commonly known as the Pillar of Fire.'

'That is beyond me,' Roger confessed.

'Don't you see, you silly man? A cloud of smoke by day, and a pillar of fire by night—a bedroom at night and a boudoir in the day-time. That object with the blue cover and the cushions is my bed, brushes and things pop out of the drawers of that table and turn it into a dressing-table, and the washstand's behind that screen. *Bon?*'

'Very *bon*,' Roger approved.

'Like the colour-scheme?'

'Ripping! I congratulate you.'

'Topping!' said Alec dutifully.

'That's all right, then. Now you can tell me the news. Sit down somewhere, the bed's the comfiest—I beg its pardon, the divan. There's a box of cigarettes on the mantelpiece. Don't mind me going on ironing, do you?'

'Not at all,' said Roger, seating himself in an armchair by the window and modestly averting his gaze from the object of Sheila's ministrations.

He proceeded to tell her the results of his two interviews during the morning, his suspicions of Mary Blower and the gist of his conversation with Alec on the way home. Sheila listened with lively interest. When Roger had finished, she delivered her verdict with certitude and decision.

'Mrs Bentley didn't leave her arsenic and lemonade on the chest-of-drawers, because we've made up our minds that she was innocent, and she couldn't have been innocent if she had. That washes out an accident on Mary Blower's part. Mary Blower didn't do it deliberately, because she probably wouldn't have the guts; these servants talk a lot, but when it comes to doing anything, they just give notice and flounce off. Allen didn't do it, because he wouldn't be such an idiot. Mrs Allen got the arsenic and asked her husband to give it to Bentley and tell him that story about it being some wonderful cure; that gives her her revenge on both of them, you see, her husband and Mrs Bentley. Probably she thought they'd both be accused together. That's what happened.'

'So now all we've got to do is to go round to the police and have Mrs Allen arrested,' Roger said admiringly. 'I do wish I had your faculty of disentangling complicated threads in two seconds and putting my finger right on the heart of the mystery without any hesitation whatever, Sheila. It's a wonderful gift. You ought to apply for a job at Scotland Yard; you're wasted at the ironing-board.'

'Oh, you can laugh,' Sheila said equably. 'But that's how it'll turn out in the end, believe me.'

'Sheila,' Alec interposed suddenly. 'You're getting uppish again. It's time you were scragged.'

'Now you leave me alone, Alec, or I'll throw this iron at you. I swear I will!'

'Peace, little children!' Roger intervened hurriedly. 'Alec, stop growling and lie down. I want to talk to Miss Purefoy. Seriously, Sheila, admire though I do your powers of penetration and insight, and aghast though I am before your grasp of the situation, there are one or two little things that have got to be done before we can arrest Mrs Allen, and most of them concern the lady's husband. Now, I've got a little job I want done that'll just suit you.'

'Good! Spit it out.'

'I want you to go off the very minute after lunch and find out all you can for me about this man Allen—where he works in London, what he does, what his habits are, what sort of reputation or character he's got (make allowances for prudery and local prejudice), and anything else you can ferret out about him. I think you said you knew some people who knew them. Can you manage that—between lunch and tea, if possible?'

'I'll have a jolly good shot at it,' quoth Miss Purefoy. 'In fact, if you're in such a hurry I might try one or two people straight away, before lunch; it's not half-past twelve yet, is it? I'll just finish off this chimmy, and the other things can wait.'

'Admirable devotion to duty,' Roger said warmly. 'All things considered, I shall have to think about a little promotion for you, Detective Purefoy. There might even be some germ of an idea in the theory you propounded just now, in spite of its incoherent improbability.'

Sheila's reply was pointed and pithy, and it had better not be printed.

During the afternoon Roger went out with Dr Purefoy on his rounds; he took a novel and a rug with him and obtained plenty of fresh air with a minimum amount of exertion. Alec allowed himself to be bullied by Mrs Purefoy into accompanying her on some calls which she professed to be quite unable to face without his support; he spent the afternoon sitting about in dismal silence in half-a-dozen drawing-rooms and sternly avoiding the quizzical glances which his cousin continued to throw at him.

As it happened, Dr Purefoy was due to give an anæsthetic at the local hospital at half-past four. Mrs Purefoy and her victim being still in the throes of that most fell of all social duties, Roger and Sheila had tea together alone.

Sheila arrived a quarter of an hour late, threw off her furs and gloves and sat down behind the tea-tray. She was wearing a little brown velour hat with a feather in it pulled well down over her head, and a trim brown coat and skirt; her cheeks were flushed with exercise in the keen air, and she looked particularly delightful. Roger even paid her the tribute of wishing for one fleeting moment (a) that he was not a good seventeen years older than she was, and (b) that he did not find bachelordom such a very pleasant mode of existence.

'Well, I don't know that I've got a frightful lot for you, Roger,' she said. 'You do take milk and sugar, don't you? I dug up about a dozen people altogether, pumped them briefly but efficiently, and then went out and wrote down against their gateposts as much as I could remember of what they'd told me.'

'Did you? Good girl. It's the only way. Let's have a look. Bread-and-butter?'

'Thanks. Oh, you couldn't make head or tail of it. I'd better give you a sort of *precis* of the whole lot. Did you ever have to do *precis*-work at school? Most awful rot. Wait a minute 'til I've had a cup of tea, which I'm simply dying for, and then I'll hold forth.'

She hurriedly ate two pieces of bread-and-butter and a rock bun, gulped down her tea and poured herself out another cupful, and then extracted from her handbag a much creased and rather grubby piece of paper which she proceeded to study with close attention.

'Ronald Whittaker Allen,' she announced; 'born eighteen ninety, and still going strong—very strong. Business, motor-car dealer; business address, 33 Orange Street, New Bond Street, W. Tall, burly, fair, red-faced; small, close-clipped moustache; jovial, jocular, hearty, cheery; a little loud, a little coarse; not nearly good enough for Mrs Allen, much too human for Mrs Allen, much nicer than Mrs Allen, not nearly so nice as Mrs Allen; drinks somewhat, but not too much; wears a diamond ring; thoroughly good-hearted, thoroughly bad-minded; rather like a superior kind of bookmaker. There! That's the whole lot, just lumped together.'

'Thanks most awfully, Sheila,' Roger said warmly. 'That's extraordinarily good; just exactly what I wanted to know. I feel as if I'd known the man for years. You couldn't possibly have done better. Great work!'

Sheila flushed with pleasure. 'Good! I was afraid you'd think it a bit scanty. More tea? Help yourself to food. These rock buns aren't half bad. Well, what are you going to do about him?'

Roger glanced at his watch. 'I'm going up to town at once to catch him before he leaves business. He'll be easier to tackle that way, I think. I shan't let on that I'm interested in the case, or that I'm staying down here, or anything like that. If I'm right in the type I think he belongs to, I shan't have to work very hard to make him talk; if I can only get him to take a fancy to me, all I shall have to do is to sit and listen, and just put in a sympathetic remark or a pertinent question here and there.'

'I do wish I could come with you,' Sheila said frankly.

'My dear, this interesting conversation will probably take place in the private bar of the Green Pig or the Crossed Horns or whatever the gentleman's particular fancy in hostelries happens to be; and emancipated though you are, I hardly think you'd like to follow us in there.'

'Why not?' said Miss Purefoy defiantly. 'I wouldn't mind a bit.'

'No? Well, I should. Now, would you be a good little detective and sleuth me a favourable train in the timetable? I want to arrive in Orange Street a few minutes before six o'clock.'

CHAPTER XVII

MR ALLEN TALKS

The offices of Automobiles Exchange and Sale, Ltd., joint proprietors, R. W. Allen & H. S. Titheridge, consisted of the entire spacious ground-floor of 33 Orange Street. Sliding doors permitted very nearly the whole width of the frontage to be thrown open during business hours, and within one caught a glimpse in passing of half-a-dozen or more glistening cars of all makes and sizes. Beyond the main-floor-space, at the back of the showroom, were the private offices, one for the typist, one for the manager, and one, the largest, for Messrs. R. W. Allen and H. S. Titheridge. The latter was the technical man of the firm, and as such nearly always cloistered in the basement whither middle-aged cars and cars past their first youth descended by lift, to return to the upper air a few weeks later in glistening glory and radiant with health and strength as if by the operation of some automobile monkey-gland; R. W. Allen looked after the business side of affairs.

Into R. W. Allen's sanctum, therefore, was shown at five minutes to six that same evening a strange customer who had confided to the manager his intention of buying a car but who wished to have a chat with one of the partners first regarding terms of payment, references and such important details; the strange customer had mentioned a preference for the company of Mr Allen, mentioning casually that he thought they had one or two friends in common, but this had really not affected the issue either way, for into Mr Allen's presence he would have been shown in any case.

Mr Allen rose and shook his visitor's hand with considerable warmth; he was a big, burly man, with a red face and a jolly smile, just beginning to run to flesh, and he spoke in a round, full-throated voice.

'You want to buy a car, Mr—'—he glanced at the visitor's card which had preceded him—'Mr Sheringham? That's fine. Sit down there and let's talk it over.'

'I'm afraid I'm a little late in the day, perhaps?' Roger said apologetically, seating himself in the big armchair which stood at the side of Allen's desk.

'Not a bit, not a bit! Time's immaterial to me. I'm often here 'til all hours.' He glanced at the card again. 'Mr Roger Sheringham, Vauxhall Club. Surely you're not Roger Sheringham, the great novelist, eh?'

'Very kind of you to put it that way,' Roger murmured.

'That's fine,' said Mr Allen with enthusiasm. 'My wife's got one or two books of yours.'

Roger began to feel that he rather liked this large, red-faced, very slightly vulgar man. At any rate he was honest; he did not pretend to have read books which he hadn't just because he happened to be talking to the author of them, as, in Roger's experience, ninety-nine people out of a hundred did. Roger recognised that Allen had already made a favourable impression on him.

'I'm glad to hear that,' he smiled. 'I'm always glad to hear of people who actually possess copies of my books instead of depending entirely on the libraries. So much better for their author, you know.'

Allen laughed hugely. 'Better business, eh? Well, I guess you're right, Mr Sheringham. Authors have to live just as much as motor traders, haven't they? So I'll tell you what—you buy one of my cars, and I'll buy one of your books. That's a fair offer, isn't it?' He laughed hugely again.

Roger laughed also.

They proceeded to business. Roger knew exactly what he wanted, for he had gone into the matter with some care during his journey up to town; he wanted a car which would do sixty miles an hour on the flat, at least thirty miles to the gallon, not be more than twelve horse-power because of the tax, must be a four-seater and fitted with a saloon body, must be able to take all but the very worst hills on top because Mr Sheringham disliked changing his gears, must have all the latest gadgets, accessories and improvements, and must not cost a penny more than two hundred and fifty, or, at the very most, three hundred pounds. Roger told Mr Allen what he wanted. Mr Allen groaned patiently as if he were not altogether unused to this sort of thing, and endeavoured to instil a little hard reason into Roger's requirements.

They went on talking

Half-past six came and went. Seven o'clock. Still they talked.

At ten minutes past seven Roger jumped to his feet. 'Look here, this is abominable!' he said. 'I don't know about you, but I've talked myself quite hoarse. Come out and have a drink.'

Mr Allen had no objection at all. They went. Allen tried to draw Roger into a cosy little public-house almost opposite, but Roger, alleging that there was a particularly favourite one of his own only a few streets away, refused to be drawn. He had no wish to share Allen among half-a-dozen of the latter's own cronies; he wanted him to himself. In the end Roger found a quiet little place in a quiet little street over a quarter of a mile away, and hailed it readily as their goal. They passed into a comfortable and deserted private bar. Roger ordered whisky.

Three minutes later Allen ordered more whisky. Not to be outdone, three more minutes later Roger ordered again. Allen did not want to be outdone either; also he hoped to sell Roger a car. Time, and whisky, passed.

At last Roger, who had managed without being seen to empty most of his share of the libations into the coal-scuttle, judged that the hour was ripe. 'By the way, Allen' he said very airily. 'I've been reading about a namesake of yours lately. That

Wychford Poisoning Case, you know. Not a relation by any chance, is he?'

Allen turned a slightly dull eye upon him. 'Relashion? No. Why?'

'Oh, I was only wondering. I know several people in Wychford myself. There's a Dr Purefoy there, and a Mrs Saunderson. She's mixed up in the case too, I see.'

'You know Mrs Saundersh—Mrs Shaunderson?'

'Oh, yes; quite well. She's rather a friend of mine. That's why I was wondering whether you happened to be any relation of that poor chap Allen who seems to have got into such a hole over it.'

Allen contemplated him gloomily. 'You're a good f'la, Sheringham,' he said with considerable emotion. 'A dam' good f'la. I'm not going to deshieve you. Not going to deshieve a dam' good f'la like old Sheringham. No!—Besides,' he added earnestly if a trifle vaguely, 'a rolling stone gathers no moss, does it? Gathers no moss, a blessed rolling stone doesn't, does it?'

Roger hastened to clear the rolling stone of any such imputation. 'Certainly not!' he agreed with emphasis. 'Most decidedly not.'

'Thash right,' Allen nodded wisely. 'Gathers no moss, a rolling stone. I'm a rolling stone, old f'la!—but I've gathered a lot of moss!' he added with some surprise. 'A hell of a lot of moss!'

Roger endeavoured to lead the conversation back into its former channel. 'There must be exceptions to every rule,' he said gravely. 'But what is it you don't want to deceive me about?'

Allen laid a hand on the other's shoulder and looked down upon him with an expression of intense seriousness. He was a good three inches taller than Roger, and his hand was a heavy one, having most of Mr Allen's weight behind it, but Roger stood his ground; his face reflected the earnest gravity of his burden's.

'No, I'm not going to deshieve you,' enunciated Allen a trifle thickly. 'You're a dam' good f'la, Sheringham, and I'm *not* going to deshieve you. I'm the f'la!'

'You're the Allen of the Wychford Case?' exclaimed Roger with excellent surprise. 'You don't say so!'

'I do!' returned Mr Allen sadly. 'And why? Because I'm not going to deshieve a good f'la like you, Sheringham. Thash—that's why. Yes, damn it, I'm the f'la!'

Roger dexterously shifted the weight from his shoulder on to its own feet and steered it to a chair in the corner of the little room. He drew another chair close up beside it.

'So you're the Allen of the Wychford Case! Well, well.' Roger paused to determine his line of attack. 'Do you know, I met Mrs Bentley once, I believe, at Mrs Saunderson's,' he went on with bland untruth, 'and I should never have considered her capable of a thing like that. Never! And I flatter myself that I'm a pretty good judge of character too.'

'Nor should I, old man,' returned Allen dolefully. ''Pon my word, I never would. It beats me altogether—absolutely whacks me! Can't make head or tail of it.'

'I thought her a particularly nice woman,' Roger prompted.

'So she is. Topping little woman! Wouldn't hurt a fly, you'd say. I'd never have believed it of her. Can't understand it.'

'Ah, well, it's extraordinary what a woman will do for love, isn't it?'

'But she *didn't* love me! Thash the whole point. She didn't love me any more than I loved her. Knew that all the time. Both of us knew it.'

Roger's eyes gleamed. 'She didn't love you? But that's supposed to be her motive for the whole thing.'

'I know it is! Too dam' silly for words. I've told the police time and time again, but they won't take any notice. Told the reporters too, but they won't print it. Supposed to be a great passion, y'see, or some nonsense like that; creem pashonelle, or whatever they call it. Dam' fools, the whole lot of 'em. I told her solicitor, but even he didn't seem to believe it! He's a dam' fool too. *Everybody's* a dam' fool!' added Mr Allen with fine impartiality.

'But this is extraordinarily interesting. It throws a different light on the whole affair. You say neither of you loved each other? You didn't love her either, then?'

'Course I didn't,' said Mr Allen with simple dignity. 'I love my wife. F'la must love his wife, mustn't he? Monkeys about a bit, p'raps; but only loves his wife really.'

'It doesn't always hold good,' said Roger mildly.

'Well, it does with me. Don't know why I'm telling you all this, but you're a good f'la, Sheringham. You're different somehow from the other f'las. Can't talk to them about it. Fact is, I want to talk to somebody. Worried to death about the whole thing. Jacky must've been mad, y'see. Assolutely mad! Been wondering what I ought to do about it. My fault in a way, y'see. Look here, Sheringham, you know about these things; think it'd be any good me going to the police and telling 'em I did it, eh? Been wondering. Must get Jacky out of it if I can, y'see.'

Roger glanced at his companion with sympathetic interest. This coarse, rather vulgar man, slightly drunk and superficially most unattractive, was offering, unheroically and in cold blood, to perform the greatest sacrifice that any man can for a fellow-creature. Roger came to a sudden decision.

'Look here, Allen,' he said, 'I'm going to tell you something. It's my belief that Mrs Bentley is innocent, and I'm trying to prove it. I'm going to get you something to sober you up a bit, and then I'm going to ask you a devil of a lot of questions. If you want to help Mrs Bentley, you'll answer them.'

Allen was not so drunk that he could not comprehend this surprising statement. 'Innocent?' he repeated without hope. 'Wish to hell I could think so. Still, I'll answer anything you like. Yes, I am a bit near the edge. Spot of Worcester sauce's what I want. Don't you bother. I know. Order it myself.'

He heaved himself up and rapped on the counter. An

intimate conversation with the stout lady on the other side of it ensued.

'Now then, let's go somewhere and have a bit of dinner,' Roger suggested, when the pick-me-up had been duly mixed and swallowed. 'Some quiet place, where we can talk.'

'I know one,' Allen agreed, walking just a trifle unsteadily to the door. 'Other side of Orange Street. Have lunch there sometimes. It'll be pretty empty at this time. Come 'long. Walk'll do me good.'

He lumbered out into the street, and Roger followed. As they walked along Allen's speech became gradually less thick, his gait more assured. By the time they had reached their destination and seated themselves in a big, almost empty room at the back of the decidedly superior hostelry into which they had turned, he was a comparatively sober man.

'Now then,' Roger began, when they had given their order, 'I've got a confession to make to you. I don't want to buy a car in the least. I came up to town to see you today and I deliberately took you out and tried to put you a little bit over the edge in pursuance of these inquiries I'm making into Mrs Bentley's case. I'm acting entirely on my own, I haven't the faintest shadow of authority from anybody at all, and I'm doing it entirely for my own personal satisfaction and interest; but, right from the beginning, I had an idea that Mrs Bentley might be innocent and, as I said, I'm trying to prove it. I can't tell you what I've been doing or what I've found out, but I will tell you this—I'm more certain than ever that I'm on the right tack!'

'You really think so?' Allen asked eagerly. 'Good God, I only hope you're right, Sheringham. I'd give anything to see Jacky out of this rotten business, she's such a dam' good little sort. Go ahead and ask me anything you like; I'll only be too glad to tell you.'

'I warn you, some of my questions will be extraordinarily intimate and unpleasant for you to answer to a complete stranger!'

'What's the matter? You go ahead. I know I can trust you. I'm a bit of a character-judge too (have to be in business, y'know), but your reputation's good enough for me in any case. I know you wouldn't be the sort of chap to fake up a cock-and-bull story. Well, what do you want to know?'

'This, first of all,' Roger said deliberately. 'Why, if you love your wife, did you embark on that affair with Mrs Bentley?'

Allen reddened slightly. 'Oh, well, you know how it is. I liked the kid, and I was sorry for her; she had a rotten time of it with that little worm, always interfering with her and ordering her about and yapping about his infernal imaginary illnesses. It was a bit of a lark, taking her out, both of us having to keep it so dark and all that; sort of exciting. We got on well together too. She was my sort—jolly and full of fun and that sort of thing. The rest just sort of followed naturally. You know how it is with a chap.'

Roger nodded. 'She was your sort?' he asked significantly.

Allen caught his meaning. 'You haven't met my wife, have you?'

'Yes, I have.'

Allen's flush deepened a little. 'Well, you can see she's a cut above me, to put it bluntly. And she's different from me too. She's the only one I've ever been really fond of, but—well, I know it sounds a bit rotten, but one *does* want a rest from dignity and that sort of thing occasionally. She's a real good sort, and I can tell you, Sheringham, I'm most damnably sorry about it all now for her sake nearly as much as anybody else's (she took it like a real sport)—but she *is* a bit of an ice-box, Edith is. Not the jolly kind, like me or Jacky.'

Roger smiled faintly. 'Jolly' was just about the last word in the whole dictionary that one could apply to the superb Mrs Allen.

'Yes, I understand. To put it crudely, when one's had nothing but grouse for a year or two, a little homely mutton becomes rather a relief.'

'By Jove, yes; you've hit it exactly. It's pretty rotten, I suppose, but it's the way we're made. Can't sort of help feeling like that, can one?'

The arrival of their steaks interrupted the conversation for a few minutes. When the waiter had gone, Roger took up the thread again.

'Now, how do you know for certain that Mrs Bentley wasn't in love with you, Allen?' he asked. 'Sorry to press you over this, but it's a very important point.'

'Oh, well—I've knocked about pretty well ever since I was a youngster. It's easy enough to tell whether a girl's really got it badly, isn't it? When you know each other pretty well, I mean.'

'You don't think that she might just have been pretending when she realised that you weren't in love with her, to save her pride?'

'Oh, Lord, no. Sure she wasn't.'

'Then why did she behave as she did? That may not always mean a frightful lot to a man, but it usually does to a woman; and in respectable society love is generally the only excuse for it.'

'She was French, y'see,' Allen said vaguely.

'You mean that the French can't be expected to have a moral sense?' Roger smiled. 'Don't you believe it. That's just as much a silly popular fiction as that they live on snails and boiled frogs.'

'Oh, I know all about the French. I was with a motor firm in Rouen for a couple of years before the war. That was another reason for her taking to me, by the way, me being able to talk her language; that and me being so different from John. No, that isn't what I mean a bit. It's difficult to explain exactly, but you might put it like this. It isn't as if the French haven't got any moral sense. I know that; but that they don't take that sort of thing so seriously as we do here. Look at their comic papers; it's the only sort of joke they've got. Well, Jacky was a passionate kid, y'see, and she wasn't any too fond of her husband by that time; and I suppose she was grateful to me for taking her about, and—well, anyhow, it didn't go against the grain, so to speak, and it certainly didn't *mean* as much to her as it would to—well, say Edith. That's the only way I can explain it. And of course you've got to remember that she wouldn't feel she owed John anything.'

'Oh? Why not?'

'Don't you know about him? Oh, well, John was a pretty poor sort of little specimen, but he wasn't a puritan by any means as far as the girls were concerned. Anything but!'

'You mean, he'd given his wife cause for divorce?'

'Well, it sounds politer to put it that way.'

'Why hadn't she divorced him, then?'

'She was a Catholic. She didn't believe in divorce.'

'Oh!' Roger helped himself to more fried potatoes with a distinctly thoughtful air.

For some minutes they ate in silence.

It was not until their plates had been cleared away and two large helpings of apple-pie and cream had been set before them that Roger continued his examination.

'I think there's only one more thing I want to ask you about,' he said. 'You remember that on the Monday before he died you spent the evening with Bentley in his bedroom. Can you remember whether there was a small packet wrapped in white paper on the table by his bed then, or not?'

Allen looked up quickly. 'The packet with all that arsenic in? No, I'm sure it wasn't. There was nothing there but a book and a vase of flowers. I'm positive about that.'

'You are? Thanks. Oh, and was there a glass of lemonade on the chest-of-drawers, did you notice?'

'I can't remember. Couldn't say, I'm afraid.'

'You don't remember noticing any lemonade in the room at all? A jug, perhaps, or anything like that?'

Allen shook his head. 'No, I couldn't possibly say, one way or the other. But, Sheringham, look here: I wish you'd give me some idea of why you think Jacky mightn't have done it after all, can you?'

Roger went on to mention some of the points which he had put before Alec in their very first discussion by the little trout-stream.

CHAPTER XVIII

MR SHERINGHAM LECTURES ON ADULTERY

ROGER returned to Wychford by the last train. It was a slow train, and it stopped at every single station on the way down, but Roger did not notice the time drag. He entered a brown study the moment the porter closed the carriage-door on him at Charing Cross, and he did not emerge from it 'til somebody came and turned him out on Wychford platform—fortunately the train's ultimate destination; otherwise Roger might have woke up an hour or two later to find himself at Dover or similarly unhandy spot.

As on the previous night it was past one o'clock when he got back, and once more Alec was waiting up for him. But this time he was not alone; Sheila had already crept downstairs to share his vigil, clad as before in her black and silver kimono, though not now in those other garments which had prompted Roger's derision.

'Hallo, Roger!' she greeted him cheerfully. 'No, you needn't look at me like that. I'm a perfect lady and I've got a nightie on, so you can't be sarcastic this time.'

'The way this young person continues to throw her more intimate garments in our faces strikes me as nothing less than indecent,' observed Roger sadly to the young person's cousin. 'No, don't bother about mixing me a drink tonight, thanks, Alec; I've seen about as much whisky this evening as I want to look at for quite a long time.' He dropped into a vacant chair and regarded his colleagues benignly.

'He's got news!' Sheila cried. 'I know he has!'

'Have you, Roger?' Alec demanded.

'Children, I have,' Roger beamed. 'Your noble-minded

superintendent, oozing devotion to duty at every pore, has walked off with the coconut once more. The man Allen is struck off the list of suspects. I have spoken.'

'I told you so!' Sheila crowed, wriggling in her chair with excitement. 'I told you so at tea, didn't I?'

'You did, my dear. You shall have a portion of the coconut. The milk. Milk's very good for infants, they tell me.'

'Shut up, Sheila. Go on, Roger. Why have you struck Allen off? I thought you were suspecting him rather strongly. Have you been with him all this time?'

'I'll tell you all about it. Exercising my well-known low cunning and acting upon the admirable *dossier* compiled for me by Detective Purefoy, I went to see the man, alleging that I wanted to buy a car. From his office I lured him into a place of refreshment (remember the presence of the young, Alexander) and made him slightly drunk.'

'Oh, I *do* wish you'd let me come up with you, Roger!'

'Hush, little babbler!—Well, it really was rather pathetic,' Roger went on with one of his swift changes of mood. 'The poor chap had no objection at all to getting slightly drunk, none at all; I think he even welcomed it. There's no doubt that he's been worried to death about the whole business, and there's equally no doubt that, according to his lights and out of business hours, he's an honest man. Anyhow, I got him to own up to being the Allen of the case, and within two minutes he was asking me perfectly seriously whether I thought it would be any good for him to go to the police and confess to the murder in order to save Mrs Bentley.'

'*Sportsman!*' cried Sheila warmly.

'Humph! Might be a bit of eye-wash, mightn't it?' queried her more sceptical cousin.

'No, I'm quite sure it wasn't eye-wash,' Roger rejoined seriously. 'Allen's a rough diamond all right, but he's a genuine one. And he was slightly drunk, don't forget; that always tends to induce truthfulness. No, I'm quite sure he was being honest, both in that and something very important indeed of which he informed me at the same time, namely that he and Mrs Bentley had never been in love with each other and knew perfectly well that they weren't in love with each other!'

'Oho!' said Alec with considerable interest. 'Exit motive, then?'

'Exactly. And I may as well tell you here that not only has my interview with this gentleman cleared Allen himself in my small opinion, but it confirms twenty times over our main theory of Mrs Bentley's innocence. For instance, not only am I quite prepared to accept the fact that she wasn't in love with Allen (there were confirmatory details, by the way, but I can't go into those just at present, always remembering the presence amongst us of the young of the species), but—'

'Don't be such an idiot, Roger!' the young of of the species interrupted with some indignation. 'I'm not a child!'

'But he was very emphatic about her character as well; he mentioned, in fact, that she wouldn't hurt a fly. Why is it, I wonder, that flies should always be selected as the supreme test of a humane disposition? Why not fleas, or wood-lice, or cater-pillars, or wasps? I suppose there must be something about a fly which brings out all one's evil instincts. They ought to make a scientific thing of it. Lock your suspected person up in a small room furnished only with a single fly, and supply him with a swatter; if at the end of a fixed period, to be determined according to the individual's estimated reactions to flies, the animal is found to be unscathed, innocence on the part of the suspected person may be confidently presumed. If on the other hand the fly is found to be suffering from a black eye or a cauliflower ear, then—'

'What did Allen himself think about the case? Did *he* think Mrs Bentley was innocent?'

'Very well; I'll develop this thesis later. Allen? Oh, no; that doesn't seem ever to have occurred to him. But he was extraor-dinarily puzzled about it; in fact, he confided to me that he couldn't make head or tail of it. Now that, I think, is another interesting point. Why this invariable head or tail that has to be identified for everything? Not all things have a tail. You, for instance. In those cases I suppose one has to—'

'Roger! For goodness' sake stick to the point. What's the matter with you?'

'I'm a trifle elated, I'm afraid, Alec,' Roger apologised. 'This has been a very successful day, you see, and I'm—yes, I'm undoubtedly a, little elated.'

'Well, take a lesson from Sheila. Even she's being serious for once.'

Sheila, curled up in her chair, her feet tucked away under her and her small chin resting on her hand, smiled faintly. Roger looked at her and smiled also.

'I'll try,' he promised.

'Well, get on and tell us the rest. You don't seem to realise that we're jolly keen to hear about it all.'

Roger bowed his head. 'Ticked off,' he admitted. 'And quite properly too. Well, let me see; there really isn't very much more to tell you. We gassed a lot, but only a few more points of any importance emerged. Oh, I ought to have mentioned that after I'd made up my mind that the chap was genuine and genuinely worried to death, I took him into my confidence and told him straight out that I was working to prove Mrs Bentley's innocence.'

'The devil you did!'

'Yes, I thought it would pay us. And it did; I put all sorts of deuced unpleasant questions to him, and he answered them all like a sportsman. These are the main things I got out of him; that he's really in love with his wife, whom he acknowledges to be a cut above him, and whom he characterises with respectful regret as an "ice-box"; that he was just amusing himself with Mrs Bentley by way of a change, and that Mrs Bentley was similarly amusing herself with him, both being of a jolly and cheerful disposition and recognising a kindred spirit in the other and neither being in the least serious about the affair; that John Bentley, in spite of his rat-like properties, was a bit of a lad in some ways and his wife knew it; that he is quite certain the packet of arsenic was not on the bed-table when he spent that Monday evening with Bentley; that he doesn't remember seeing any lemonade about, either in a glass or a jug, but can't swear to there having been none; and that Mrs Bentley wouldn't hurt a fly. All that is in favour either of him or her, you see. Against it one point emerged in Mrs Bentley's disfavour.'

'What's that?'

'Well, it's not really very important, but it's the sort of thing that the prosecution would be almost certain to twist into a significance far greater than it deserves. She's a Catholic, and she doesn't believe in divorce.'

'Oh! Yes, I see what you mean.'

'And that's really all. So up with you, Sheila, to bed, my infant, while your uncles have one final cigarette in virtue of their greater years.'

'In other words,' retorted Sheila, uncurling reluctantly, 'so that you can talk about the spicy bits with me out of the way. All right, I suppose I shall have to go then. Though it really is damned silly, you know. I'm not a kid.'

'What would your mother say to this theory?'

Sheila giggled. 'Oh, she'd have kittens, of course. But all mothers do that if they think their idiot daughters can put two and two together and make four instead of three.'

Roger rose and opened the door for her. 'This peculiar property of mothers has quite escaped my notice,' he remarked with interest. 'The chief authority on mothers, their ways and habits, the American film industry, is singularly silent on the point. Goodnight, Miss Purefoy.'

'Goodnight, you old idiot. 'Night, Alec!'

Roger closed the door. 'I wonder whether that young lady really does know as much about certain aspects of life as she is rather inclined to insist,' he remarked as he resumed his seat.

'Oh, I expect so,' Alec replied calmly. 'There's not much girls don't know nowadays. Jolly good thing too. I'm all in favour of it. Bringing a girl up in blinkers never did anybody any good, least of all herself.'

'Alexander, I quite agree with you. But it does go to their small heads a little, doesn't it? Well, now about Mrs Bentley and Allen; the point I want to put to you is this—Allen's statement about their not being in love with each other isn't going to carry the slightest weight with either judge or jury, you know. To us it almost clinches the fact of her innocence; in court it's going to have the exactly opposite effect. He's already told the police, by the way, and they simply laughed in his face. They would.'

'I don't quite get this,' Alec said. 'Why isn't it going to carry any weight with judge and jury? I should have said it was extraordinarily significant.'

'That's because you're a person of common-sense. But it's no good looking for common-sense inside a law-court; the motto over the door is "Abandon any common-sense ye may once have had, all ye who enter here to serve in the jury-box, on the bench, and nearly always in the capacity of counsel." I was talking about something like this the other day, wasn't I? In connection with our dear old friend, the legal mind. Well, this is just another example of the same thing.'

'Explain,' said Alec, leaning back in his chair and puffing contentedly at his pipe.

'Well, let me put it like this. In the first place, this affair with Allen is terribly prejudicial to Mrs Bentley's case, you understand. To the legal mind, as I pointed out before, everything is either one extreme or the other, black or white; no shade of grey can be recognised. A faithful wife, of course, is white all through; an unfaithful wife correspondingly black. Love legalised by marriage is blamelessly white; and illicit love black as pitch. Extenuating circumstances which might produce a grey effect can't be admitted for a moment. In other words, an irregular love affair can never kindle a single spark of sympathy in a court of law. Prosecuting counsel talks piously about the sacredness of the marriage-tie, and the judge refers to "this guilty passion," while the jury look down their noses in the good old hypocritical way—as if there was a single person, from judge through counsel and jury to the constable at the door, who hadn't had his own private lapses from the blameless purity they're all making such a fuss about! Though that, of course, makes them all the more intolerant of other people's. Anyhow, you see, hopeless, irrational prejudice at once, and the firm conviction in everybody's British mind that from adultery to murder is only the shortest possible step.'

'Yes, but if she *doesn't* love him—!'

'I'm coming to that. Well, that's the state of things when an unfaithful wife has the misfortune to be standing in the dock. We know she's black all through, because infidelity admits of no compromise. But supposing, to top all this iniquity, she actually hasn't got the excuse of *loving* her partner in sin! Could anything be more abominable than that? Why, it's monstrous! It's inhuman! The woman simply can't have any moral sense at all! She must be a complete monster! What would murder be to a person like that? Why, obviously the most ordinary, the most natural, the most inevitable thing in the world! Gentlemen, my learned friend has submitted to you that the fact of this abandoned creature not having even the excuse of love for her conduct (if *love* it would have been called in any case) destroys the motive which we impute to her for taking her husband's life. Gentlemen, my learned friend has a reputation second to none for brilliance and plausibility, but surely in this suggestion he has overstepped himself. Destroy the motive! Gentlemen, when we are considering such incredible—nay, I will go further!—such *revolting* conduct, need we trouble to look for a mere *motive*? If you will allow me to paraphrase an old saying, I would simply make this reply to my friend's suggestion— actions speak louder than motives!'

''Struth!' said Alec.

'Well, you see what I mean. That's the construction counsel would put upon it. And I'd bet a hundred to one that the silly old judge would back him up. Judges *are* silly old men, you know; nearly always. Sense on the bench is as rare as it is delightful: recognition, I mean, of human beings as they are, and not as they ought to be. And this is just precisely the sort of case that seems to make a judge hurry to shed any elements of native sense he may be blessed with.'

'You seem to feel rather strongly about all this, Roger.'

'Well, I do. I've read so many trials, you see, and so many summings-up, and the amount of really wilful stupidity in so many of them leaves me simply gasping. Some judges seem to go absolutely out of their way in order to deliberately blind themselves to human nature, whereas a close knowledge of psychology ought to be the very first requirement in any applicant for a judicial position. Dear me, I am getting worked up; I've murderously split, maimed and maliciously damaged one perfectly good infinitive. By the way, of course there *are* plenty of sound humanly minded judges; I'm not condemning the whole judicial tribe. But unfortunately they're very decidedly in the minority.'

'I see what you mean. Yes, that certainly is a point. But good Lord, do you really mean to say that these lawyers would twist the thing round like that?'

'My dear Alec, it wouldn't be twisting to their minds. That's the first way they'd look at it. The law lives on axioms, you see. All adultery is founded on guilty passion; all faithful wives are blameless; all unfaithful wives want their husbands dead; every individual is either thoroughly good or thoroughly bad—that sort of thing. To suggest that any of these axioms may be based on false premises is simply to be laughed at. It'd be worse than useless to put forward the idea, for instance, that a good and faithful wife may be a far more harmful member of the community than a bad and unfaithful one, or that adultery is not synonymous with a desire to transform an inconvenient husband into a convenient corpse. In private life a barrister or a judge might go so far as to admit that there might be something in this revolutionary idea; but in court, facing a British jury and with the legal mind in full working order, he simply wouldn't understand you.'

'I shall have to confront you with a lawyer one day, and let you fight it out,' said Alec with a slight grin.

'Don't. He'd wipe the floor with me in argument, of course; that's his job. But just consider once more—what hope would Mrs Bentley have of being believed at all if she were to get up in court and tell them she wasn't in love with Allen? That she didn't commit adultery with him out of infatuation or dear old "guilty passion," she just did it because her husband bored her rather stiff and she wanted a little mild amusement? Good Lord, what a hope! They simply wouldn't believe her for a second. If they did, of course they'd consider her even more depraved and abandoned than before; but they wouldn't. And yet if one only went into it, that's the cause of nine-tenths of the adultery that *is* committed.'

'You seem to know a devil of a lot about this subject, Roger. Been studying it too?'

'Adultery? Of course. That's my business. You can't write novels in these days without a very intimate knowledge of that particular phenomenon, its cause, cures and general ramifications, my dear Alexander. Don't think I'm defending adultery, by the way, because I'm doing nothing of the sort; we all know it's very naughty indeed, and, even more important, economically quite unsound. But because one condemns it in principle, that doesn't say that one must side with the law in refusing to recognise how very easily, and for what apparently trivial causes, we poor feckless humans can be driven into it; and of these trivial causes the most powerful, the most frequent and the most easily comprehensible (always outside a court) is a lack of sympathetic understanding in the second member of the triangle and the presence of it in the third. Anyhow, you see how it is in this instance. A judge and jury simply wouldn't be able to understand the very first thing about the psychological condition of either Mrs Bentley or Allen himself which resulted, without the least talk of love or infatuation or anything like that, in their being unfaithful to their respective spouses out of a combination of sheer fun, good spirits, devilry, mutual understanding and boredom. And for Mrs Bentley to put it forward, or for Allen to try and explain it, is simply to throw her to the lions. You and I and any other sensible person may realise that it knocks the bottom out of the whole case against her (unless any other motive could be brought forward, of course; I mean the case as it stands); inside a court it would be taken as tantamount to complete proof of her guilt. I have spoken.'

'You have,' Alec agreed admiringly. "Mr Sheringham then delivered a short lecture on adultery." No, but seriously, Roger, that really is extraordinarily interesting about Mrs Bentley. I should never have dreamed of looking on it that way, but I see you're probably quite right. Well, all this naturally makes me a good deal keener on proving her innocence. What's the programme for tomorrow?'

'I'm not sure yet,' Roger said thoughtfully. 'I've got two more people to see, haven't I? Brothers William and Alfred. The former, as I told you, strikes me as a bit of a hysterical ass and I don't think I shall waste much time on him. But Brother Alfred—!'

'Yes?' Alec asked, knocking out the ashes of his pipe.

'Well, Brother Alfred does interest me. Quite considerably!'

CHAPTER XIX

INTRODUCING BENTLEY BROTHERS

ROGER spent the following morning at Wychford. He took the opportunity after breakfast of taking Mrs Purefoy aside and giving her some clearer idea of the reason for his and Alec's visit to town, not mentioning his belief in Mrs Bentley's innocence but simply saying that he was acting for the *Daily Courier* in a special capacity to see if he could bring any new facts to light; he felt he owed his hostess this by way of some excuse for his repeated absences and for treating her house as an hotel. Mrs Purefoy smilingly told him not to bother about anything like that, but simply to come and go just as he liked; they were delighted to have him, and Alec was a good companion for Sheila in the absence of that young lady's brother and sister.

Later on, Dr Purefoy being confined once more to the local hospital by an operation, as happened very nearly every afternoon, Sheila demanded and obtained the car and took them both for a little run into the country. Earnest attempts on her part to extract information regarding the turn taken by the conversation after her departure the night before were met with stern rebuffs.

'I say,' Sheila said suddenly, at last abandoning her endeavours in despair. 'I say, Roger, what about that other maid at the Bentleys'? There were two of them who saw the fly-papers, you know. She's left now, I found out yesterday, but she ought to be easy to trace. I can't remember what her name was, but—'

'Nellie Green, you mean?' supplied Roger, who was sitting beside Sheila on the front seat. 'Why, what about her?'

'Well, you made such a fuss about seeing Mary Blower. Oughtn't you to see the other one as well?'

'And the cook,' Roger said thoughtfully. 'Well, strictly speaking, I suppose I ought. But their evidence before the magistrates didn't strike me as affecting the case one way or the other; just about the Bentleys' home life, and corroborating Mary Blower's story of the fly-papers and that sort of thing. No, I don't really think I need bother about them.'

'Well, if either of them turns out to have done it, don't say I didn't tell you,' said Sheila. 'And what about the Saunderson? I suppose you've dropped her like a red-hot coal now you've got all you wanted out of her.'

'I have!' returned Roger heartily. 'And that reminds me. I believe I'm supposed to be going there to tea today. Will you ring her up at about four o'clock and tell her I've been called off suddenly to see a woman about a cat in Singapore or Cape Cod or somewhere equally plausible.'

'I will,' Sheila undertook with enthusiasm. 'And I'll add that you therefore won't be staying any longer in Wychford to see a cat about a woman, that mission having already been most successfully accomplished, shall I?'

'You can tell her anything you jolly well like,' Roger said generously.

At lunch Roger remembered something that he had been intending to ask the doctor. In view of the way in which the case had developed during the last twenty-four hours, it no longer held quite the same importance as before, but Roger preferred to have everything cut and dried.

'By the way, doctor,' he remarked, 'has arsenic any value as a cosmetic?'

The doctor's eyes twinkled. 'Are you forecasting Mrs Bentley's defence, Sheringham?'

'Part of it, yes. I expect you've read of the Madeleine Smith case, haven't you? That was the defence set up for the possession of arsenic there, you know, and it's been put forward in other cases since then. I shouldn't be at all surprised if Mrs Bentley does the same. Is there anything in it?'

'Oh, there is, undoubtedly. Arsenic is prescribed internally in certain cases where the skin is affected; it makes the skin softer and would eradicate pimples or anything like that. It's good for the complexion too, I believe, but don't let Sheila hear me say that, or she'll be the next one to buy fly-papers.'

'Thank you, father. I'm perfectly satisfied with my schoolgirl complexion as it is.'

'It does wear pretty well,' Alec said critically, 'considering the amount of paint and muck you wear over it.'

Under cover of the resulting wrangle, Roger pursued his inquiries further. 'Internally, you said. And would it be any good applied externally instead?'

'Oh, yes, I think so. It isn't the sort of thing one could order, of course, because of the danger; but I should say that Mrs Bentley would have no difficulty in making out a perfectly legitimate case for its use in that way.'

'I see,' said Roger with satisfaction. 'Yes, that was my idea too.'

Shortly after lunch Roger announced his intention of running up to town for an hour or two. Sheila offered to drive him down to the station, and Alec once more accommodated himself in the dickey.

'Though this is absolutely the last time,' he said plaintively. 'I'm so sore already that I can hardly sit down. It's your turn next, Roger.'

'One sore person in a household is generally quite enough,' Roger pointed out. 'I don't think you ought to be unreasonable, Alec.'

'So you're going to tackle Brother Alfred, are you?' Sheila asked, when they were under way. 'I think you'll find him a rather tougher nut to crack than Mr Allen.'

'I'm afraid I shall. And I've really got nothing to crack him with, like I had Allen.'

'How are you going about it?'

'Well, I don't see what else I can do except send in my name as the *Courier*'s representative. He's given one or two interviews already, so I may have luck.'

'But what do you want to find out from him?'

'Oh, there's nothing exactly that I want to find out from him; no information, or anything like that. I just want to get an impression of the man himself.'

'To see whether he's capable of murdering his own brother?'

'If you like to put it so bluntly, yes.'

'Well, I shouldn't be a bit surprised if he did. He sounds just like the sort of man you're always saying a poisoner usually is—hard and cold and calculating and all that.'

'Yes, I must admit that's how he struck me too.'

'Better buy a pair of handcuffs before you get there,' Sheila advised, bringing the car round in a broad sweep in front of the station-entrance.

Alfred Bentley, as Roger had already discovered, was the manager of a big paper-manufactory in the south of London. He had begun at the very bottom of the business when he was eighteen years old and worked up to the position he now held. His age was thirty-six.

Roger gave his name at the little pigeon-hole marked 'Inquiries,' mentioned that he represented the *Daily Courier* and made his request for an interview.

Three minutes later the girl who had taken his message came back with his answer. 'Mr Bentley is very sorry, but he is not seeing any more interviewers.'

Roger was not unprepared. 'Will you tell him that I have some very important information not yet known to the police which I should like to discuss with him,' he said with a bland smile.

The girl disappeared again.

This time Roger's strategy was rewarded. 'Mr Bentley can give you two minutes, sir. Will you come through, please.'

She led the way down a short corridor and tapped deferentially on a door. 'Mr Sheringham, sir,' she said, opening it in response to a curt summons to enter. Roger stepped past her into the room.

Mr Alfred Bentley looked younger than his years. His face was lean and clean-shaven, his hair short and dark, his eyes a peculiar shade of light blue—'flinty' was the epithet which sprang at once into Roger's mind. He did not rise.

'Good afternoon, Mr Sheringham,' he said, in curt, brisk tones. 'Sit down, will you? I had not intended to see any more interviewers, but you say that you have information of special importance not yet known to the police?'

'Yes, Mr Bentley,' Roger said easily, seating himself in a chair by the big desk. 'I have.'

'I can conceive of nothing important which the police do not already know. May I ask you to tell me what it is? But please remember that I am a busy man and I can't spare you more than the two minutes I mentioned.'

'That will be ample. This is my information—that your sister-in-law and Allen were not, as we understand the phrase, in love with each other.'

Roger had been watching his man closely as he spoke, but Alfred Bentley did not change countenance; only a very faintly contemptuous expression appeared on his impassive face. 'That must be a matter of opinion,' he said shortly. 'Really, if that is all you have to tell me—!'

'My information is reliable.'

Bentley's mouth closed in a hard line. 'I'm afraid I must decline to discuss the question with you. The interest is of a purely personal nature. In any case, your information is clearly mistaken.'

'I don't think you quite appreciate the importance of it, Mr Bentley,' Roger said, leaning forward a little. 'The interest is not purely personal. The question affects the basis of the whole case. It destroys entirely the motive imputed to Mrs Bentley for the crime of which she is accused.' He paused for a moment. 'It really makes one wonder whether she *is* guilty!' he added deliberately.

If Roger had expected to read any dramatic revelation in Bentley's face at this doubtless startling statement, he was disappointed. The only emotion registered there was a slight impatience.

'She hasn't been tried yet, I might remind you,' he said laconically. 'If there is anything in this information of yours, no doubt you will lodge it with its proper recipient and it will receive any attention due to it at the trial. In any case, I must repeat that I cannot discuss it with you, I'm sorry.' He rose to his feet and held out his hand. 'Good afternoon.'

'Good afternoon,' said Roger, and quitted the presence.

In the passage outside he glanced at his watch. 'Two minutes and three seconds,' he murmured. 'A methodical gentleman, Brother Alfred; and evidently a man of his word as well.'

He emerged into the street and stood for a moment on the pavement in thought. It was nearly half-past four, his watch had told him. Coming to a sudden decision he hailed a passing taxi and gave an address to the driver.

The offices of Thomas Bentley and Sons, Ltd., Import and Export Mchts., as their door-plate put it, were situated in the neighbourhood of Gracechurch Street, where land is worth goodness knows how many thousand pounds a square foot. Thomas Bentley and Sons, Ltd., occupied one large and two smaller rooms on a first floor, and no doubt they paid extremely highly for the privilege. Twenty-five minutes after shaking hands with Brother Alfred, Roger was again lifting the flap of a little porthole labelled 'Inquiries' and sending a message to Brother William. This time, however, he played his card of important information in the first round instead of the second.

When Brother Alfred had not denied himself, who was Brother William to do so? 'Mr Bentley will see you, sir,' said the girl in the words of her predecessor. 'Will you come this way?' Roger followed her.

Whereas Brother Alfred had been lean to the point of cadaverousness, Brother William was plump, very nearly stout; his hair was thinner than his brother's and decidedly greyer; his eyes were blue, but it was a paler blue, a watery, indeterminate, uneasy blue; in place of the other's air of dry, hard impassivity he wore a petulant look of resentful dissatisfaction with the world in general. He was the sort of person whom one might expect to cherish, instead of bees, a swarm of grudges in his bonnet.

He rose with obvious reluctance as Roger entered the little room. 'Good afternoon, Mr Sheringham,' he said in a peevish voice. 'I was expecting you.'

The devil you were! observed Roger to himself in considerable astonishment. Aloud, he repeated surprisedly, 'You were expecting me, Mr Bentley?'

'Yes, and I must tell you at once that I must decline to discuss this—er—this information you say you have obtained.'

'But I haven't told you what it is yet!'

'That is—er—immaterial. Certain information has already reached me that—er—that—In any case, I do not wish to discuss it. I might have refused to see you—I was very strongly tempted to do so—except that I should like to put a question to you myself. Where—er—that is, from what source did you obtain this precious information of yours?'

Roger looked at him with growing amazement. William Bentley was obviously ill-at-ease. His hands were trembling as he rested them on his desk, and his face was flushed; he had clearly been picking his words with considerable care, and, to Roger's eyes at any rate, the expression on his face indicated a barely concealed anxiety. Roger decided swiftly to see whether he could force him to show his hand a little more plainly.

'Well, Mr Bentley,' he said slowly, 'if you decline to discuss the matter with me, I hardly see that I can tell you where I obtained my information.'

Bentley's attitude seemed to become tenser. 'I must tell you, Mr Sheringham,' he said with obvious constraint, 'that we—that I, have a particular reason for asking this. I am not prompted by idle curiosity. I have—er—a particular reason for asking.'

'I'm sorry to have to refuse, Mr Bentley,' Roger said courteously, 'but I hardly see how I could tell you without betraying somebody else's confidence, and that I am not prepared to do.'

'But damn it, man!' Bentley snapped. 'We're the lady's brothers-in-law, aren't we? We're more closely concerned than anybody else. If anybody is spreading stories about her or pretending to supply information about her, we have a right to know who it is, haven't we?'

'That, I'm afraid,' replied Roger gravely, 'must be a matter of opinion.'

Bentley sank into his chair. 'Sit down, Mr Sheringham,' he said testily. 'Sit down. Let's talk the matter over. I know perfectly well what this information of yours is. I wanted to know where you got it from in order that I could judge whether there may be any truth in it or not. But if you think you have a right to withhold that, it's obviously no good pursuing the matter.'

'I'm sorry,' Roger murmured.

'Well, what do you propose to do about it? Are you going to publish it?'

'I haven't decided yet'

'Because I must tell you at once that there isn't a vestige of truth in it. Can't be! I only wish I could think otherwise; perhaps in that case my sister-in-law might not have—er—acted as she did. As things are—well, it stands to reason. You must understand that I am influenced only by consideration for my poor brother's memory. This case is terrible for us—terrible!'

'I can believe that,' Roger put in sympathetically.

'I am only anxious to stop the source of any further scandals connected with his good name, you must quite understand that. This is the particular reason for asking you the question to which I referred just now. There has been enough publicity given to the actual facts of the whole dreadful business, without adding anything further in the way of sheer baseless rumour.

Both my brother and myself are quite agreed upon that. We have to take those facts as—er—as they are, but we are determined to take every step to prevent my sister-in-law's case from being prejudiced by completely untruthful—er—tittle-tattle—every step in our power!'

'But would my information have that effect?' asked Roger with considerable surprise.

'Ask yourself, Mr Sheringham! Ask—er—ask yourself! Her position is bad enough as things are. What would it be if you inform the police of this idea? From a—h'm—a morally guilty wife, but with the excuse of a guilty passion, she becomes nothing less than a—er—h'm!—an ordinary loose woman. That is a thing which my brother and myself will combat with all the means in our power against a member of our own family— for, having married into our family, we accept her as a member of it. Whether she is or is not guilty of the terrible crime for which she is to be—er—tried, we are determined to set our faces against the stirring up of any more—any more moral mud, so to speak, in connection with her.'

'What you mean is, if the Allen motive is destroyed, other motives of a similar description might be brought to light?' Roger asked quickly.

Bentley's jaw dropped slightly. 'Certainly not!' he said loudly. 'Nothing of the sort. I must decline to discuss the matter with you further, sir.'

'Or perhaps you meant,' Roger remarked chattily, following the other's lead in rising to his feet, 'that the mud might not be so much concerned with your sister-in-law, as with a male member of the family instead?'

Bentley stepped back a pace, struck the back of his knee against the seat of his chair and sat down heavily, gasping like a fish out of water. His watery eyes stared at Roger from a white face. Roger followed up his advantage. It was rather like hitting a fallen man, but fallen men had to be sacrificed in the interests of truth.

'You are afraid, I take it, that something might be unearthed to show that Mrs Bentley's husband had been carrying on an intrigue under her very nose with somebody very inferior to himself in station?'

The effect of his words was curious. The unmistakable fear in Bentley's face gave place, first to equally unmistakable relief and then to anger. His flush returned and he jumped to his feet once more, pointing a quivering finger at the door.

'Now then, you—you get out, see?' he cried shrilly. 'You get out, and take your filthy lies with you. And if you have the impudence to publish a word or—or hint of them in your beastly rag, I'll—we'll—I'll have you up for libel, see? Criminal libel! Get out, damn you!'

Roger got out with what dignity he might.

'Well, I'll be damned!' observed Mr Roger Sheringham, self-elected detective for the defence. Which was apparently no less than the truth. Mr William Bentley had already attended to that point.

Roger had another very thoughtful journey back to Wychford an hour or so later.

CHAPTER XX

MR SHERINGHAM SUMS UP

It was not until after dinner that evening that Roger had a chance of laying his new discoveries before his colleagues. Sheila gave him the opportunity.

'I'm going to take Roger and Alec upstairs now, mum,' she announced soon after they had returned to the drawing-room. 'We're going to smoke cigarettes and discuss life for an hour. Then I'll bring them downstairs again to talk like little gentlemen to you and father.'

'Very well, dear,' Mrs Purefoy aquiesced, with a smile at Roger.

And so it was.

'Now, then,' Sheila demanded, as soon as they were settled round the fire in her cosy little room. 'Now then, what had Brother Alfred to say for himself?'

'I thought you were going to keep quiet about Mrs Bentley and Allen not being in love,' Alec remarked, when he had finished.

'Well, I did intend to; but I had to put something pretty startling up to the man to watch whether he blanched or paled or did anything interesting like that, and that was the only really startling thing I could remember. Unfortunately not a blanch resulted.'

'But what did you *think* of him, Roger?' Sheila wanted to know.

'I think,' Roger replied with some care, 'that Brother Alfred is a very exceptional man. He gave nothing away to me by so much as a bat of an eyelash. Whether that was because he had nothing to give or whether it was because he *is* a very exceptional man, is one of the chief points we shall have to consider.

The only definite thing I can tell you is that he showed no eagerness at all to receive news which might go some way to exonerate his sister-in-law, and perfectly conflicting conclusions can be drawn from that. Brother William, on the other hand, was decidedly more communicative.'

'Oh, you saw him, too?' asked Alec.

'Yes, I was intending to go round to see him here this evening, and then I luckily remembered what Mary Blower told us about Alfred staying in Wychford at present, so I jumped into a taxi and went off to see him. I'm now going to describe the interview as exactly as I can just as it happened, and please don't interrupt me. Then we'll go into the obvious points that arise.'

He proceeded to recount the conversation which had taken place in Brother William's office.

'Alfred had telephoned to him, of course,' Sheila remarked the moment he had finished.

'Of course. But why? Just as a matter of general interest—or because he suspected that I should be calling there and wanted to put Brother William on his guard? From the particular words William used, I very much suspect it was the latter.'

'Yes, I agree with you,' Alec nodded.

'Then again—why? Why had Brother William to be put on his guard? One thing seems pretty obvious to me, and that is that it was Alfred who had told him to try and find out where I'd got my information from. Was that the sole reason for ringing him up? Was William speaking the truth when he insisted on his and Alfred's desire to protect what shreds are left of Mrs Bentley's good name? Was that enough to put him so plainly ill-at-ease—distaste at speaking of delicate family matters with a complete stranger? Was it enough, again, to make him so very anxious that I should neither publish this information, nor communicate it to the police? It's all *possible*, and as far as the last question goes, actually plausible; he was practically taking the words out of my own mouth, you remember, Alec. But I don't know! It doesn't seem satisfying, somehow.'

'I should jolly well think not!' Sheila interjected with much scorn. 'Of course those two know something. It stands to reason.'

'Oh, yes; there's no doubt about that. William certainly knows something. What I can't make out is whether it's just private family immorality or something worse. The end of the interview showed clearly enough that he knows something. When I suggested that further inquiries might bring to light something connected with a male member of his family, he looked scared to death; when I identified the male member as Mrs Bentley's husband, he was considerably relieved and proceeded rather hysterically to lose his temper. It's quite plain that Master William has some naughty little secret up his sleeve that he's terrified of anyone learning; and from Brother Alfred's action, I should be inclined to think that he shares it.'

'Well,' Sheila remarked brightly, 'what it all amounts to is this—do you think Brother William did it?'

'Hark at the little bull charging its gate! No, Sheila, I don't. And for why? Because I shouldn't say that Brother William's psychologically capable of murder. Brother Alfred, yes; a hundred times over. But William's a weak, feckless, squashy sort of person; he might have the desire, but I'm quite sure he wouldn't have the resolution. At any rate, that's how he strikes me.'

'They might have been in league, though,' Alec suggested.

'Yes, I'd thought of that. But that presupposes Alfred as the moving spirit taking William into his confidence, and that I can't see for a minute. You know, there's a pretty close parallel for that situation in Mr and Mrs Seddon. Seddon was, fundamentally, not at all unlike Brother Alfred; and Mrs Seddon and Brother William have a good deal in common. I could never see Seddon taking his wife into his confidence on a matter of such vital importance as intention to commit murder, and I can't see Brother Alfred doing so either.'

'Supposing if Alfred had planned and carried it out alone, and William had found him out?'

'Ah, that *is* an idea, Alexander! Yes, certainly that's feasible enough. We must bear that in mind. Well, we've learnt now about as much as we can of the people in our list of suspects, and I think the time's come to sum up for and against each one separately, both psychologically and with regard to the facts. I made a list of them in the train coming down, and jotted down a few notes for each. There are seven of them, and we'll take them in turn.'

'Wait a minute, Roger!' Sheila intervened. 'Who are the seven? Just tell me over again?'

'You ought to have all that sort of thing in your head, Detective Purefoy,' Roger rejoined severely. 'William, Alfred, Allen, Mrs Allen, Mary Blower, Mrs Saunderson and Mrs Bentley.'

'Oh, counting her. Yes. All right; fire away.'

'First, William. Behaviour decidedly suspicious, first-class motive, plenty of opportunity; on the other hand considered by our psychological expert to be doubtful as a potential poisoner. On the third hand, *is* he the ass he seems—or is he a very clever man indeed? Remanded for further investigation, I think.'

'Audited and found correct,' murmured Alec.

'Secondly, Alfred. Very suspicious indeed. First-class motive, haste to get the new will executed, arsenic found in the thermos flask after he had visited the office (though that tells equally against Brother William, by the way), just the sort of man John would have believed about the wonderful new cure, and seems to have done his best to rub Mrs Bentley's guilt well into everybody concerned; self-reliant, rather grim, stern, avaricious, hard as nails. Oh, very suspicious indeed. In his favour I can't find anything except that he has an honest look about him, which means exactly nothing: he could share that with the greatest criminals.'

'Guilty!' said Sheila promptly. 'I'm positive he did it.'

'Are you, Sheila? I wish I was. Thirdly, Allen. Is he genuine, or is he uncommonly cunning? Is his story about Mrs Bentley and himself true or not? We must remember that the story does not destroy only Mrs Bentley's motive; it destroys his own motive equally for wanting Bentley out of the way. Was I taken in by him? Further, if I was, is he capable of standing aside and letting an innocent woman take the blame and the punishment for his crime? Or again, were Allen and Mrs Bentley in collusion to murder Bentley? Ever so many questions crop up here. Personally, I'm quite convinced that he is absolutely and entirely innocent.'

'Pass Allen,' Alec agreed. 'I think so too.'

'So do I,' put in Sheila.

'Exit Allen, then. Fourthly, Mrs Allen. She's decidedly suspicious; motive a little mixed, but understandable enough; opportunity perfect. It seems to me that everything with her hinges on the question as to how far she was disposed to condone her husband's peccadillos. My impression of her would lead me to think that she'd be absolutely uncompromising in this respect, filled with cold disgust and fury; would feel herself insulted and humiliated beyond words. I should also say that she'd be vengeful; though to what lengths she'd be prepared to go in that respect I haven't the least idea. On the other hand, we have Allen's word for it that she took it all like a sportsman, and listening between the words one would gather that she had guessed at other infidelities before this and passed them over in silence. Is Allen shielding her? Supposing he knew that she was guilty (the woman he really does love, remember!) and that Mrs Bentley was innocent. His position would be an extraordinarily difficult one. Another thing—how far does that calm, collected, great-lady manner express her real character? Is that what she really is, or is it a pose? Is she actually off the top shelf, or is this super-refinement? These are a few of the questions that occur to me with reference to her. In any case, she must certainly be detained pending further inquiries.

'So that brings us to, fifthly, Mary Blower. Did she intend to murder Bentley with that lemonade she was giving him? If we're satisfied that she did, and that it was the preparation of lemon and arsenic that Mrs Bentley had made for a cosmetic (I wish I knew more about the history of that mixture, by the way, between the time Mrs Bentley brewed it and the time when it was found in her trunk)—if we're satisfied on those two points, there's an end of the case. Mary Blower had motive both against Bentley himself and Mrs Bentley; she hated both of them, and she's about as low a type as one could get. But I don't know. She struck me, when I tackled her on that point, as a good deal more like frightened innocence than conscious guilt; and I don't think she'd be much of an adept at concealing her real feelings either. It's quite possible I'm mistaken, however. If she *wasn't* actively trying to murder him, was Bentley's death pure accident, resulting from Mary Blower's mistaken administration to him of his wife's cosmetic? That's perfectly possible, but I don't think it's at all probable; as I pointed out before, it's almost incredible carelessness to leave a tumbler of lemonade and arsenic about in an invalid's bedroom. And we're assuming that Mrs Bentley did not do so with deliberate intention. Lastly, about Mary Blower, a new theory's just occurred to me—did she steal a little of the decoction of fly-papers at the time it was lying about with the intention of using it on Bentley, making good the deficiency with water (the easiest thing in the world), and did she, in fact, administer this in a preliminary small dose and a subsequent large one, just as Mrs Bentley is said to have done?'

'That's an idea!' Alec exclaimed.

'Well, I'll tell you what put it into my head, and that is the fact that it was Mary Blower herself who was the one to call the attention of the others to the fly-papers, thereby fixing the subsequent crime once and for all on Mrs Bentley's shoulders. That's a thing you very often get in criminals of a low type, this calling attention to the actual means of the crime in connection with some other person, with the hope of shifting suspicion from themselves. It very rarely turns out successfully, but that doesn't say it might not have done in this case; and it wouldn't have needed any more low cunning than Mary Blower may be reasonably said to possess to have thought of it. Anyhow, it's yet one more interesting theory that we shall have to keep in mind.

'Sixthly, Mrs Saunderson. Well, I think we might dimiss her. She had opportunity, but no conceivable motive; and nobody commits murder without a motive except a homicidal lunatic, and I think Mrs Saunderson, singularly repellant little person though she is, might be exonerated from that suspicion. Seventh and lastly, then, Mrs Bentley. Well, all I'll say about her is that of course she remains under terrible suspicion, though we've already gone a long way in lessening it. And that's the lot.'

'Humph!' observed Alec. 'Well, we've got some possibilities, haven't we?'

'We have indeed!' Roger groaned. 'They're absolutely endless, even with just those seven people. I'd never realised before quite how many there were. I thought that summing-up was going to clarify the case. But it seems only to have made it more impossible than ever.'

'Run through the other possibilities, Roger,' Sheila suggested, 'while we're about it. Outside those seven.'

'Well, they seem to me to fall under three heads: (1) Any single unknown person—business rival, private enemy, and so on; (2) a combination between one of our seven and an unknown, or else a hitherto unsuspected combination between two of our seven; and (3) any two persons, as we touched on once before, both trying unknown to each other to put an end to Bentley and both using arsenic for the purpose. Also, of course, there's always the possibility of accident, either, as we've already seen, through the agency of Mary Blower or else by some other train of circumstances. But what's the good of going on? We could suggest fresh theories all night, it seems to me, without repeating ourselves, and still get no nearer the main question—*Why* was Bentley killed?'

'Don't despair, Roger!' Sheila urged.

'I'm not despairing exactly, my child; but I really can't help wondering, after that review of the case as a whole, whether we haven't bitten off rather more than we can masticate with our own amateur jaws. In other words, whether it wouldn't really be better to lay the whole thing before Mrs Bentley's solicitor (what we've actually discovered, what deductions we've been able to draw and what we have good reason to suspect), and let him carry on. After all, what we set out to do was to get Mrs Bentley's innocence proved, not necessarily to do the whole thing off our own bat; and if the job's proved too big for us, then somebody else had better take it over.' Roger's mercurial spirits had evidently suffered a severe fall.

But his lieutenants were made of sterner stuff.

'Superintendent Sheringham!' exclaimed Miss Purefoy in scandalised tones. 'I'm surprised at you. Are these the words I should expect to hear from my superior officer's lips? Constable Grierson, I appeal to you.'

'I stand by the ship, admiral, till all the rats have fled. No, seriously, Roger, we mustn't chuck it just yet. There's crowds of time to hand it over later if we really can't get any further ourselves, but we must have another cut at it first.'

'And you've done so *awfully* well so far, dear Roger!' Sheila cooed.

Roger brightened a trifle. 'Well, that's certainly true,' he had to admit.

'That's right then,' Sheila said soothingly. 'Feeling better now? Don't cry, and mother'll kiss it well again. There's a good Superintendent! Now then, tell me this, Roger—who in your heart of hearts do you *really* think did it?'

'Well,' Roger smiled, 'it's my perfectly personal, private and quite libellous opinion that it lies between Brother Alfred and Mrs Allen, with the probabilities pointing decidedly to Brother

Alfred, with, possibly, but I'm not at all sure about that, Brother William as accessory after the fact.'

'That's all right, then,' Alec took up the tale briskly. 'In that case we'd better concentrate on those two first of all. Let's see if we can't hammer out some sort of a plan of campaign.'

'I wonder after all if we *have* been devoting too much attention to the personal side and not enough to the material,' Roger mused, prodding the fire absently with a little brass poker. 'And yet there's so jolly little of the material, isn't there? All tangible clues seem to point straight to Mrs Bentley. If one could only spot something to follow up that might lead us in some other direction!'

Three brains were duly racked.

'Look here!' Alec exclaimed suddenly. 'What idiots we are! That packet of arsenic—what about that? If we could only find out who bought that, we'd know at once who was the criminal!'

'I'd thought of that,' Roger nodded. 'But it seems almost impossible to do anything with that. It might have come from anywhere in the whole of England, you see—or out of it! The label's gone, and it seems to have been wrapped in just ordinary white paper. Scotland Yard might possibly be able to trace it, but I don't see how we could. It couldn't have come from any chemist in this neighbourhood, by the way, or he'd certainly have reported the sale of it.'

'Oh!' said Alec, somewhat dashed.

'All we know is that the label had a squiggle in one corner and the inscription "C.3." As I said, some part of a chemical formula, no doubt.'

He pulled his notebook out of his pocket and, opening it at the page on which Mary Blower had made her drawing, studied the latter a little absently.

'There's one thing,' Sheila remarked. 'The police don't seem to think much of it, do they? At least, nobody said anything before the magistrates about finding out where it had come from. I suppose the fact that Mrs Bentley had it was good enough for them.'

'Looks like it,' Alec agreed.

For a minute or two there was silence. Then:

'Idiot!' exclaimed Roger suddenly and with intense bitterness. 'Oh, ass, dolt, fool, goop and *mutt*!'

'Are you talking to me, Mr Sheringham?' Sheila inquired carefully.

'No, I was soliloquising. Oh, would you believe it? Here I've been carrying about with me for thirty-six hours the clue to the whole blessed business! Of *course* we can trace that packet of arsenic. Oh, *bonehead*!'

'We can? How? What is it?' exclaimed Alec.

'You've discovered something?' exclaimed Sheila.

'Why, that "C.3" which I've been assuming all this time to be part of a chemical formula isn't anything of the sort! It's part of "W.C.3." or "E.C.3." of course. Why, heaven love us this is going to be child's play!'

CHAPTER XXI

DOUBLE SCOTCH

'Now then,' said Roger Sheringham, as he and Alec stepped through the ticket-barrier at Charing Cross the following morning. 'Where to first?'

'Anywhere you like,' responded Alec largely. 'Right-ho! Follow me, then.'

After his discovery on the previous evening, Sheila had plunged downstairs to interview her father and returned in triumph a few minutes later with a telephone Buff Book. Half an hour's work had resulted in a list of all the chemists in W.C.3 and E.C.3 in their estimated order of importance, and armed with this Roger and Alec had departed for London immediately after breakfast in order to set about a little routine work.

To describe their morning's adventures would be to repeat the same tale two dozen times over. From shop to shop they made their way, in each of them Roger showed the man behind the counter a fair copy of the squiggle Mary Blower had depicted and asked whether they used labels with that pattern, in each the man told them that they did not and good morning. Lunch found them weary but undismayed.

'I'm sick of E.C.3,' said Roger frankly, as he set down his empty coffee cup and prepared to face another toilsome round. 'Let's have a shot at the other for a change.'

'All right,' Alec agreed equably. 'Warton's is the first on the list, isn't it? Manufacturing chemists, or something.'

'Warton's it is,' said Roger, and reached for his hat.

And then their luck, in the curious way luck has after a change or a break, turned abruptly. Warton's *did* use labels with a scroll in the corner. Roger gazed at a specimen with happy eyes; it was, if not the brother, at any rate, the first cousin of Mary Blower's artistic effort.

'I want to see your manager,' said Roger, quivering with excitement.

The manager was unenthusiastic. To Roger's introduction of himself as a special correspondent of the *Daily Courier* he was politely inquiring; to Roger's request to be informed at once whether a two-ounce packet of arsenic had been sold over the counter during the last fortnight in June or at the beginning of July he was courteously blank; in answer to Roger's entreaty to be allowed to see the poisons' book for that period the manager replied a little proudly that Warton's was a wholesale house, not a retail chemist. The manager then began to hint ever so politely that he was a very busy man and what about good afternoon?

'Damn all managers!' said Roger impartially as he emerged into the passage once more.

'Quite so,' Alec agreed. 'What about trying at the counter ourselves?'

The ground floor of Warton's covered a large area. It was like a shop and yet curiously unlike a shop. Broad, low counters ran about like long fat snakes in all directions and men in long dull-yellow overalls stood about very occasionally behind them. There was an air of repose over the whole place which was not unpleasing.

Roger tackled one of the men in the long dull-yellow overalls. 'Good afternoon,' he said brightly. 'I want to make some inquiries about arsenic.'

'Over there, sir,' said the man, pointing to a distant counter. 'Just to the right of that pillar. No, not that one—the one on the left of the clock.'

With some difficulty Roger presented himself at the right counter.

'Arsenic, sir?' said the elderly assistant, in a marked Scotch accent; he was a little dried-up man with a straggling grey beard and gold-rimmed spectacles. 'Would it be the pure arsenic or the commaircial ye're wanting?'

'Are you the man who looks after all the sales of arsenic here?' Roger asked.

'Yes, sir. I attend to all the orders for arsenic.'

'And I suppose you sell it in buckets, so to speak?'

'We sometimes sell a verra large quorntity at a time,' the little old man admitted in a somewhat puzzled voice.

'But if one wanted to buy a sample, just a couple of ounces say, you could let a customer have that over the counter?'

'Weel, I should want yere business card, of course, sir. Ye'll understand that we only supply the trade here. Or maybe ye want it for a manufactory process?'

'I don't want it at all,' Roger said confidentially. 'As a matter of fact I'm acting for the *Daily Courier* and I want to ask you some questions about a small packet of arsenic which was bought here a short time ago.'

The assistant looked dubious. 'I doot ye'd best see Mr Graves, sir,' he said. 'He's the manager. Or maybe one of the directors. I misdoot whether I ought to tell ye myself.'

'Well, I'd much rather see you, because you must be the man who sold it. And also,' Roger added cunningly, 'if you can give me the information I want (which I'll undertake to treat quite confidentially if you prefer), the *Courier* would be prepared to pay very handsomely for it indeed.'

The little old man brightened visibly. 'After all, perhaps there wouldn't be any harm in me just hearing yere questions, sir. What would it be ye were wanting to know?'

'Either during the last fortnight of June or the first fortnight of July, probably the latter, somebody came in here and bought two ounces of arsenic. Now, does that convey anything to your memory?'

The man shook his head regretfully. 'Is that all ye can tell me, sir? There's a terrible lot of people come in here for sma' samples like that.'

'Well, now, supposing it was a woman—would you remember then? Did you serve any woman with two ounces of arsenic during that period?'

'It wusna a wumman, sir; I can tell ye that. I don't mind that I've served a wumman with arsenic for twelve months or mair.'

Roger exchanged glances with Alec.

'You're quite positive of that?' he asked.

'Pairfectly! I can take my oath it wasna a wumman.'

'Lay you doon and dee, eh?' said Roger happily. 'Well, that's something anyhow. Now, how are we to get at who it was? Do you keep any sort of a record of these small sales?'

'Oh, aye. I enter them all up in ma cash-buke. But not the names, ye see.'

'Well, what about having a glance through your cash-book and seeing how many two ounces of arsenic you sold at that time? You never know; there might only be this one, and then seeing it in the book might help you to remember the circumstances.'

'It's not verra probable, I must tell ye,' muttered the little old man, but produced a bulky ledger nevertheless and began to run his finger down its columns.

A customer arrived, and Roger stood aside; the customer departed, and the search continued.

Three customers later the little Scotchman closed the ledger and laid a slip of paper in front of Roger. 'Five times, between the fifteenth of June and the fifteenth of July, sir,' he said. 'Two of them I mind, on the twenty-thirrd of June and the fifth of July; customers I know. The ither three might have been onnybody.'

Roger pounced on one of the dates. 'July the seventh! That's our man. July the thirteenth is too late, and June the seventeenth probably too early.' He pulled out his pocket-book and extracted his copy of the time-table of the case which he had made out the evening before leaving for Wychford. 'Yes, July the seventh—look, Alec! See?' He stubbed excitedly with his finger at the items immediately below and pushed it into the other's hand. 'That was a Tuesday,' he said, turning back to the counter. 'Now then, can't you remember who bought that two ounces of arsenic on Tuesday, July the seventh? What he looked like or—or whether he wore glasses or anything like that?'

The little Scotchman turned his eyes dutifully up to the ceiling and proceeded evidently to rack his brains, while Roger watched him in an agony of anxiety.

'Ah doot ma mind's a pairfect blarnk!' he said at last, turning them down again.

They gazed at each other in dismay.

'Try again!' Roger urged, and up went the eyes once more.

With difficulty Roger refrained from dancing with impatience.

'It's nae use at a',' confessed the assistant, his accent becoming broader every minute as he saw the *Courier's* generosity eluding his clutches. 'Ah canna mind onnything at a' aboot it.'

'But this is awful!' Roger groaned. 'We've got our finger right on the crux of things. We *must* hoick it out of him. Alec, try the effect of his native language, and see whether that jabs his memory.'

Alec and the assistant eyed one another Scotchly.

Then Alec gave tongue. He said, quite calmly:

'Didn't you say something just now about business cards? Couldn't you get a hint from that?'

Roger sank on to the counter. 'I resign!' he moaned. 'The death of Superintendent Sheringham. Superintendent Grierson, I hand it to you.'

'Would he be a chemist, this gentleman?' the assistant wanted to know.

'Go on, Alec,' said Roger. 'You answer him. I'm not here any longer.'

'No, he wouldn't,' Alec replied. 'He'd be—What would he be, Roger?'

'God knows!'

The little old Scotchman was burrowing happily under the counter. 'If he's not a chemist, I'd have his caird, ye see,' his voice floated up. 'Chemists' cairds I juist have a luke at, but if the customer isna a chemist I keep his caird and mak' a note on it of the sample he bocht, so that we can follow up wi' a le'er la'er on if we don't get an orrder from him, ye see. I thocht a' the time that yere gentleman maybe was a chemist. Here's the cairrrds!'

He reappeared with a cardboard box in which little bundles of business-cards were held together with elastic bands. With maddening deliberation he at last selected one of these, pulled off the band and began to turn over the cards. Roger watched him breathlessly, and even Alec looked decidedly interested.

'Here we aire!' said the assistant with much satisfaction at last, holding one of the cards up to his spectacles and looking at it intently. 'Two ounces of best white arsenic, on the seventh of July, wanted for a manufactory process in connection wi'—I canna richtly read for the moment what—'

'L-let me have a look at it!' Roger interrupted unsteadily, stifling an insane desire to hurl himself upon the bleating little old man, and tear the card out of his grasp.

But that individual was not a Scotch business man for nothing. With an unmistakable gesture of caution he stepped back from the counter arid regarded Roger over the top of his spectacles.

'Wull I get the *Courier's* money if I show you this cairrd?' he asked carefully.

'You wull,' Roger choked. 'By the nine gods I swear it. And I'll name a trysting day if you like. Only for heaven's sake hand it over!'

'Hoo much?'

'Oh—oh, whatever you like!'

'Five poonds?'

'Five poonds? Lord, yes, I'll see you get five poonds. Honest to goodness, I will. Oh, tell me a Scotch deity to swear by, Alec!'

'Ah'll get five poonds if I let you tak' a luke at this cairrrd?' repeated the assistant, who clearly preferred things quite cut and dried.

Roger leaned over the counter. 'You'll get five pounds if you let us look at that card; and if you don't hurry up, you won't need it, because you'll be dead.'

'Then Ah'll tak' it noo,' said the assistant with simple dignity.

Roger tremblingly counted out five pound notes. A moment later the precious card was in his hands. He stared at it with bulging eyes, while Alec peered over his shoulder. Printed upon it plain for all men to read were these words: 'Thomas Bentley & Sons, Ltd., Import and Export Merchants.'

'Well, I'm *damned!*' said Roger.

'Good Lord!' said Alec.

In silence they turned their eyes upon the little old assistant.

'Do you ever read the newspapers?' Roger asked him reverently.

'Aye. Whiles I do.'

'You *do?*'

'Aye. Whiles. I hae the *Peebles Gazette* sent on to me maist every week by ma dochter. But I dinna always read it, ye ken; I dae verra little licht reading.'

In silence Roger and Alec turned their eyes back to each other. In silence they turned on their heels and marched out of the barn-like place.

'Hey! Hech!' cried the little old assistant after them, rendered since the receipt of his five pounds almost incoherently Caledonian. 'Hooch! Ah wornt thart cairrrrd barck!'

They paid no heed. It is doubtful whether they even heard him.

On the pavement outside they halted and faced one another.

'The Wychford Poisoning Mystery is solved,' said Roger in hushed tones.

'Who'd have thought it of the blighter?' grunted Alec.

'*Brother William!*' intoned Roger and Alec in unison.

CHAPTER XXII

ENTER ROMANCE

'But what an *ass*!' exclaimed Roger for the tenth time. 'To do it under his own trade card! I can't get over it. What on earth's the use of tearing off the label, if he leaves his business card behind to be identified by? Well, I said right at the beginning, if you remember, that Brother William was an ass, and my hat, he is!'

They were sitting in a little tea-shop, discussing their tremendous discovery over a very early cup of tea. The next move had not been decided. Alec was for laying their case before Mrs Bentley's solicitor, holding that they had now done all that might be reasonably expected of them; but now it was Roger who demurred at this. Moral certainty, he pointed out, is not the same thing as legal proof; and it was legal proof he wanted before he allowed the conduct of affairs to pass out of his hands.

Alec's next question bore on this matter. 'Well, what's the next move?' he asked. 'Can we do anything more today?'

'What's the time?' said Roger, glancing at his watch. 'Five past four. Yes, I can just do it. The next step, obviously, is to get William properly identified by that compatriot of yours, and the only way we can do that is with a photograph. Now, Alexander, let me test your powers of observation. Where have you seen a photograph of Brother William lately?'

'I never have seen one,' Alec replied promptly. 'Haven't the least idea what the blighter looks like.'

'For a detective-constable, you're singularly unobservant,' Roger said, shaking his head reprovingly. 'There's a photograph of Brother William, excellent Alexander, in Mrs Saunderson's drawing-room, as you ought very well to have noticed. One to me, I fancy.'

'Wait a bit!' Alec retorted. 'I've never been inside the place, curse you!'

'Oh!' said Roger, somewhat taken aback. 'I was forgetting that.'

'For a detective-superintendent,' observed Alec nastily, 'you've a rotten memory.'

'I am humbled and abashed,' Roger murmured. 'And for the second time during the last hour, too. It's getting quite a habit. Well, shelving the question of my humility and abashment for the moment, this is what I propose to do—scud back to Wychford; find out by telephone whether the Saunderson is in; if she isn't, scud round and feloniously steal, purloin and illegally confiscate her portrait of Brother William; scud back to town again, and get it identified before Warton's close. Then, having obtained our legal proof, we can spend this evening discussing pleasantly what to do about it.'

'And if the Saunderson is in?'

'Then I shall have to wait my opportunity tomorrow morning. Anyhow, get your hat down and let's make a move.'

They passed into the street and turned in the direction of the nearest underground station.

'What rather beats me,' Roger observed thoughtfully as they walked along, 'is the question of motive.'

'I thought you decided ages ago that Brother William had a motive?'

'Oh, yes; he had. To get his brother's share of the business. But dash it all, that hardly seems a big enough motive for murdering one's own brother, does it? It isn't even as if he were hard up; he must have had a perfectly comfortable income for a bachelor.'

'But if William had a screw loose?'

'Yes, there is that,' Roger admitted, though not in very satisfied tones. 'But it would have to be a jolly big screw, and I must say that my impression of the man didn't go as far as that at all; he might be eccentric and badly balanced, even cranky, but he certainly didn't strike me as a criminal lunatic—and that's how he seems to be emerging. Still, we shall certainly have to accept that motive, in the absence of any stronger one.'

By a stroke of good luck a train was on the point of leaving for Wychford when they arrived at Charing Cross, and they just managed to catch it. Roger talked a good deal on the way down. Arrived at Wychford Station, he entered a telephone booth and rang up Mrs Saunderson's house.

'She's out,' he announced, rejoining Alec a moment later, 'and not expected back till after six, so that's all right. I didn't give my name, of course, so I shall go round there right away, express consternation and sorrow at hearing the maid's news, and ask to write a note in the drawing-room; for a person of my criminological education, the rest will be easy.'

'And what do you want me to do?'

'You can go home and enjoy yourself with breaking the news to Sheila. I shall fly back here to catch the next train for London, but there's no earthly need for you to come up as well. It's only a formality. I shall be back for dinner. So long!'

They went their respective ways.

A quarter of an hour later Roger's strategy was being rewarded, and Mrs Saunderson's drawing-room door was in the act of shutting respectfully behind Mrs Saunderson's parlourmaid. Roger waited till the sound of her retreating foot-steps had disappeared: then he made for the photograph of Brother William which reposed in a chaste silver frame on Mrs Saunderson's grand piano (Mrs Saunderson was one of those people who keep photograph-frames and silver vases on the tops of their pianos).

'Not that I'm really a thief,' he murmured, as he extracted it from its frame, 'for I fully intend at present to send somebody to restore it when I've finished with it; and after all, intention is everything.'

He replaced the frame on the piano and stood for a moment examining the portrait. It was a good likeness, and the photographer had not only caught something of Brother William's expression of peevish resentment but had even refrained from eliminating it in the touching-up process. Before slipping it into his pocket and making good his escape, Roger turned the thing over and glanced idly at the back. The next moment he started visibly and uttered a single expletive, not unconnected with life after death; for on the back of the photograph was written, 'For my own darling Mona, from her William.'

'Good Heavens!' exclaimed Roger aloud, ringing a change on the same topic.

He dropped into a chair and stared at the words, his brain racing madly.

How did it affect the situation? That it did in some way Roger felt as sure as that he and Alec had that afternoon solved their main problem. Brother William and Mrs Saunderson! Did they intend to marry? There was not the least rumour coupling their names together; if there had been, it would certainly have come to Roger's ears in the course of these exhaustive inquiries, either directly or, more probably, through Sheila. Why, then, were they keeping their affection so dark?

Did they intend to marry? Surely! But if so, didn't that go a very long way towards removing William's motive for his brother's death? Mrs Saunderson was a wealthy woman. Even without William's income from his business, she must have an ample sufficiency for two people. How in the world, then, could this matter of marriage make it necessary for William so largely to increase his own resources? It could hardly be that he disliked so intensely the idea of living on his wife's money: Brother William was not that sort. And to dislike it to the extent of murdering his own brother in order to obviate it! Oh, no; out of the question. What, then? It *must* be something connected with the project of marrying Mrs Saunderson, and it *must* be something connected with money. How could these two be made to combine?

Gazing with unseeing eyes at the carpet, Roger allowed his mind full play.

Suddenly he stiffened. Ah! *But supposing that—*

The sound of the front-door opening and closing with a bang startled him out of his reverie. He heard light footsteps crossing the hall and held his breath. Mrs Saunderson must have returned, nearly an hour before she was expected; and Roger did not want very much to meet Mrs Saunderson just then.

The footsteps passed the drawing-room door, and Roger sighed with relief. Evidently she was going straight upstairs. He would have plenty of time to get away, the precious photograph safe in his pocket.

Then came an interruption. The footsteps ceased, and other footsteps, it seemed, drew near. There was the soft hum of feminine voices.

'Damn!' said Roger bitterly.

The next moment the drawing-room door opened and Mrs Saunderson tripped in, a smile on her lips and both hands stretched eagerly forward. 'Mr Sheringham!' she fluted. 'I thought you'd *quite* deserted me!'

In the instant between his expression of regret and Mrs Saunderson's entrance, Roger had taken a swift decision. He advanced to meet her and caught both her small hands in his.

'Mrs Saunderson,' he exclaimed, a little throatily, 'I want to ask you just one question. You must forgive me—I can't help myself!'

'Oh, Mr *Sheringham*!' murmured the little lady, dropping her eyes below the brim of her hat, and waited expectantly.

'Does your income cease with your re-marriage?'

Mrs Saunderson's head jerked abruptly up. 'Why, y-yes!' she stammered, considerably taken aback.

Roger dropped her hands and struck an attitude. 'Then all is over between us!' he exclaimed dramatically, and fled for his life.

At the station he found that he had to wait ten minutes for a train. His desire to impart the information with which he was bursting drove him into a telephone-box. He gave Dr Purefoy's number and, when the maid answered him, asked for Alec.

'Alec!' he exclaimed, directly that gentleman intimated his presence. 'Tremendous news! I've found Brother W's big motive. It's positively romantic. He wants to marry Mrs S., and her income ceases on her re-marriage. What do you make of that?'

'I say!' Alec exclaimed quite enthusiastically. 'Is that so? That alters matters.'

'Intensifies them, you mean. Yes, rather! I'm as pleased as a dog with two tails. I think we've collected pretty well all we want now (I've got evidence of this new fact in my pocket, by the way), so I shall probably spend the evening writing out a statement, and we can lay one copy before the solicitor tomorrow and post the other off to Burgoyne, as I promised. Alec, this is a triumph!'

'Rather!'

'And look here, what about there being a bit more in it even than that? What about the lady having taken a hand herself?'

'Good Lord! You don't think that, do you?'

'Well, it's on the cards. Decidedly on the cards! Do you think he'd have had the guts all alone? I very much doubt it. That's what struck me as so curious this afternoon, as well as the motive question. I don't think he would have, you know. I've said so all along.'

'But what about her? Is she capable of it?'

'Capable of inciting, most certainly. And remember how very emphatic she was about the other lady. Oh, yes, I shouldn't be at all surprised if there may not be some *very* interesting developments indeed!'

'Well, I'm damned! I say, can I tell Sheila about this? She's here now, simply burbling with curiosity.' Sounds as of scuffling made themselves heard over the wire.

'Yes, tell her by all means. Point out what a clever man her Uncle Roger is.'

'You *are* a clever man, Uncle Roger!' came an admiring feminine voice. 'Do tell me what all the new excitement's about. I'd much rather hear from you than Alec. He's awfully stodgy to hear exciting things from.'

As guardedly as he could, Roger told her. Ecstatic noises floated into his ear-piece.

'The bad lad!' Sheila exclaimed happily. 'Must run in the family, mustn't it? Well, well, well! Will all our names be in the papers, Roger? Can I have a photograph on back page? I'll go to the photographer's tomorrow; this is too good a chance to miss. "Detective Purefoy in her new green crepe marocain." "Detective Purefoy, pinching her father's two-seater for a joy-ride." "Same lady with gloves on." Oh, Roger, will Mrs Saunderson—'

'Goodbye, Sheila!' Roger exclaimed hastily. 'Telephones have ears, you know.' He hung up the receiver and made his way to the platform.

During the journey up to London, Roger occupied himself with making copious notes for his forthcoming report, and enjoyed himself a good deal. He also spoilt a perfectly good page in his notebook in the following way:

A BALLAD OF WYCHFORD GAOL

'Yes, William's my commonplace name, sir,
And Arsenic's the means I prefer;
Maybe it's not playing the game, sir,
But—well, sir, I did it for *her*!

'Yes, all for the love of a lady—
That's what has brought me to this;
And maybe my conduct *was* shady,
But I'd do it again—for her kiss!

'Have *you* known what it can be to love, sir?
Have *you* known how it comes up (de dee)
Behind you and gives you a shove, sir?
The Saunderson came and shoved me.'

? Work up for *Spectator*, *Church
Times*, or *Good Housekeeping*.

It was a few minutes before seven when Roger got back to the Purefoy's house that evening. With a somewhat absent air he hung up his hat and coat and listened while the maid told him that Sheila and Alec were upstairs and would he join them as soon as he came in.

Sheila flew to him the moment he opened the door of her room and grasped his sleeve. 'Enter the conquering hero!' she exclaimed. 'Well, any more news?'

'Yes,' Roger answered. 'I have. And I'm afraid something seems to have gone wrong a little with the conquering hero's works. I showed Brother William's photograph to the man at Warton's and he swears blind that he isn't the man who bought that arsenic!'

CHAPTER XXIII

FINAL DISCOVERIES

'Isn't the *man*?' repeated Alec and Sheila in unison.

Roger dropped into a chair by the fire. 'No. Isn't that annoying? Of course it's just the sort of low trick one would expect Brother William to play.'

'Is the chap quite sure?' asked Alec in perturbation.

'Absolutely. He says he never forgets a face, and he's perfectly certain he's never had dealings with Brother William's.'

'Oh!' exclaimed Sheila. 'But suppose he disguised himself?'

'Yes, I thought of that.'

'You did?' said Sheila disappointedly. 'What a nuisance you are, Roger! You think of everything.'

'Not *everything*,' Roger replied modestly. 'Business cairds, for instance. No, but we did go into the question of disguise. I covered up bits of the face, chin and so on, in case he'd been wearing a false beard, forehead, all the rest of it. But it wasn't any use; the little chap's quite positive it wasn't Brother William.'

'This is a bit of a body-blow,' Alec murmured. 'What are you going to do about it?'

'Well, I shall try him with photos of Brother Alfred, of course, and Allen, and anybody else I can think of. This does complicate the case rather infernally, though. You see, a business card isn't necessarily the wonderful clue we first thought it. Anybody could get hold of the Bentleys' business card, and it's my belief that it's rather a cunning blind. If the police had taken the trouble to get as far as we have, you see, the obvious inference for them, not knowing as much as we do, is that Bentley bought the stuff himself for some purpose connected with his business, took it home and had it stolen from him by his wife. That all goes to throw suspicion still farther away from the real culprit.'

'And on to Mrs Bentley?'

'Yes, as it happens. But I'm not saying that that was the culprit's intention. I'm rather inclined to think that it's just the way things have turned out. And there's a little job for you again, Sheila. Can you get hold of photographs of those two for me? I want to spend tomorrow in town if I can?'

Sheila wrinkled her forehead. 'That's a bit of a problem. I don't know where—Oh, yes, I do! Good enough! I've got some old copies of the *Daily Pictorial*; kept them, in fact, because of the pictures. They've got photos of pretty well everybody in the whole case there. I'll look them out for you now.'

She went over to a drawer, pulled out half-a-dozen newspapers and began to turn the pages rapidly.

'Here we are! "Mr Alfred Bentley, brother of the deceased man." "Mr R. W. Allen, whose name has been mentioned in connection with the case." Look! That the sort of thing you want?' She spread them across Roger's knee and leaned on the back of his chair as he looked at them.

'Excellent,' Roger approved. 'Not a very good one of Allen, but quite good enough. Yes, that's fine.'

'I'll cut them out for you,' Sheila volunteered, and busied herself with doing so.

Roger pulled out his pipe and began to fill it slowly.

'There's another thing about the purchase of this arsenic that's struck me since I saw you last, Alec,' he said slowly. 'It was bought on the seventh of July. Well, if you consult that admirable little table of dates which I drew up, you'll see that this was actually the Tuesday *after* the picnic. After Bentley's first illness, in fact. Therefore, whatever it may have been due to, the first attack was not caused by the arsenic in the packet.'

'Yes,' Alec nodded. 'I see that, of course.'

'What did cause it, then? The police say it must have been caused by arsenic, because of arsenic being found subsequently in his hair and skin and so on; and I must say that does sound damned reasonable. But if it wasn't arsenic from the packet, what was it?'

'There's only one other lot of arsenic we know anything about,' Alec pointed out.

'Yes, I know, bother it! It looks nasty, Alec; very nasty! I wonder if she really was trying to poison him all the time, and somebody stepped in and finished the job for her? Upon my word, it does begin to look uncommonly like it.'

'He might have got it into him by accident, Roger,' Sheila called out from the table by the window. 'Supposing he thought the arsenic and lemon-juice was concentrated lemonade, or anything like that. He might have been thirsty, and mixed some with water. How about that?'

'It's possible, of course,' Roger agreed. 'And yet—! I don't know. Lemonade in a medicine-bottle? And again, would she have left it lying about? It's no good disguising it from ourselves, there *are* difficulties.'

'I say, you're not coming round to the idea of Mrs Bentley's guilt after all, are you?' Alec wanted to know.

'Oh, no; I think we've proved that that's out of the question. But I do think we ought to keep in view the possibility that she may at one time have had a guilty intention, whether she gave it up later or whether somebody else nipped in before she could carry it out. I don't know that I think it's altogether probable, mind you; but—well, I do find this question of how arsenic got into the skin and nails an uncommonly difficult one to answer.'

'Isn't there any way it might have got there without anyone having given him arsenic at all? Any natural way?'

'Funny you should have mentioned that,' Roger replied, holding a match over the bowl of his pipe. 'There are one or two questions I want to ask the doctor about that very point after dinner this evening.'

'And talking of dinner, there's the gong,' Sheila put in.

'Damn—these papers have made my hands simply filthy! Here are the photos, Roger. I must fly.'

After dinner Roger detained Dr Purefoy as he was about to follow the others out of the dining-room. 'I say, just a minute before we go into the drawing-room, doctor. I want to ask you two more questions about arsenic.'

Dr Purefoy smiled. 'I shall have to begin thinking of a padlock for the surgery door if you go on like this, Sheringham.'

'It is rather an obsession, isn't it?' Roger laughed, 'But I think you know what I'm doing down here. I told Mrs Purefoy under pledge of the most terrific secrecy.'

'For an artist in words,' said Dr Purefoy mildly, 'I think you might have put that a little better.'

'It didn't sound very well, did it?' Roger admitted. 'But one never expects a wife to have any secrets from her husband, however terrific; that's understood. Rather neatly got out of, I fancy. Well, what I wanted to ask you was this; could one reasonably expect to discover arsenic in the nails and hair and skin of anybody who had died from—who had died a perfectly natural death?'

'That depends,' said the doctor cautiously. 'One would want to know what sort of medicine he'd been taking, and that sort of thing.'

'Well, let me put my question in a different way. Does the presence of arsenic in the extremities like that point decisively to an attempt at poisoning?'

'Oh, dear, no! A sufficient quantity of any medicine containing arsenic would quite account for that. A little arsenic goes a very long way in the human body, you know.'

'But it must have come from a medicine, you would say?' Roger persisted.

'In other words, the medicine Bentley had been taking didn't contain arsenic, and is there any other way in which it could have got into his system? That's what you mean, isn't it?'

'You read me like an open book,' Roger murmured, and they

both laughed. 'I'm just worrying about the arsenic in the extremities for the moment; not the fatal dose in his tummy.'

Dr Purefoy leaned against the back of a tilted chair and stroked his jaw thoughtfully. 'Well, with an ordinary person I should say no; with Bentley, it's impossible to say one way or the other. You see, one doesn't know in the least whether the medicines prescribed for him were the only ones he took. He might have been dosing himself with a tonic containing arsenic of which there's no record at all.'

'Ah!' Roger observed. 'Arsenic is used in tonics, is it?'

'Oh, very largely. Nearly all tonics contain arsenic or strychnine, and often both.'

'That,' said Roger, 'is very interesting. I believe you've given me an idea.'

In the drawing-room a few minutes later he bent over Sheila. 'I say,' he said in a low voice, 'you might cut me out a photo of Bentley from those papers of yours too, will you? I think I can find a use for it as well tomorrow.'

For the rest of the evening the Wychford Poisoning Case was allowed to rest silently on its laurels.

Directly after breakfast the next morning Roger was conveyed once more to the station, Sheila again acting as *chauffeuse*. Having a busy but dull day in front of him, as he expected, he was going up alone, leaving Alec in the care of Sheila and her mother.

At half-past six that evening he returned, weary but not ill-pleased with himself, to discover Alec sitting over the drawing-room fire with a book.

'Hallo, Alexander,' he said. 'All alone? Where's the other member of the trio?'

'Goodness knows! Haven't seen her since lunch-time. Some lad came round in a red car and wanted to take her out to golf, and that was that.'

'Gross dereliction of duty!' Roger said warmly. 'She left you to look after yourself?'

'Oh, well,' Alec grinned, 'they did ask me to go too, but they weren't very pressing. Besides, I hate playing gooseberry. Well, any news?'

'Yes and no.' Roger replied, holding his hands to the fire. 'Jolly parky tonight, isn't it? That little compatriot of yours refused to acknowledge either Brother Alfred or Allen as the purchaser of the arsenic, and quite emphatic he was about it too.'

Alec whistled. 'I say! And we know it wasn't a woman, don't we? That exhausts our whole list of suspects.'

'Yes, it really is most awkward; and when we thought we were getting along so nicely too. Still, I've got a bit of good news to offset that. I've discovered how that arsenic got into Bentley's hair and so on, and it *wasn't* through the criminal administration of it on the part of anybody else.'

'By Jove, that's a good bit of work. Mrs Bentley's cleared of that, then. Good! How did it come there?'

Roger pulled a chair up to the fire and sat down. 'Well, I asked the doctor-man a few questions last night, and he mentioned the word tonic. That set me thinking. Bentley had a poor physique, hadn't he? But on the other hand, he was fond of his fling. What more natural, then, than that he should treat himself now and then to a tonic, such tonic containing in all probability arsenic? I've therefore been spending most of the day carting that photograph of him round to all the chemists in the neighbourhood of his office, and asking them whether they remember supplying tonics containing arsenic to that sort of face. And sure enough, in the end I struck oil! Quite a small shop, in a dingy little back-street. The proprietor told me that he knew the man by sight well, though he'd never heard his name (I'd taken good care to cut the name off the bottom of the photo, of course), and that he had been in the habit of coming into the shop quite often, at least three or four times a week and sometimes twice in a single day, and asking for a special pick-me-up of his own devising. That pick-me-up, I need hardly add, contained among other ingredients arsenic. The amount of arsenic he would have collected in his body in that way would amply account for its presence in his toenails and eyebrows. So there we are!'

'I say!' Alec exclaimed. 'Could that be the cause of his death, do you think? A—a surfeit of arsenical pick-me-ups?'

'Oh, Lord, no! There'd only be a tiny amount of arsenic in each. I went into that; about three-fiftieths of a grain. It's a perfectly ordinary thing. No, there's no question of anything like that. You'd have to drink something like fifty pick-me-ups straight on end to get a fatal dose that way. Its only interest is to show how he got the arsenic into his extremities.'

'And very interesting too,' Alec agreed. 'You really are rather a marvel, Roger, the way you seem able to dig these things out.'

'Oh, there's nothing much in it,' Roger said carelessly. 'Just a small modicum of sense, a small modicum of obstinacy and a very large modicum of good luck. Anyhow, I don't seem able to dig out the identity of the blighter who bought that arsenic— in other words, the real criminal. You see, we've got to examine such a dreadfully wide field now that our six particular pet suspects are eliminated. Good Lord, it might be anyone Bentley had ever known! I'm going to get Sheila to cut out for me every single person connected with the case whose picture appears in her papers and try that assistant with them tomorrow—everybody! Doctors, servants, women—'

'But if he said it wasn't a woman?'

'How do we know it wasn't a woman disguised as a man? Mrs Allen, for instance. Mrs Allen, I feel sure, would make an excellent boy, with the addition of a small moustache and a billy-cock hat on her shingled—'

'Hallo, you frowsters!' cried Sheila, bursting without warning into the room.

Roger twisted round in his chair to look at her as she pulled off her hat and gloves and tossed them on to a chair. Her cheeks were pink with rushing through the cold air and her eyes sparkling.

'Where have you been, you bad girl?' he asked sternly.

'Playing golf,' said Miss Purefoy innocently.

'Who with?'

The pink in Miss Purefoy's cheeks deepened slightly. 'What's it got to do with you?' she demanded aggressively.

'Charlie Braithwaite, the gent's name was,' Alec supplied.

'Why did you leave your poor little guest all alone and forlorn while you went off and enjoyed yourself with Charlie Braithwaite?' Roger continued with much enjoyment.

'I didn't, you ass! He had mother to talk to. Besides, we asked him to come and he wouldn't.'

Roger eyed her with mock severity. 'And why not? Because he doesn't like playing gooseberry! And quite rightly too. Oh, Sheila, I wouldn't have thought it of you. I thought you were a *good* little girl!'

'Roger, you perfect idiot, I don't know *what* you're talking about!' returned Miss Purefoy with tremendous dignity, the effect of which was somewhat spoilt by the positively flaming effect of her cheeks.

'Oh, Sheila!' Roger grinned maliciously. 'Oh, *Sheila*! And I thought you were not only a good little girl, but a truthful one too. I thought—'

But Miss Purefoy had fled.

The conversation at dinner that evening turned quite a lot upon the absent Mr Charles Braithwaite. In the end, a pudding-plate having been broken, a tumbler of lemonade upset over Sheila's frock and the entire contents of the water-jug cascaded over Alec's devoted head, Mrs Purefoy had to prohibit any further use of the fatal name that evening. It is amazing in how many ways one can say a name without ever saying it at all.

Armed with his sheaf of photographs, Roger departed the next morning as usual. But this time he was not long absent. Within two hours he was back again and entering Sheila's room, where its owner and Alec, in expectation of his early return, were ready waiting for him, the latter reading a novel over the fire, the former busy at her ironing-board.

Roger closed the door behind him and looked at them moodily. Alec had never seen his mercurial friend so serious before. In the end it was Sheila who broke the silence.

'You haven't found him, Roger?' she cried, putting her iron on its rest and gazing at him through the thin steam which was rising from the board.

'On the contrary,' Roger said sombrely, 'I have. And it's the very devil!'

'You've found out who bought that arsenic?' Alec demanded, slewed round in his chair. 'Who?'

Roger stared at him for a moment. 'Bentley himself!' he said gravely.

CHAPTER XXIV

VILLAINY UNMASKED

For a full minute there was silence in the little room, while the other two tried to grasp the significance of this startling information. Then Alec said:

'So Mrs Bentley did do it after all!'

'Mrs Bentley? Of course she didn't!' Roger snapped, walking over to the fireplace and taking up a position with his back to the fire.

'It was an accident!' cried Sheila.

'No, my child,' Roger said more gently. 'That it certainly wasn't. It was as deliberate a thing as you can imagine.'

'I'm lost,' Alec confessed.

'So am I,' said Sheila.

Roger surveyed them in turn, his spirits beginning to lift a little already. 'You are?' he said, with either real or pretended surprise. 'Dear me, I should have thought it was obvious enough.'

'Look here, Roger,' Sheila observed, 'let's get this right. Have you solved the mystery?'

'Lord, yes! I've solved it all right; just as the train was leaving Charing Cross, to be exact. That's nothing. The devil of it is going to be to prove it—and that *is* going to be the very devil himself! A more diabolically ingenious little plot I've never struck.'

'Oh, Roger!' Sheila wailed. '*Do* tell us!'

'Well, I will,' Roger grinned, now completely restored once more; 'having kept you in suspense for a few minutes for the good of your little souls. Now, consider. All this time we've been considering only two alternatives, haven't we? Murder or accident—with the accent decidedly on the former.'

The other two nodded.

'There was a third possibility staring us in the face all the time, and we never caught a glimpse of it. Can't either of you see what it is now?'

Alec looked blank. Sheila shook her head.

'Well, perhaps I could hardly expect it. You have to have a very nimble brain indeed for this sort of thing. To put it briefly, Bentley was neither murdered, nor was his death an accident; he committed suicide.'

'*Suicide!*' repeated the astonished audience.

'Yes. The reasoning's pretty obvious. There are only two deductions to be drawn from the fact of Bentley having bought the arsenic himself, you see; one is that Mrs Bentley is guilty after all, and the other that Bentley committed suicide. Having already arrived at the conclusion that the former is a psychological impossibility, the latter must hold good.'

'That seems fair enough,' Alec conceded.

'Yes, but that isn't all. It isn't just a case of plain, straightforward suicide. We know that because of the arsenic in the medicines and the thermos flask.'

'What is it then?' Sheila demanded. 'Do get on with it, Roger!'

'Gently, gently, child; don't hurry me. The *clou* of the matter, I was going on to tell you, is that Bentley was bent on having his revenge on his wife, and *that* we know from the way he altered his will to cut her out of it altogether. I'll try and reconstruct the situation as I see it. To put the thing in a nutshell, Bentley had discovered his wife's infidelity.'

'Oh!' breathed Sheila.

'Now we know what sort of a man he was—morbid, fussy, self-pitying, highly strung, unbalanced; and naturally this came to him as a terrible shock. He brooded over it. Just as naturally he didn't consider for a minute what excuses his wife might have had or what the moral aspect of his own married life had been. At first, no doubt, he was full of agonised self-pity, and felt that he had never before loved his wife so well as he did now that he had lost her—the usual state of affairs at this kind of juncture, I understand. But by degrees his love, in the dramatic way found both in melodrama and in real life, turned to hate, and to a remarkably substantial, vengeful hate at that. He began to wonder how he could have his revenge, possibly upon Allen, certainly on his wife. He wasn't man enough to tackle the job out of hand, you see; he must go about it in a sneaking, underhand, cunning little way. Well, what does he do? Turns of course to that invariable refuge of ill-balanced minds, suicide. Life for him is over now; to go on living would only be to inflict unnecessary torture on himself; better end the whole thing and have done with it. That sort of thing; and all combined with a now absolutely maniacal hatred of his wife. It's all so utterly understandable with a man of his rotten little temperament, isn't it?'

'Lord, yes,' Alec agreed.

'Go on, Roger!' Sheila implored, gazing at him with round eyes. 'This is too *thrilling*!'

'Well, having these two ideas uppermost in his mind, obviously he sets about combining them. How can he work in with his suicide the revenge for which his petty little soul is aching? And then comes the great idea—arrange his death so that, again Allen if possible, but certainly his wife, will be accused of it—arrested for it—tried for it—*hanged* for it! That's a pretty juicy revenge for any wronged husband, isn't it? So he sets about his preparations. Buys his arsenic openly in his own name, leaving his own business card, and knowing that his identification will be perfectly easy; spills it about all over the place—in his medicines, in the thermos flask, in everything with which his wife could be connected. Oh, it really was magnificently planned.'

'But the fly-papers, Roger,' Alec put in. 'Was that pure coincidence?'

'Possibly; and mustn't he have hugged himself over it if it was? But I shouldn't be at all surprised if he hadn't somehow contrived it himself. It would be so easy to lead the conversation round one evening to cosmetics, and slip in the suggestion so casually that Mrs Bentley would never realise afterwards that it was he who had made it. She'd know all about arsenic as a cosmetic, you see; just the idea of getting it out of fly-papers would be all he'd have to put forward. In any case, whether the suggestion came from him or not, he took very sound advantage of it; the first dose of arsenic, of course, he administered to himself on the afternoon of the picnic. And after that—! Really, you know, I do take my hat off to Bentley: I think we must accord him the fictional title of Master-Criminal. If any criminal in fiction ever deserved it, Bentley does in real life.'

'But you can't call him a criminal, exactly,' Sheila objected. 'It isn't a crime to commit suicide.'

'It is,' Roger retorted. 'It's a felony. But let that pass. You're missing the whole point, little one. Can't you see that Bentley is planning all this in order to murder his wife? M-u-r-d-e-r— *murder* her! By causing her to be wrongly accused and executed for his own death!'

'Gawd!' remarked Sheila with respect.

'And good Lord, even that isn't all!' Roger continued excitedly. 'How is he going to commit his suicide? Why, great Scott! by actually *causing* his wife to murder him! That's the real sublimity of the plan. No arranging the stage first and then killing himself, but actually arranging to *be* killed! Why, it's— For the first time in my life, words fail me.'

'Well, I'm damned!' quoth Alec, though on account of which wonder he did not state.

'Fancy planning one's own murder!' Roger went on a little more calmly after a moment's pause. 'The nerve of it! Just try and imagine the man's state of mind. Of course he was mad; stark, staring, raving mad—and yet how diabolically sane! Handing over to his wife the packet of poison, not merely asking but *imploring* her to put it in his food, racked with agony and the most damnable physical discomfort, vomiting, retching his soul out, half-mad with pain—and then begging and praying for more! Really, it absolutely beggars description.'

'Well, I'm damned!' said Alec again.

Sheila sat down suddenly, her face a little white. 'Don't, Roger!' she said a trifle unsteadily. 'Not quite so—so graphically.'

'Good Lord, I'm awfully sorry, my dear,' Roger exclaimed contritely. 'I was getting quite carried away by my own eloquence. The details are pretty beastly, I admit.'

'I wasn't meaning the details so much as the—the *realness*. I could almost see the horrible man going through it all.'

'Let's talk about something else, then, quickly,' Roger urged. 'Don't want you dashing up and down the house all night having nightmares. Alec, think of something nice and soothing! Bees, beeswax, bandits, Birmingham, bracers, boils, boots, botany—stop me when I reach something that appeals to you—boulders, bibliographers, blackmail, barrels, bath-bricks, basilisks, bashfulness, bagpipes—'

'Roger, you idiot!' Sheila laughed. 'Have you got B's on the brain?'

'Oh, no; only in the bonnet. Feeling better?'

'Much, thank you.'

'Feeling up to carrying on with the discussion?'

'*Roger*! I won't be ragged!'

'The lady is restored. Well, anyhow, there we are. That's the solution of the Wychford Poisoning Case, as the papers call it. What do you think of it?'

'Damned ingenious,' Alec grunted.

'That's not the right thing to say, Alexander. I don't want it to be ingenious; all I want is that it shall be satisfying, fit the facts, and leave no reasonable doubt in your minds as to its correctness. Does it do all those things?'

'Oh, I should think it's correct enough. Must be.'

'Of course it's correct!' Sheila cried.

'Well, that being so, we come to the real problem, which is—how in the world to prove it! There's not a word of proof

in what I've been saying, you see; it's all pure assumption—
psychological deduction if you like. How are we going to
substantiate it sufficiently to take it into court and secure Mrs
Bentley's acquittal on it?'

'*Won't* it do that as it is?' Sheila asked.

'Indeed it won't! Just imagine prosecuting counsel dealing
with it. The first thing he'd do would be to call it a farrago of
baseless assumptions and impossible inferences (Bentley being
a wronged husband is white all through in court, remember; it's
impossible that he can have done anything even smudgy). The
next thing counsel would do would be to point out this simple
fact—if Bentley bought that arsenic himself, then it practically
clinches the fact of his wife's guilt; all she had to do was to steal
a couple of nips when he wasn't looking; that there could be any
possible truth in her own explanation that Bentley actually *asked*
her to administer that powder to him, knowing it to be arsenic,
is simply too ludicrous for words. You see. The plain truth that
Bentley was causing his wife to murder him would be simply
laughed out of court. And without a shred of evidence to support
it, really for once I can't altogether blame the legal mind.'

'But how on earth *can* we prove it?' Alec asked helplessly.

'That's just what I'm blessed if I can see. But if we don't
find a way, you can depend on it that Mrs Bentley will be
hanged!'

'Oh, Roger!' cried Sheila. 'This is awful!'

'It is indeed,' Roger agreed. 'I went over and over it in my
mind coming down in the train, but I can't see even the faintest
glimmer of a loophole. It looks as if Bentley's been too clever
for us.'

'What about putting it before her solicitor?' Alec suggested.
'Hasn't it reached the stage when special knowledge is wanted?'

'Well, if we can't think of anything ourselves, of course we
shall have to do that. But I'm not keen, if it's humanly possible
to avoid it. How would he take it, you see? Not very seriously;
I can't help feeling. Dash it all, one can't blame him! We've

been led up to it gradually, so it doesn't strike us in quite the same way; but put it before some fresh person, and it must seem too utterly fantastic and impossible. No, I can't think that we must hand it over to Mrs Bentley's solicitor except as a last despairing resource. And as yet we're not so pressed for time as all that.'

Alec smoked in silence, Sheila picked up her cold iron and absently scrutinised its bottom, Roger stared at the ceiling and went on toasting the back of his legs.

'Oh, somebody do say something!' Sheila implored, when the silence had lasted a good three minutes. Three minutes can be a remarkably long time when minds are a little taut and nerves a little strung.

'All right, I will,' Roger smiled. 'As far as I can see, there's only one possible hope and that is to unearth evidence of insanity on Bentley's part. If we can't prove fact, we must try and prove state of mind.'

'That's a scheme,' Alec approved warmly, and Sheila nodded her agreement.

'I don't know how far it will take us, but it's worth trying because it seems to me it's the only thing we *can* try. Now, I said just now that we're not pressed for time. Well, from one point of view we're not; from another, we most decidedly are. Anyhow, in order to save some of it I propose that we split forces and utilise our full strength; there are hundreds and thousands of inquiries waiting to be made, so let's split up and make them separately instead of together. You, Sheila, look after Wychford, and you, Alec, London. That is to say, get into touch with as many people as you can who knew Bentley, knew of Bentley, knew people who knew Bentley, and knew the second cousins of people who had once lent Bentley a match—that sort of thing; and from all of them find out, as tactfully or as blatantly as you like, whether Bentley had ever shown signs of being what you might call "queer." Your Superintendent has spoken; he knows you will not fail in your duty to the dear old flag.'

'And what about the Superintendent himself?' Sheila wanted to know.

'He,' said Roger proudly, 'is going to Paris. This very afternoon!'

'Paris?'

'Yes. Bentley spent twelve years there. Who knows what one might not pick up there? And an Englishman isn't so guarded in Paris as he is in London.'

'Hark at the man!' Sheila cried admiringly. 'Talk about hustle. You ought to have been an American, Roger. But what I want to know is, how are you going to discover Bentley's old haunts and friends and all that?'

'Oh, but too simple, my infant. I shall go straight to the firm's Paris office, talk at them in an official way and obtain in exactly half-an-hour every bit of the information I require.'

'Do you know, Roger,' said Alec with not altogether willing admiration, 'I really believe you will!'

'Of course I shall. So that's settled. I'll go up leisurely after lunch, pop round to my flat and collect passport and so on, and cross this evening. Perhaps I'd better go along now and throw my things into a bag before the bell goes. I like these sudden and soul-shattering decisions; they make one feel so important. You'll take me to the station and see me off, Miss Purefoy?'

'Oh, yes,' said Miss Purefoy very airily. 'Father'll run you down all right.'

'*Father?*' Roger repeated, wheeling round from the door. 'Did I hear you say "father"? Why not you?'

Miss Purefoy flushed brightly. 'Well—'sa matter of fact I promised to do something else this afternoon. Of course, if you *particularly* want me, I could cut the other thing. But I should think father—'

'Cease this babbling!' said Roger sternly. '*What* are you doing this afternoon, woman?'

'Playing golf, blast you!' retorted Miss Purefoy uneasily.

Roger turned back to the door. 'Ah me!' he observed sadly. 'We have our day, don't we? We have our day—and cease to be. 'Tis better to have been loved and got lost than—'

'Damn you, Roger! Shut *up*!' screamed Miss Purefoy hotly.

CHAPTER XXV

ULTIMA THULE

So Roger went to Paris.

Alec had a letter from him a couple of days later, written on the morning after his arrival, and stating that he had already got into touch with the Paris branch of the firm, who were proving very willing and helpful, and that he was in process of making a lifelong friend of the manager. There was also a note enclosed for Sheila, containing a number of quotations bearing upon the word Charles, including a reference to a line in a well-known Jacobite song. Mrs Purefoy also had a letter to thank her for her hospitality and hinting that important developments would be accruing therefrom before very long.

With earnest endeavour Alec proceeded to tackle the task which had been assigned to him. Every day he went up to London and pursued his inquiries among the business friends and acquaintances of Bentley. The name of the *Courier,* which he used freely, was a passport that carried him into all fastnesses and caused tongues to wag and brains to be racked to a quite satisfactory extent; for each and all of the artless businessmen cherished the hope of obtaining a little free publicity for themselves and their businesses by being able to contribute some item of information which should cause their names to be starred in the powerful *Courier.* Unfortunately, however, not a single one of them could produce the least evidence of Bentley not being all that a sane man might be expected to be.

Nevertheless, to look on the bright side of things, the experience was certainly a very excellent one for Alexander Grierson. Never before in his life had he held converse with so many strangers as he did during those days, and in a very short space of time he had learned how to emerge, when the situation demanded it, so far from his habitual taciturnity as to become on occasions almost chatty. A remarkable tribute to his devotion to duty.

Nor did Sheila in Wychford have any better luck. Stifling nobly her new-found passion for golf, she threw herself heart and soul into the chase. It is true that she did not have to work quite so hard as Alec, as there was fortunately no necessity for her to proceed on foot from place to place. A large red car conveyed her conveniently and expeditiously from one house to another, and waited patiently outside while she interviewed the occupants. Friends of the dead man, tradesmen, employees, workmen, anybody with whom she could discover that he had ever come into contact, she questioned patiently and tirelessly; but from none could she extract anything of any real importance. It became only too plain that both she and Alec were battering at the wall across a blind alley. They wrote a joint letter to tell Roger so.

Roger's reply took the form of a series of telegrams at short intervals. The first one ran as follows:

'Don't worry on the track of big things here.'

The next, a few hours later:

'Tremendous discoveries expected.'

On the following morning:

'Hopes confirmed revolutionary developments.'

The same afternoon:

'Oh children triumph of your Superintendent.'

And lastly, the next evening:

'Case ended Alec can go home shall be here some time highly confidential will write later collecting affidavits love to William and Saunderson.'

Then followed a maddening silence for a whole fortnight. Alec went home, and from both Dorsetshire and Wychford Paris was bombarded with letters and telegrams demanding news, at first politely, then peremptorily and at last with considerable pithiness. To all of them Roger replied not a word. As a matter of actual fact he never got a single one of them, having changed his hotel in Paris and in his excitement quite forgotten to notify the first one of his new address; but this did not transpire till considerably later.

At last, three weeks or more after Roger's departure for Paris and only ten days before the date of the assizes at which Mrs Bentley was to be tried, Alec received a long typewritten document from his late colleague accompanied by a letter. It arrived by the first post, and Alec spent the whole of his breakfast time in reading it, with intervals for ejaculations to Barbara, passing the marmalade, and automatic absorption of food.

It was at Alec's breakfast-table that the whole business had had its beginning, and it is at Alec's breakfast-table that we finally take leave of it with Roger's letter. The letter ran as follows:

'DEAR ALEC and SHEILA (I'm sending copies of this to both of you, my infants, to save typing it out all over again), I know you'll both have been cursing me like blazes for leaving you in outer darkness all this time, but it simply couldn't be helped. I've been engaged in most delicate and confidential negotiations with solicitors, lawyers and all manner of similar persons, and also with people of no less importance than the Solicitor-General and the Home Secretary themselves (imagine your Roger entering the latter's room on all fours and kissing the homely secretarial boots; it was a great sight!) and I've been put under the most awful vows of secrecy until everything was finally out of the wood. That moment has now arrived, and I can at last give you an account of things.

'I am enclosing a copy of the report which I was finally able to draw up in Paris, copies of which I sent at the time to (*a*) Mrs Bentley's solicitor, (*b*) the Director of Public Prosecutions, and (*c*) in accordance with my promise, Burgoyne of the *Daily Courier*. You will see everything set out in orderly form there, and most of it is known to both of you already; this letter is just to point out for our own private edification where we were right, where we were wrong and what I finally discovered in Paris.

'In the first place, then, we were perfectly right all the time in our main assumption of Mrs Bentley's innocence. Where we were chiefly wrong, at the beginning, was in our thoughtless agreement with the rest of the world that murder had, in fact, been committed. We altered our opinion about this at the end, of course, but even then we were no less wrong in setting it down to suicide and an attempt on Bentley's part to put a noose round his wife's neck. I must say I'm rather sorry about this, as I proved it so very convincingly and the whole idea (to say nothing of my subsequent elucidation of it) was so delightfully ingenious. However, we must be truthful: the whole beautiful structure your superintendent erected had no more basis upon fact than had the original theory of the police about which we were all so refreshingly ironical.

'To come straightaway to the heart of the matter, there was one possible explanation of Bentley's death which, hardly surprisingly, simply never occurred to us at all. We considered that he might have been murdered, we touched on the idea of accident, we founded a pretty case upon the theory of suicide; what we never dreamed of for one moment was that he might have died from natural causes. And that is the explanation of the whole mystery. Mr John Bentley, my children, *did* die from natural causes.

'I'm putting the cart before the horse, you'll understand, because I'm telling you first of all my conclusion before the discoveries which enabled me to form it. These are the discoveries, or rather, the discovery, for they all boil down to this one fact—Bentley was an arsenic-eater! There! That, you see, is the explanation of everything. It explains the more than ordinary fatal dose found in his body (the three grains that would kill any ordinary person were just by way of a snack for Bentley), the presence of arsenic in the medicines and so on, his purchase of it, everything; and it is supported, one might add, by that habit of imbibing arsenical pick-me-ups with such regularity, as I discovered. I'm sorry to have to provide such a tame ending—disappoint you of a dastardly criminal, a full-dress trial and a subsequent execution; but so it is. Real life is one anti-climax after another, you know.

'By the way, in case you don't know what an arsenic-eater is, I'll explain that he is a gentleman who makes a practice of taking arsenic in surprisingly large quantities (twice an ordinarily fatal dose, for instance, and followed up perhaps by another equally large one the next day) because he thinks that it bucks him up and puts new life into him, as in certain cases undoubtedly it does. The big doses are worked up to very gradually, of course, habit inducing greater and greater immunity. The classic example of arsenic-eaters are the peasants of Styria, who, as far as I can make out, practically live on it, with the most beneficial results; a sturdier body of men, they tell me, you won't find anywhere. Never having myself been to Styria and not even yet possessing the faintest idea where Styria may be, this must be taken as hearsay evidence.

'There's no need to go through the various steps by which I established this singular hobby of Bentley's; you'll find it all set forth in the enclosed document. What it all amounts to is that quite early in my investigations over there I noticed that the word "arsenic" was beginning to crop up with increasing frequency, and I simply followed it to its logical conclusion; nearly all the rest of the time I spent in getting the affidavits that are incorporated in the report, sixteen of them altogether, from the various people I was able to unearth who had either seen Bentley taking arsenic in large doses or to whom he had actually spoken with reference to the habit he had formed.

'In Paris, it appears, Bentley (very luckily for his wife) seems hardly to have troubled to conceal his fad, was more proud of it, in fact, than anything else; that is, before his marriage. After it, he was a good deal more reticent, and evidently neither his wife nor his brothers ever had the slightest idea of it. Back in England, he appears never to have said a single word on the subject. Personally, I shouldn't be at all surprised if he wasn't trying during the last few years to break himself of the habit; and probably he found it very much more difficult to get hold of the stuff than in Paris. Then, when he felt so bad before his last illness, he had one more shot at it, rather in despera-tion I should judge, considering that he bought it quite openly on his own business card.

'Anyhow, that's the long and the short of it. Bentley died from natural gastroenteritis set up either by the chill he had caught at the picnic or by impure food, and possibly (one might say, probably) aggravated by the arsenic with which he at once proceeded to treat himself. And in this connection you must remember that, what with the arsenic itself and all the other numberless things he had been dosing himself with, his stomach must have been in a very bad state and you could say that he already had a predisposition to gastroenteritis.

'Of course this clears Mrs Bentley completely. She *was* speaking the truth when she gave her own explanations of what had happened, you see, as we very intelligently decided to assume. Of course if one wanted to do so, one could found on this case a long tirade against the value of circumstantial evidence, but that would be foolish. Circumstantial evidence *can* have its dangerous side, of course; and it *can* lead to a wrongful conviction—as it certainly would have done in this case. We shall hear shrieks in the press about it without doubt, and the columns of the newspapers will be filled for some weeks with hysterical letters from ridiculous people demanding the exclusion of circumstantial evidence from all murder trials, or at the very least the quashing by the court of appeal of all verdicts for the prosecutions obtained on circumstantial evidence alone.

'They might just as well demand the abolition of all trials for murder. For every murder case that can produce direct evidence, at least five hundred have to rely entirely upon circumstantial; and against every mistaken verdict obtained by the latter, at least a thousand correct ones can be set. Whenever I see this old controversy about circumstantial evidence cropping up, I always think of the remarks of Sir Robert Collier, the Solicitor-General, at the trial of Frank Muller—the first railway murder, as you probably don't know. The murderer took his victim's hat away with him by mistake and left his own behind. Sir Robert said: "If you discover with certainty the person who wore that hat on that night you will have the murderer, and the case is proved almost as strongly against him as if he was seen to do it." That this is not in itself a full answer to the arguments against the danger of relying entirely upon circumstantial evidence, I know perfectly well, but I won't pursue that subject here. All hobby-horses to be kept strictly under control.

'Well, about Mrs Bentley; all this evidence I've collected has been put by Mr Matthews (Mrs Bentley's solicitor) and myself before the Director of Public Prosecutions, and he saw at once that it alters everything. In fact, with the defence bringing it forward at the trial Mrs Bentley's innocence would be definitely established and a conviction quite impossible. So after a good deal of chin-wagging, and consultation with the Home Secretary and all that sort of thing, it has now been decided that the Crown will not continue the case; in other words, when Mrs Bentley is brought up for trial a *nolle prosequi* will be entered on behalf of the prosecution.

'And that, I think, is really all there is to tell you. It was an interesting little exercise in psychology, and the amazing thing is how right we were and how wrong. I think the conclusions we formed about each one of those seven people was perfectly right from the psychological point of view, only in the cases of Allen, Brother William and Mrs Bentley herself were our deductions therefrom equally correct. Brother Alfred we maligned most dreadfully, and Mrs Allen still worse. Still more amazing was the situation—seven people with a perfectly good motive for killing Bentley, and yet he died a natural death! To my mind, this is hardly playing the game on Bentley's part. The fact of the matter was that we paid too much attention to the psychological possibilities, and not enough to hard fact; we allowed ourselves to be led away by fascinating but really quite untenable hypothesis about perfectly respectable citizens.

'For the rest, one or two things still remain a trifle vague, but as they have nothing whatever to do with the case we won't let them worry us. Brother William, for instance. He really was thoroughly alarmed that day in his office when I suggested that other unpleasant things might come to light concerning a male member of the Bentley family. It's my belief that the truth is that he has a few private peccadillos of his own on his conscience, and was terrified lest the Saunderson should get to hear of them. I suppose that engagement will be announced soon now—unless Brother William manages to retreat before it's too late. I am also inclined to believe that Mrs Bentley's affair with Allen was not the first of its kind, and both Brother William and Brother Alfred knew that this was so; but that is pure guess-work.

'All the others, of course, even Mary Blower, emerge with stainless characters—or fairly stainless; but in only one case will I recant absolutely the first estimate I formed, and that is Mrs Allen's. I've seen a good bit of Allen lately (they've had him on the carpet to be questioned and so on), and once or twice he's taken me back to Wychford to dine. Mrs Allen is a real sportsman—and a jolly shrewd judge of human nature into the bargain; she may be an "ice-box" in certain matters, but if so there's a lot to be said for ice-boxes. She takes Allen exactly as he is, has quite forgiven him what he did and is altogether a most admirable person and wife; I like her immensely. She's one of the few women I've ever met who are able to take a man as the Lord made him, and not try to re-model the pattern herself. A very rare gift, my dear Sheila!

'Well, *au revoir, mes enfants* (you see the effect of my recent visit). Sheila, I shall be coming to Wychford shortly to pay my respects to your excellent parents and thank them for what they did, and I shall expect you to cancel any engagements with a red motor-car that you may have for that day; please show them this report so that they can see that their sufferings were not in vain. Alec, kindly give my humble devotion to Barbara and ask her if I may come to Dorsetshire in the near future and finish my visit before I have to buckle down to my next confounded book; and as her answer will certainly be "yes," please thank her for me at the same time.

'Your late Superintendant, and still Superior,

'ROGER SHERINGHAM.'

THE END

Also available

The Silk Stocking Murders

Anthony Berkeley

Investigating the disappearance of a vicar's daughter in London, the popular novelist and amateur detective Roger Sheringham is shocked to discover that the girl is already dead, found hanging from a screw by her own silk stocking. Reports of similar deaths across the capital strengthen his conviction that this is no suicide cult, but the work of a homicidal maniac out for vengeance—a desperate situation requiring desperate measures.

Having established Roger Sheringham as a brilliant but headstrong young sleuth who frequently made mistakes and trusted the wrong people, Anthony Berkeley took his controversial character into much darker territory with *The Silk Stocking Murders*, a sensational novel about gruesome serial killings by an apparent psychopath bent on targeting vulnerable young women.

'Anthony Berkeley is the supreme master not of the "twist" but of the "double-twist".'

THE SUNDAY TIMES

Also available

Ask a Policeman

By Members of The Detection Club
including Dorothy L. Sayers & Anthony Berkeley

Lord Comstock is a barbarous newspaper tycoon with enemies in high places. His murder poses a dilemma for the Home Secretary: with suspicion falling on the Chief Whip, an Archbishop and the Assistant Commissioner for Scotland Yard, the impartiality of any police investigation is threatened. Abandoning protocol, he invites four famous detectives to solve the case: Lord Peter Wimsey, Mr Roger Sheringham, Mrs Adela Bradley and Sir John Saumarez. All are on their own—and none of them can ask a policeman . . .

This unique whodunit involved four of the 1930s' best crime writers swapping their usual detectives and indulging in sly parodies of each other: thus Dorothy L. Sayers' instalment features Roger Sheringham, Anthony Berkeley writes for Lord Peter Wimsey, and Gladys Mitchell and Helen Simpson swap Mrs Bradley and Sir John Saumarez.

The book is introduced by Martin Edwards and includes an exclusive preface by Agatha Christie, 'Detective Writers in England', in which she discusses Sherlock Holmes, Hercule Poirot and her Detection Club colleagues.